Spirit Ridge

by

L. A. Kelley

Spirit Ridge

Cover Art by *Kristian Norris*

The Wild Rose Press, Inc.
PO Box 708
Adams Basin, NY 14410-0708
Visit us at www.thewildrosepress.com

Publishing History
First Cactus Rose Edition, 2016
Print ISBN 978-1-5092-0747-3
Digital ISBN 978-1-5092-0748-0

Published in the United States of America

"Never reckoned you smart enough
to figure the truth. The Mick's reward ain't for fetching you alive." His tongue flicked in and out again. "Please me, and I'll make it quick."

Tears sprang to Daisy's eyes. "Sweet Jesus, help me."

Bart's callous chuckle encased Nell's heart in ice. "Ain't no God nor man gonna help a whore."

"Get away from her this instant!" Nell stepped into the alley, right hand hidden in the tunic, finger on the trigger.

Bart raised the gun to meet the new arrival. "Where'd you come from? Best be on your way. This ain't no concern of yours."

Nell strode toward them through the fog. The gaslight shone on her white wimple and the scapular under the veil.

Daisy gasped. "She's a nun, Bart. You can't shoot a nun."

"Shut up," he barked, backhanding her across the mouth. "For five thousand, I'll shoot anyone."

"Get out of here, Sister," Daisy moaned. "Please, don't get hurt on my account. I ain't worth it."

"Release her." Nell's tone betrayed not a single tremor. "If you beg trouble, sir, let fly. I guarantee you won't live long enough for regrets."

Bart's thumb pulled back to cock the trigger. "Your words don't cut nothing. The devil claimed me as his own long ago."

"Then perhaps," she responded coolly, "the time has come to meet your maker and beg forgiveness in person."

A shot rang out. Daisy shut her eyes and screamed.

Dedication

For John

A special thanks to my editor, Lara Parker,
the guru of grammar.

Chapter One

Daisy Tremaine had no experience in subterfuge. She scampered like a spooked deer, casting wide-eyed glances over a shoulder. Even a casual observer could see fear of pursuit clung as tight as a knotted apron, but passersby were rare at night. Especially in a rough part of San Francisco in 1885. Here the fog cloaked all manner of evil, along with the movements of two people who spied on Daisy from across the street.

"Damnation," muttered Arthur Hollingsworth. "You're right, Nell. She's on the run."

"Haven't you accepted by now I'm always right?" whispered Nell Bishop, "and mind the rough language." In reality, Arthur's outburst amused rather than shocked her. Unless rattled, profanity never dropped from the lips of the editor of *The San Francisco Dispatch*.

Arthur grunted, but whether an apology or another curse, was beyond Nell's determination. He peered left and right. "No witnesses. We can snatch her easy."

Nell eyed him askance. "Do you honestly believe she'll cooperate after being manhandled off the street?"

"It's not as if the girl has another choice. It's only a matter of time before The Mick catches her."

"No, Arthur. With any wild thing, trust must be earned before cooperation is solicited. We'll do it my way."

"Your way nearly got me shot last time."

"You exaggerate as usual. I explained the trajectory of Foster's carbine always drew to the left. That alone should have been ample enough information for you to escape unscathed."

Arthur gaped at her. "Breeze kissed my ear as the bullet whizzed by."

"Yet, your head is still intact," said Nell. "Ergo, I was correct. No one appreciates a nitpicker, Arthur."

"Has anyone ever suggested you remain at home embroidering tea cozies, or whatever occupies the time of proper young ladies?"

"Constantly, but I pay them no mind." Nell bunched up the heavy tunic to prevent a single rustle or even a betraying rattle from the beads. "You'll send the wire?"

"I'll send the wire," Arthur grumbled. "He'll be waiting."

"The Mick has men at the telegraph office. Any mention of Daisy—"

"I'll be discreet."

"Don't be petulant, Arthur," she chided. "I've the utmost faith in you, but can the marshal be trusted? You haven't had contact in years, and the poisonous corruption of Colin Doyle spreads far into the West."

Nicknamed the Mick, Doyle controlled his criminal empire from the shadows. To local society, he was a successful businessman, but the underbelly of San Francisco knew no one who crossed him ever escaped alive. Nell resolved Daisy Tremaine would be the first.

"No man is more straight-up than Frank Tanner," Arthur stated with confidence. "He'll help, but the Arizona Territory is rough country. Doyle is cozy with men who run the railroad. Many frequent his establishments to take their pleasures. He surely has his operatives, and those of the railroad, spying on the depots. You might think twice—not that you ever do."

For good reason. If I waited for men to act, nothing would be accomplished.

Nell swallowed the retort. She had no time tonight for verbal jousting with Arthur. "I'll keep a sharp eye. Our escape route is designed to throw off pursuit. Once free of San Francisco, we'll take a train across the mountains. On the other side, a series of stagecoaches will transport us to Spirit Ridge. From there, the distance is a day's ride to Fort Braddock and the cavalry. Within the walls of the fort, The Mick can't touch us."

"I still say we hide Miss Tremaine here and contact the authorities," he muttered.

Nell sighed. *Will the man never concede an argument?* "We tried to spread the alarm, and the authorities sent us packing. Doyle hid his activities and bought a raft of powerful friends. Proof of his treachery won't be found in San Francisco in time."

"You're not even sure of his plans or know this girl can help."

"I have a gut feeling."

Arthur relinquished the struggle with a final grunt. "Then I'll stand by for word and keep watch on The Mick. Don't bother to protest. If you're hellbent on this mad scheme, I'll see it through."

"I won't protest. Prolonged arguments never sit well with you, Arthur. That vein in your temple already throbs." Arthur grumbled another unintelligible comment as he slipped from her side.

Nell moved without a sound, keeping the girl well

in sight. Daisy Tremaine had been hard used. Trust could be won, but releasing her from Colin Doyle's poisonous web first was essential. Human nature most certainly made her wary of any intervention, but as Aunt Agatha often reminded Nell, mankind's most sacred duty was to rise above human nature's dismal shortcomings.

The girl turned a corner toward the train depot. Nell's brow furrowed. "Foolish," she murmured under her breath. "Doyle's men surely lie in wait nearby."

As if in response, a figure stepped from an unlit doorway. Time had run out for Daisy Tremaine. An unladylike expletive escaped Nell's lips, and she gave silent thanks Arthur wasn't there to give her due comeuppance.

The stranger grabbed Daisy from behind and shoved her down an alley. Without a sound, Nell gathered her skirts tight around her body and followed. The alley was a dead end. The man backed Daisy against the brick wall.

"Didn't think you'd skip so easy, did ya?" he taunted.

The terrified girl clutched the shawl covering her thin shoulders. "I weren't going nowhere, Bart."

His foot kicked the battered portmanteau Daisy had dropped at her feet. "Sure looking you planned to make tracks. The Mick put a fair amount of coin on your head. Five thousand gold is a mighty haul for a right common little tease."

Nell's hands clenched as Bart's eyes scaled Daisy up and down like a newly honed blade. Her heart went out to the poor girl. Daisy flinched and pulled the shawl tighter as if the measuring glance tore right through her thin frock.

Bart pressed against her. "What'd you do that's worth good coin to The Mick? His likes could buy the favors of a dozen of you twice over for the price of a steak dinner."

Nell wrinkled her nose as Bart's sour stench wafted from the alley; a putrid mixture of whiskey, tobacco, and unwashed body.

Daisy wore a forced smile. "Nothing, I swear. It-it must be Doyle's joke."

Bart snorted. "Shouldn't swear, Daisy. T'ain't ladylike. The Mick never jokes about money, especially his own." Rough hands strayed to her breasts. "Course I might be persuaded to forget I seen you for a taste of what The Mick savors." His tongue flicked out against his lips like a snake.

Anger flared in Nell, but she fought the urge to charge forward. Men such as Bart were always armed and trigger-happy. Instead, one hand slipped inside a hidden pocket in the tunic. Her fingers touched cold hard steel. Even from her position, she noted Daisy's tremble. "Easy, girl," Nell whispered, "a snake strikes when it senses weakness."

Daisy glanced at Bart's crotch and flashed a coquettish smile. "I have my cycle," she said sweetly, "but I reckon we can work something else out."

"Well, now I see why The Mick holds you in such high regard." Bart ripped off the shawl. He pushed Daisy to her knees and then fumbled for his belt buckle.

Daisy's small hand knotted in a tight fist. Nell nodded her approval. One swift punch to Bart's manhood would incapacitate him for several seconds. Fear would give Daisy's feet wings, and she could easily hightail away before he recovered. Nell slipped the derringer from her pocket. She'd cover the girl's escape from the alley and then lead her to safety.

Bart reached under his jacket. The gaslight reflected a dull metallic glint. He pulled a revolver from his belt and pressed the barrel against the side of Daisy's head.

"Don't be getting no ideas now," Bart growled. "Don't bother to scream, neither. In this part of town, screams don't fetch the law. We'll finish our business, and you can go."

Daisy swallowed hard. "You won't tell Doyle you seen me?"

Bart yanked at the top buttons on his drawers and shoved a hand inside. "I swear. Let's get to it."

Daisy peered into his eyes. "Liar."

Surprise shot through Bart's expression. "Never reckoned you smart enough to figure the truth. The Mick's reward ain't for fetching you alive." His tongue flicked in and out again. "Please me, and I'll make it quick."

Tears sprang to Daisy's eyes. "Sweet Jesus, help me."

Bart's callous chuckle encased Nell's heart in ice. "Ain't no God nor man gonna help a whore."

"Get away from her this instant!" Nell stepped into the alley, right hand hidden in the tunic, finger on the trigger.

Bart raised the gun to meet the new arrival. "Where'd you come from? Best be on your way. This ain't no concern of yours."

Nell strode toward them through the fog. The gaslight shone on her white wimple and the scapular under the veil.

Daisy gasped. "She's a nun, Bart. You can't shoot a nun."

"Shut up," he barked, backhanding her across the mouth. "For five thousand, I'll shoot anyone."

"Get out of here, Sister," Daisy moaned. "Please, don't get hurt on my account. I ain't worth it."

"Release her." Nell's tone betrayed not a single tremor. "If you beg trouble, sir, let fly. I guarantee you won't live long enough for regrets."

Bart's thumb pulled back to cock the trigger. "Your words don't cut nothing. The devil claimed me as his own long ago."

"Then perhaps," she responded coolly, "the time has come to meet your maker and beg forgiveness in person."

A shot rang out. Daisy shut her eyes and screamed.

Nell clapped her hand over Daisy's mouth. "Silence," she ordered. "No matter what Bart said before, sound can draw interest—and we must avoid attention, now, more than ever. Nod your head if you understand and will do as I say."

The girl's eyes went wide, and she nodded. Nell removed her hand. In her other was the smoking derringer. Daisy gasped. "Y-You ain't dead?"

"Hardly." Nell's gaze flicked to the body. "Although, I can't say the same for him."

She gulped. "Sweet Jesus, you killed Bart."

"When justice is done, it is a joy to the righteous, but terror to evildoers. Proverbs 21:15."

Daisy rose to her feet, gaping at the corpse. "It ain't that Bart will be missed, but you're a nun. They're all peaceable-like. I didn't think shooting people was allowed."

"Not generally," she said with the trace of a smile, "so if anyone asks we know nothing of the wretched sinner's untimely demise." Nell gazed at Daisy. The girl was but a few years younger than herself. Her heart filled with both compassion and steely resolve. *One unfortunate turn of events and any girl's life could end in this alley.* "I bring no harsh judgment to you."

Daisy's expression flickered with hope. "Thank you, Sister."

Nell picked up the shawl and wrapped it around Daisy's thin shoulders. "You're in trouble, aren't you? You need a safe place."

Daisy shuddered. "There ain't none. He'll find me."

"Colin Doyle?"

"H-How'd you know his name?" Her face paled. "Are you an angel? I called out to Jesus for help, but didn't reckon he'd be so forthright."

Nell tucked the derringer into the voluminous folds of her habit. "I'm no angel," she said with undisguised amusement. "Even dear Aunt Agatha will attest to that. You have been ill-used, Daisy, but no more. Now, you have a choice. Come with me and leave this life of degradation. I promise a chance to start fresh. Only death waits on the streets." She eyed the girl sharply. "What is your answer?"

"I-I can't lie to you, Sister. I won't make a good nun. I ain't religious, and I done things." Daisy's chin trembled. "Sinful things."

"Unkindness and cruelty forced your choices." Nell linked her arm with Daisy's. "Difficult days lie ahead, but all I require from you is courage. Do you have it?

Will you trust me?"

Daisy squared her shoulders. "Yes. I ain't gonna be no man's whore any longer."

Nell suppressed a cheer. She had been right about Daisy all along. "We must go. Talking here is dangerous. The eyes and ears of Colin Doyle are fixed throughout the city."

Daisy grabbed the handle of the battered portmanteau at her feet. She cautiously sidestepped the crumpled figure of Bart, buttons on his pants half undone, blank eyes staring at the sky. She sucked in a breath. "The Lord sure works in mysterious ways."

"Amen, Sister Daisy. Amen."

****

Deputy Marshal Sam Tanner dropped low, belly flat against the rocky outcrop. He inched forward, careful not to disturb a single pebble. Sam froze at the top of the rise. Sharp eyes scanned the vista. He stilled his breathing, slow and steady, and inhaled deeply, drawing in the scent of the surrounding earth. Sam had discarded his hat and duster below to make movement easier and keep a low profile. Rays of sun, still warm in October, beat on his naked head. He shrugged off any discomfort and focused on the terrain.

At first glance, the land was empty of life, nothing but heavy brush, red rock boulders, and pebbly dirt mixed with sand for miles. The leaves on an alder stirred in the breeze. Sam's eyes narrowed as a scrub jay alit on a juniper bush. It cocked its head and then with a *caw* flew to roost in the tree.

Sam shifted his gaze to a cluster of red rock jutting from the earth. Across the wash, came the *tick-tick-tick* of pebbles tumbling down an incline. He'd seen and heard enough. Without a sound, he returned to the three men eager for his report.

A man with iron gray hair and ice-blue eyes that could freeze a rattler mid-strike stepped forward and handed Sam his hat and coat. Sunlight reflected off the marshal's badge pinned to his chest. "What did you learn?" he whispered.

Sam shrugged on the duster and adjusted the Stetson to shade his dark brown eyes and high cheekbones. "McLaren and the rest are sitting tight."

Marshal Frank Tanner rubbed his chin. "All of them?"

"Same tracks we picked up earlier: Reese McLaren, Gates, and both Sutton boys. They must have tied up their horses on the other side of the notch." Sam's brow creased in bewilderment. "Funny them passing near Spirit Ridge. I thought after that shooting over the county line, they'd hightail straight to Mexico. Where the hell are they headed?"

"Can't say." The marshal glanced at the rise as if to weigh their limited options. The posse left town in a hurry after a report of the sighting. Out this way, fresh water for the horses was scarce. If they lost the outlaws now, they'd have to head back. "I reckon they won't come quiet-like, especially McLaren. Not with the price on his head."

"Best not make it easy for them." Sam grabbed his rifle, a Winchester lever-action repeater resting against a boulder. "I'll draw them out."

The marshal nodded in agreement and then turned to the two other men in the posse. "Jeb and Earl, come with me. We'll circle round and get between them and the horses. We can take them by surprise on the other side of the wash." He turned to Sam. "Be careful. Each man is well armed, and McLaren is a crack shot."

"I remember," said Sam tersely. "We've crossed paths."

"Your granny won't forgive me if her baby comes home with a scratch on his pretty face. Don't need any Apache curse dogging my trail."

Sam shot him a dark look as the other men cracked grins. His grandmother's over-protectiveness was a sore point. With a soft chuckle, Marshal Tanner and the posse slipped away.

Toting the Winchester, Sam headed to the wash; soft footfalls betrayed not a whisper of sound. The posse needed several minutes to get into position. Concealed by brush, he cast a trained eye over the lay of the land. A mass of sandstone to the right offered an excellent vantage point. His rangy muscular body crept across the rough ground, moving furtively from bush to boulder.

Now and then, Sam paused to listen as his grandmother taught him. Her demanding voice rang in his head. *Steady, It'sa. Let your feet brush the earth. Move as if wings lift you from above. Leave no path for enemies to follow.*

Only the soft rustle of a few dead leaves skittering across the ground broke the silence. The scrub jay watched from its perch, cocking its head in interest. Sam gave the bird a wide berth. Any jittery flight instantly betrayed his position to an experienced tracker. Like Sam, McLaren had once been a cavalry scout. He had been good. Damn good.

Sam reached the outcrop. The others should now be in position. From above, a few well-placed shots would draw the gang's return fire. With luck, he'd have their positions marked and keep them penned until surrounded by the posse.

The scrub jay took off. Sam threw himself into the dirt. A bullet grazed the rock where his head had been moments before. He rolled across the earth, heart pounding as a volley of bullets kicked up soil. His eyes caught a glimpse of a black shirt before he made it to safety behind a boulder, blood close to boiling. Close…too close. If it hadn't been for the bird's warning, McLaren would have gotten the drop.

Sam placed the rifle aside. He whipped the pistol from the holster and cocked the trigger, drawing in a steadying breath. From nearby, the sound of gunfire drew the outlaws' attention. He darted behind another boulder. Shots rang out, but his ears marked the position. Sam grabbed a stone and flung it at the outcrop. It hit the surface, causing a cascade of pebbles as if a careless man tried to scramble to the top.

Leaves rustled in the scrub. Sam sprinted from the safety of the boulder. Sunlight caught the glint of gunmetal steel as he fired. From the thick mass of vegetation came a muffled grunt and then silence. He crept forward and parted the brush. Gates was dead, shot through the heart.

Rifle fire closed on his position. Sam snatched the Winchester and clambered to the rocks. His keen eyes tracked the landscape for any elusive trace of the enemy. All was quiet, and then came gunfire and shouting voices. Sam cursed under his breath. Something was wrong. He dashed to the wash. Jeb had one arm around Earl who limped with a bloody bandana tied around his leg.

Marshal Tanner trailed behind, leading four horses. "The Sutton boys got the jump on Earl, but they won't cause any more trouble."

"T'ain't bad," Earl grumbled. "Just hurts like hell. What about Gates?"

"Body is over there," said Sam. "McLaren?"

"Must have slipped past," said Frank. "Won't get far without a horse."

Sam frowned. "Why the hell were Gates and the Suttons traveling with McLaren? They're train robbers. He's strictly gun for hire."

Frank grunted. "Maybe business for McLaren was slow. No range war in this part of the territory. Robbery might be more to his liking now."

"No rail lines through here and no one worth killing—not that I know of," Sam said wryly. "The last sighting of McLaren was months ago in Oklahoma, and now he's riding past Spirit Ridge with thieves as company? Ain't nothing that way except the hills. It made more sense to hightail it to Mexico directly."

"Both Suttons wore those black shirts, too," said Jeb.

Sam shook his head. "So did Gates. Don't make sense."

"Outlaws don't necessarily make sense." Frank peered closely at the crown of Sam's hat. He jabbed a finger through a bullet-sized hole at the very top. "McLaren near had you in his sights. Your grandma's gonna let you have it, boy."

"Naw, Marshal," jibed Earl. "She's gonna let his grandpa have it for getting her little angel scuffed up. Lookee, he done dirtied his pretty face."

"My rifle is still loaded, Earl," drawled Sam, much

to the amusement of the other men. Above their laugher, came the snap of a twig.

"Down!" Sam yelled.

A tight cluster of bullets tore through the brush and spooked the horses. All the reins except for those of a wild-eyed roan snapped from Frank's hand. The rest bolted.

Sam caught a glimpse of movement. *McLaren.* He dodged shying horses galloping hellbent along the wash and then fired into the rustling leaves. "Give it up, McLaren!" Bullets pinged off a nearby rock, and Sam dove for cover.

"That you, Tanner? Well, ain't this a small world? Come in and get me."

Jeb darted beside Sam. "Circle round?" he whispered.

"Grab the horses, first," Sam murmured. Jeb nodded tersely and edged away. McLaren couldn't get far in this harsh country on foot.

Sam noted the direction of the outlaw's voice and weaved to reach McLaren from the rear. He sidled through the brush, Winchester at the ready. Not a single track was visible on the rocky ground. McLaren was gone.

Three shots fired in rapid succession. A horse whinnied.

McLaren had drawn Sam toward him and then circled in the other direction. Sam's heart hammered as he broke into a run. The only horse nearby had been the roan.

"Grandpa!" he shouted.

Frank Tanner didn't answer. Earl sat near a crumpled body while in the distance the pounding of a horse's hooves drew ever farther away. Earl's face was pale, but not from his wound. The blood pooling in the sand didn't belong to him.

"Ambushed us." Earl's voice broke. "Took the roan. I-I'm sorry. He moved so fast I couldn't get off a shot."

Sam dropped to one knee. Tightness squeezed his chest so hard, speech was difficult. "Damn it, Grandpa, I told you to duck."

Frank's eyes fluttered open. "Not your fault," he wheezed. "Shouldn't have let him get the drop."

Jeb jogged toward them, three missing horses in hand. Sam jumped to his feet and vaulted into the saddle of a pinto mare. "Hand up my grandpa. I'm taking him for help."

"Get McLaren," gasped Frank. "Don't mind me."

"McLaren will wait. That bullet wound won't."

They gently lifted the injured man in front of Sam. The marshal's eyes closed. His head sank onto his chest. Sam wrapped an arm around to steady him in the seat.

"H'yah!" Sam jabbed his boot heels into the mare's side. She danced a skittering sidestep before bolting across the range. "Don't you die on me, old man," he muttered in Frank Tanner's ear. His grandfather made no response.

Chapter Two

Sam darted into the bedroom at the sound of a faint groan. "Grandpa? How you feeling?"

Frank's eyes fluttered open. "Better. I ain't bouncing on that damn horse." His body shifted position, and he groaned again. "Shoulder hurts like hell."

"Serves you right." An elderly woman with high cheekbones and the fierce gaze of an eagle glared at him. Foolish people might see the gray streaks in her jet-black braided hair and mistake them for frailty. If so, they lived to regret it. Frank Tanner was too smart to be one of them.

He grinned with undisguised affection. "Howdy, sweetheart. I reckon I ain't dead."

Lenna Tanner washed her hands in a basin of water. "Old man is too stubborn to die, yet. Although, I may finish what Reese McLaren started. Why is there a bullet hole in our grandson's hat?"

"Was there?" Frank gazed at the ceiling. "Do tell. I hadn't noticed."

Arms crossed, she glared with disapproval. "You should not lie to a woman who always carries a knife."

"Sam got a little cocky and nearly got his head blown off. He learnt his lesson."

"You are supposed to protect him!"

Sam rolled his eyes. "Grandma, I'm a grown man,

twenty-one years old."

"Now, Lenna," Frank said in a soothing tone. "Sam is the best damn deputy I ever had. What am I supposed to do? Carry him on my back and wipe his nose? He's stubborn. Like his grandma. Besides, the fault weren't his. Sam wanted to fetch more men, but I refused to stand down." He glanced around the cabin. "What happened to Earl?"

"He arrived yesterday with Jeb. I tended his wound and sent him on his way. You slept over a day."

Frank shifted on the bed and grimaced. Lenna rushed to his side. The fire in her eyes dimmed. Her voice filled with tender concern. "Is there pain?"

"Not so bad. I'd do better with a kiss." His wife willingly obliged. "I reckon," he murmured, "your face is the prettiest sight a man could ever see."

She ran her fingers gently through his hair. "You almost lost the chance to see it again. You are a stubborn fool."

"I've no regrets," he said lovingly. "If I hadn't been so stubborn, I never could have talked such a pretty gal into marrying me."

Sam smiled at the display of affection. "What do you say, Grandma? Will the old dog live to growl another day?"

"Who you calling an old dog?" To Sam's amusement, his grandfather's protest came out like an indignant bark.

"You," Lenna huffed. "That posse needed at least three times the number of men. McLaren is a stone cold killer with more than a dozen murders to his credit and no fear of shooting a lawman. He has done so before."

"We weren't sure it was McLaren," Sam said.

"After that shooting in Robertsville, Grandpa got word McLaren rode with black-shirted riders. When we heard a group with that description passed near Spirit Ridge, we had to go."

"McLaren ain't the type to sit on his tail," Frank grumbled. "I didn't have time to round up more men. We shot most of them," he added gruffly.

Lenna sniffed in disparagement. "Most don't count—not when Reese McLaren nearly blew both your heads off. Riding out with only four men and one of them Earl—what were you thinking? That man can't hit his own barn door in broad daylight from ten paces away with help to aim the shotgun. You won't hear the end of this for a long time."

Sam chuckled. "Surrender now, Grandpa. You can't win against her. Don't even try."

"Ain't that the truth." He reached for his wife. The storm left Lenna's eyes as she sat on the side of the bed. Frank brought her hand to his lips. "Nor do I wish to. Dear heart, forgive me for bringing on such worry."

Lenna tenderly kissed his forehead. "I am not ready to be a widow." For once, the determined voice of Lenna Tanner betrayed a slight tremble. She dabbed at her eyes with the apron and then removed an envelope from the pocket. "I almost forgot. You received a telegram. Mateo rode from town and delivered it a few hours before you and Sam arrived." She eyed her husband severely. "He was angry you did not wait until he returned to form the posse."

"I reckon I'll get it from him, too," Frank groused, good-naturedly. "Doesn't anyone have a kind word for a wounded man?"

"Yup," said Sam with a grin. "We already agreed

the old dog will live to growl another day."

Frank grunted. "Just read me the telegram."

Lenna tore open the envelope. "Passengers arriving by stage. Please render assistance. Greatest urgency." She looked at Frank. "It's signed Arthur Hollingsworth."

Frank's gaze widened in surprise. "Arthur Hollingsworth? I haven't heard from him in years. What passengers? When?"

"That's all it says." Lenna handed him the telegram. "His name is familiar."

"I've mentioned Arthur. We fought together in 1840 when Texas allied with Mexican rebels in the Yucatan. Afterward, we came to Arizona, but Arthur left directly for San Francisco. He invited me along, but I declined. City life agreed with him more than me."

"Ah, I remember. Did he not have a relative with a newspaper?"

Frank nodded. "His uncle owned *The San Francisco Dispatch.* He sent for Arthur to take over the business. Last I heard a few years back, he made a go of it. Arthur was a mite tightly wound," Frank chuckled, "but a good man nonetheless. He saved my life from an ambush once." He gave the telegram a quick scan, and his frown deepened. "I wonder who he wants me to help."

"You are not well enough to travel," said Lenna tartly. "Don't argue. I will not listen. Sam will meet the stage."

Sam yelped an immediate protest. "I can't. Now that Grandpa is on the mend, I'm going after McLaren. He already has a fair lead. I'll have to ride hard to catch him."

"Not alone, you ain't," snapped Frank. "Gathering another posse together takes time."

"I don't need a posse," he insisted. "I travel faster by myself, and, anyway, McLaren's gang is gone. He's riding solo. This is the first sighting in months. What if he reaches Mexico?"

His grandmother's eyes bored into him. "Then he is their problem and not yours. Good riddance, I say."

"He got away before."

Lenna patted his arm. "The escape was the Army's doing."

Sam's voice tightened. "He'll kill again, Grandma. His kind don't stop."

Frank gave the young man a searching look. "Forget McLaren for now. After many years, a man I'm beholden to asks for help. I can't turn my back on him, so consider it a personal favor if you meet the stage."

"And do what? Play escort to a bunch of sissified swells from San Francisco?"

"If need be. Arthur Hollingsworth was never one to ask a favor lightly. Something of great importance must have caused him to reach out."

Sam sputtered with annoyance. "I don't even know when these passengers will arrive. You expect me to meet each stage until somebody shows?"

"I do." He motioned to his bloody shirt draped across a chair. "Take my badge."

"Grandpa—"

"Take it. Bigwigs might not act kindly to only a deputy showing." He cleared his throat. "I hereby name you acting marshal of Spirit Ridge."

Sam grudgingly removed his deputy's badge and pinned the other in its place.

"Good," said Lenna. "Maybe weight of a bigger badge will remind you not to act so foolish." She grabbed a bucket and headed to the well.

"What does Mr. Hollingsworth expect me to do when the stage arrives?" Sam griped to his grandfather. "Blow kisses at all the passengers until I figure out who I'm supposed to meet?"

"I reckon they'll look for the marshal." Frank held out the telegram. "Keep it. Let the person know you work with me."

Sam touched the paper.

The coyote's brown eyes held flecks of gold. "Help me, It'sa."

No, not again! Sam blinked. The vision disappeared. A sense of impending danger tightened a hard knot in his stomach. He swallowed once, and it vanished.

Frank eyed him askance. "You all right? You went a mite peaked there for a second. Maybe you got too much sun."

Sam hazarded a glance toward the door, relieved to see no sign of his grandmother. Of course, too much sun explained the reaction. He shook off his unease. "Don't you fret over me, old man. You're the one flat on your back."

"Old man, my ass—"

"I reckon Grandma needs more firewood." With a wicked grin, Sam slipped out the door.

****

When dinner ended, Sam wandered to the porch. He had his old room inside the cabin, but for now the clear evening sky beckoned. Tomorrow, he'd return to his quarters behind the marshal's office. He drew in a deep breath enjoying the view of stars overhead instead of a lath and plaster ceiling.

Nights outdoors brought pleasant memories of hunting trips with his grandparents. They never came back empty-handed. Frank Tanner was a crack shot and trained his grandson until Sam's skill surpassed his own. While to Lenna Tanner every line in the sand, every whisper in the wind pointed out trails even the craftiest game couldn't disguise. Apache magic, his grandfather called her tracking skills. She passed those to her grandson, too.

Sam leaned against the porch railing, closed his eyes, and let his senses drift. Horses nickered in the corral, and then the sweet scent of roses tickled his nostrils. The smell brought an unbidden rush of emotion. The rosebush had been his mother's favorite, carefully tended. Born from a cutting she nurtured from the east and her own garden. Everyone told her roses never bloomed here, she once admitted with pride to Sam. They did, even this late in the year. Perhaps, he mused with a smile, the flowers responded to stubbornness. God knows, Tanner women had it in spades.

Sam had no memory of his father. Sergeant Joseph Tanner returned from the Civil War, but his injuries were grave. Death claimed him soon after arriving home. Then Alice Tanner decided she and her infant son should make the difficult journey alone to the Arizona Territory to live with Joseph's parents. Her own kin disowned her for marrying a half-breed. Except for each other, Frank and Lenna were the only family she and Sam had left. His mother may have suspected her time on earth was short, too.

Alice Tanner with her pale skin and golden hair must have been nervous to meet her Apache mother-in-law. How would a dark-skinned Indian wise woman greet her? However, she bonded at once with Lenna and Frank, united in the common grief over losing Joseph. Sam realized with a start it had been fifteen years since she died. If not for the small photograph of her hanging on his bedroom wall, his mother's image would also have faded from memory.

"You are troubled, *It'sa.*" Sam's eyes flew open. His grandmother stood in the doorway.

"I was thinking of Ma."

She sat in the rocker. "Alice had a pure spirit. It shined like her golden hair. Many women cannot accept a man whose mother wears different skin, but Alice saw beyond to a person's heart and knew their nature. You have her strength."

"Strength didn't do her much good in the end." He snapped his lips shut, not meaning for the words to come out so harsh.

"Her body failed, *It'sa*, not her spirit. No healing magic could defeat the wasting sickness that claimed her." She sighed. "Death is a part of life. It comes for us all. It came for your father and mother. Someday it will come for me."

"I reckon you'd just spit in its eye, *Shee-cho*," he teased, using the Apache endearment.

She snorted in amusement. "Perhaps, I will." Her expression sharpened. "That is not what keeps you awake, my young eagle."

Sam shifted his feet and turned his head away, unnerved by her piercing gaze. "T'ain't nothing. I'm wound up tight." He pretended to yawn. "Had a long day, best get some shut-eye."

"You had another vision."

Damn. Would he ever be able to hide his worries from her?

"No," she said as if in answer to his thoughts.

Sam stiffened. "I didn't—"

"You cannot fight the gift, *It'sa*," Lenna said. "It comes whether you wish it or not."

"What good are visions? They warn me of deaths I can't stop." His voice dropped. "I never could."

He shuddered, recalling the first vision. The image of his mother in the coffin a week before she died woke him sobbing in terror. His grandmother tried to offer comfort. She said the spirits sent a gift so he could say goodbye. To a broken-hearted six year old, the gift wasn't welcome.

Sam dreamed others through the years, lifeless faces, disembodied voices calling for help. He'd wake in a cold sweat knowing he was already too late. Eventually, a body surfaced: a rancher swept away by a flash flood, a woman killed by a rattlesnake, a prospector thrown from his horse.

The last dream came while still a scout on the trail. He'd seen the corpse of a girl, over her stood Reese McLaren with a bloody knife. When the troop reached civilization, he received word McLaren had disappeared, wanted for the murder of a prostitute.

Too late again.

Lenna sighed. "To have foreseen the death of your mother was difficult for one so young. It closed your mind to the spirits' warnings. Do not fight them, *It'sa.* Open your thoughts, and you will see into the shadows as far as my father and find a way to use the gift." She smiled at him with affection. "You may then also spit into death's eye."

"I'll try," he said gruffly.

She leaned back to stare at the sky. The rocker swung slowly to and fro. "Now, tell me what you saw."

"A coyote with golden brown eyes. She called to *It'sa* and asked for help."

"She?"

"The voice was a woman."

"Good," Lenna grunted. "It's time you claimed a wife."

"Wife?" he sputtered. "Who said anything about a wife? It was a coyote."

"And you are *It'sa*, the eagle. The day your father's letter arrived telling of his son's birth, I saw an eagle light upon a white oak tree. Keen eyes held my gaze. As the eagle screeched a war cry, I sensed the power of your spirit guide. The coyote is a good match," she added with a nod. "You are a skilled warrior, eyes sharp, ferocious with your enemies, but the coyote is smart, a trickster, one to bend the rules. A powerful ally to have at your side." She rose from the chair. Her face crinkled in a smile. "Yes, a good match. Goodnight, *It'sa*."

"Goodnight, *Shee-cho*."

Sam yawned and then headed for bed. He stripped off his clothes and settled under the blankets, amused by his grandmother's interpretation of what had obviously been a mild case of sunstroke. "Coyote wife," he chuckled. "Don't that beat all?"

He closed his eyes. Unbidden, an image of the coyote formed in his mind. The golden brown eyes drew him in, warm and soft, reflecting near-human intelligence. An unseen emotion hid in their depths, a fiery intensity hinting at passion. Sam rolled over and snorted in disbelief. "You got a wild imagination."

Chapter Three

Nell parted the curtains and peered out the boarding house window.

Daisy nervously paced the room. "Is he still there?"

"He hasn't moved from the spot by the stage depot."

"Do you reckon he's looking for us?"

"He doesn't appear to pay undue attention to anyone, but we dare not linger another day. We're barely over the California line. The longer we dally, the easier it will be for Doyle to find us."

Daisy ran a finger between the wimple and her neck. "Can't I take this contraption off for a stretch? It scratches something fierce."

"Why?" Nell teased. "I think you look charming."

"I don't think I look like much of anything," she grumbled, "except a big pile of laundry. I can barely move confined in all this swaddling."

"Which is why the habit is such an excellent disguise for both of us. Any men hunting for Daisy Tremaine will seek a lovely girl of eighteen with flaxen hair. We can't hide your blue eyes, but no one can determine your face, figure, or age in such a costume."

"I can't argue that point." She eyed the habit with a guilty expression. "You're certain we ain't breaking church law traipsing around in these getups? I don't want God taking me to task for pretending to be one of his own, now that I've turned over a new leaf."

"Whoever walks in integrity walks securely, Proverbs 10:9…Our goals are strictly for the betterment of the people in the territory. I hardly see where God sees fit to complain."

Daisy harrumphed. "I'm with you, Nell, but I reckon the Pope might not agree."

"When the Pope pays a visit to the American West, I'll directly address his concerns."

"Then, I reckon you'll chastise him for thinking women ain't good enough to be priests."

"Naturally."

Daisy cast a hopeful glance toward the window. "Are we safe, yet? We're far from San Francisco now."

"No," Nell stated firmly. "We're only one step ahead of Doyle. The reward he offered for you is substantial. I fear his men aren't far behind us."

Daisy shuddered. "I feel as if eyes bore into the back of my head."

"I agree, but we still have a long journey. I won't rest easy until inside the gates of Fort Braddock." Nell sat on the bed next to Daisy and placed a comforting arm around her shoulders. "You've been very brave throughout this terrible ordeal, but I'm afraid your courage will continue to be tested."

"This ain't nearly as bad as what I went through."

For the first time, Daisy spoke of her former life. "May I ask why you left home? If you don't wish to say…"

"I don't mind telling you, Nell. I reckon you already guessed the worst of it. Ma got sick. She could do nothing but take to her bed. When the whiskey got to Stepdaddy, he told me I had to take her place and satisfy his needs." Her voice dropped to a whisper. "Whiskey got him right often. I couldn't leave. He swore to put a bullet in Ma's head to end her."

Heat rose to her cheeks. "He'd a done it, too. Right after Ma passed, he said I was his now. I saw to her burial and then ran away. I made it to San Francisco, but had no money and couldn't find work. I near starved in the streets until I met Doyle. All I needed to do for him and his guests was what I'd done for Stepdaddy. In exchange, I'd have food, shelter, and nice things around me. I figured it was a fair trade."

Daisy hung her head. "I was wrong. Every night, I took a hot bath in his big claw-foot tub. I'd scrub and scrub and scrub, but the filth didn't wash away."

Nell's heart went out to her. "I'm so sorry. Evil men treated you cruelly."

Daisy's gaze strayed toward the window again. "They're the only kind to want me now. A man's expression changes once he learns I'm a whore. I'm tainted forever."

"Nonsense," Nell said fiercely. "You shan't return to that life, Daisy. I swear a bright future awaits with a good, kind man if you wish it."

"Maybe…" She scrutinized her with a curious look. "How come you ain't married? You're twenty-one, I reckon. Each passing year only sullies your looks."

Nell bit back a grin. "Thank you for pointing that out. It's not that I object to the married state; my parents led a contented life with each other which I freely admit brings envy. Mother was an accomplished writer. My father was a teacher and the first one to sing her praises. He never felt less of a man because of her success. They were so close," she mused, "they even seemed to know each other's thoughts."

Nell started at a sudden pang of hollow emptiness and brushed it away. "Most husbands prefer wives to be decorative and submissive. Men appear to have an irrational fear of a woman who isn't afraid to speak her mind or act of her own accord, as if those characteristics bring manhood into question. I graduated at the top of my class, and yet an education afforded me no added respect. If anything, a woman who held her own in a conversation astounded them."

"How did you end up as a reporter for *The San Francisco Dispatch*?" said Daisy.

"I returned from an exclusive eastern women's college and hoped to use my education and social connections to effect change in the plight of the city's downtrodden inhabitants." Nell sighed. "I can hear Aunt Agatha now. 'Eleanora, I promised your parents before they passed to support your education, but you continue to maintain an unhealthy interest in the most sordid affairs.'"

Daisy raised an eyebrow. "Eleanora?"

Nell cringed. "I always detested the name, but Aunt Agatha insisted 'Nell' was too common. She wanted me to concentrate on suitable marital prospects—of which I'd no interest. We got into a terrible row over Roger Weathersby, a wealthy, handsome bachelor. Whenever she invited him to call, I slipped out the kitchen door."

"Whatever for?" asked Daisy. "He sounds a catch."

"And you sound like Aunt Agatha. I loathed him. Mr. Weathersby's eyes were cold and callous. Aunt Agatha advised if his demeanor was bothersome I should direct my attention elsewhere—perhaps, a potted plant. She offered assurance she had been happily married to my late uncle Henry for over thirty years, and they hardly ever looked at each other."

Daisy giggled. "Aunt Agatha would make a right fine madam." She gasped in horror at her impolite words. "Oh, lordy, I'm sorry."

"Don't apologize for speaking the truth," said Nell with a wicked grin. "I tried to explain I wanted to have my existence count. Poor Aunt Agatha shook her head and heaped blame on the newspapers I trotted into the house, especially *The Dispatch*. She insisted it filled my head with unhealthy ideas. 'Social advocacy will never secure a proper husband' was her advice. Husbands don't approve of women who think."

Nell's eyes flashed. "At that moment, I resolved to no longer drown in the stifling rigidity of Nob Hill society and be relegated to husband-hunting. I marched into Arthur Hollingsworth's office at *The Dispatch* and demanded a job as an investigative reporter. Naturally, he was horrified, but as the niece of one of the most socially prominent women in San Francisco, he could hardly have me forcibly removed. We struck a deal. He gave me one week to write a suitable story. Poor Arthur never expected to see me again. His flabbergasted expression when I returned only five days later was quite heart-wrenching."

Daisy leaned in with an avid expression. "What was the story?"

"Roger Weathersby," Nell admitted with glee. "I disguised myself as a flower girl to talk to his washerwoman, maid, and cook. Neighborhood gossip can be extremely useful. Woman say things to other women they won't tell to men. The washerwoman noted powdery residue on his shirts. The maid said Roger often stayed out all night and returned with dilated pupils. The cook remarked on a decrease in appetite, but a new preference for Chinese tea. After investigating, I discovered he was an opium addict in league with a Chinese tong to smuggle the drug into San Francisco. Arthur hired me at once. Even Aunt Agatha gave grudging approval after viewing a sketch in *The Dispatch* of my potential husband clapped in irons by the authorities. Ah…the stagecoach approaches. Come."

As they grabbed their belongings, Nell's sense of urgency doubled. She never intended to stop, but a storm front delayed their departure, forcing them to take a room at a boarding house. The owner was a garrulous woman full of questions about where two sisters of the cloth were headed. Daisy blurted "Spirit Ridge" before Nell surreptitiously kicked her in the shin to hush.

At once, Nell stated Sister Mary was under the weather and must take to bed for rest. They stayed locked in the room, but the gossipy owner assumed "do not disturb" didn't apply to interruptions from her. The repeated attempts to glean information from Nell at the door on poor Sister Mary's condition were a continued aggravation.

Now, Nell couldn't shake the sensation danger closed in from all sides. The sooner they put this town behind them, the better. As they crossed the street to the stage depot, Nell grabbed Daisy's arm. The man lounging outside peered in their direction. "Keep your head low," she hissed. "Don't let him see your face."

As the stage departed, Nell dared a glance out the window. The man by the depot had disappeared. Nell was uncertain whether to be relieved or disturbed. Either way, she and Daisy were one step closer to Spirit Ridge.

****

Sam awoke the next morning after a dreamless night, strangely disappointed no vision of the coyote disturbed his sleep. He ate a quick breakfast, pleased his grandfather's face had regained color. Lenna Tanner's healing worked its own special magic.

When Jeb rode in with the wounded Earl, he also brought Rio, Sam's palomino stallion. Sam saddled him for the ride to town. As he gave him an affectionate pat on the neck, the young, sturdy pinto that carried Sam and Frank with ease nosed in for attention. He scratched her ear. "Happy here? Good. Your last owner has no call to complain if I keep you, seeing as how you're unbranded and he's dead and all." The mare whickered and nuzzled his shoulder.

Spirit Ridge was less than half an hour by horseback, but today's ride took longer. Sam detoured on a well-worn path to his glen. His grandparents set aside the land for Joseph and his wife and then deeded it to Sam when he came of age. He dismounted and gazed with satisfaction at the surroundings.

Cream-colored bluffs dotted with junipers and piñon pines rimmed the center range. In the spring, the ground erupted with fresh, sweet grasses to nourish Sam's own herd. He envisioned Mexican gold poppies and purple lupine spreading a carpet of vibrant colors unlike now when blazing tones of autumn tinted the leaves.

Sam ambled past a stand of dewberry trees to a natural spring shaded by cottonwoods and willows. Cool, clear water splashed from limestone rocks to a deep pond ringed by lush ferns and bracken. Sam crouched, and then cupped his hands to bring a drink to his lips. He leaned his head back, smiling as the cool liquid trickled down his throat.

He wasn't the only passerby to slake a thirst. Pressed into the dirt were the tracks of raccoon and deer. Sam ran his fingertips across fresh paw prints from a bobcat. His tracker's skill read the story etched into the ground. The creature stopped to drink and then bounded away, startled by the sound of a human's approach.

A puff of wind scattered the leaves at his feet. Sam rose and strolled straight toward the bluffs as if someone called his name. Inset against the rocks was the dale, bathed in sunshine, but protected from the harshest weather. Beneath a wooden cross in the shade of an old cottonwood Alice Tanner lay in eternal rest.

Her son removed his hat and knelt to pull a few weeds from her grave. He reached into his jacket pocket and retrieved a rose, cut that morning from the bush Alice had so carefully tended. Sam placed the bloom against the cross. He closed his eyes, enjoying the quiet serenity. His mother's loving voice was in the rustle of the breeze through the treetops, her gentle touch in the soft grass. No other place brought the same sense of peace. His grandmother said Alice Tanner's kindly spirit stayed to watch over her son. Perhaps, *Shee-cho* was right. If spirits lived after death, then surely hers resided here.

With one last wistful gaze, Sam mounted Rio and

then rode into town. He caught sight of Jeb leading a horse from the barn at Mateo's blacksmith shop. Jeb eyed the marshal's badge and paled. "Is Frank—"

"Sitting pretty at home," Sam assured him. "He's healing, but needs a few days to get on his feet."

Relief washed over Jeb's face. "That's good news. I checked on Earl this morning. He's mad enough to spit nails because Miss Lenna forbade his missus to allow him any whiskey before breakfast."

Sam snorted. "I reckon he's on the mend, too."

Jeb shook his head. "Luck was truly with us, Sam. We should never have gone after McLaren and the others with only four men."

"Every one of us is alive. That's all that matters."

"Can't argue that. The outlaws' bodies are buried in the cemetery. Gates' horse is in Mateo's barn." Jeb patted his horse's nose. "This here belonged to one of the Sutton boys. He's got no brand or bill of sale. I have a mind to keep him."

Sam shrugged. "Suits me. I'm keeping the pinto. We'll give the other to Earl's wife as payment for having to listen to his complaints. I'll wire Prescott to let them know of the deaths. We'll split any reward among us four."

"Thanks, Sam. I appreciate it."

A strident whirr from the smithy signaled the blacksmith hard at work. Sam dismounted and led Rio to the barn. Mateo Perez bent over a grinding wheel sharpening an ax.

"*Buenos dias*, Mat."

The smith called a friendly greeting. Although the same age as Sam, his heavily muscled arms dwarfed the marshal's lithe athletic build.

Mateo asked after Frank. His expression of concern lessened as Sam brought him up to date. "Jeb passed word from Miss Lenna that he'd mend, but I'll go by later today to visit. You should have stood by for my return. Earl is the worse shot in the county."

"Couldn't. Grandpa was hellbent to get going."

"Glad to hear he'll make a full recovery. Simply because I have my own business now doesn't mean you can't ask for my help."

"Your business, Mat?" Sam joshed. "Ain't you getting ahead of yourself? Or did the bank manager take one look at your charming smile and waive years of payments?"

"*Si*, my smile is most charming, but sadly, the bank manager is not impressed." Mateo looked around with pride. "My name is not on the title, yet, *amigo*, but my sweat and blood are most definitely written on the walls, so I'll call this little place my own." Mateo wiped his hand on a rag and then leaned over to open the lid of a battered storage crate. He pulled out a saddle bag and tossed it to Sam. "Belongings of the late unlamented Sutton brothers."

Sam unbuckled the strap and peered inside. "They sure traveled light. Twenty dollar gold pieces and enough food for another day on the trail, same as what the pinto's bag held."

"This, too." Mateo dug out several cartridge boxes with U.S. Army stamped on the side. "Where did they get Army ammunition? From McLaren? He used to be a scout."

"Not likely. This box is brand new, never opened, and McLaren ain't been near Army compounds for a while." Sam tossed back the saddlebag. "Keep it and the money, too. Consider it the Suttons' payment for tending to their horses. Coin won't do them any good where they rest now."

"True." Mateo crossed himself. "Money can't buy your way into heaven or your way out of hell."

Along with the forge, Mateo had stalls and a corral for boarding. Sam secured Rio and then went to the marshal's office. The one-story wooden building sat in the center of town. It had a single jail cell and a small room in the rear where Sam slept when they had prisoners or he chose to bunk in town.

No one was incarcerated at the moment, not that a place with a population of less than two hundred sported a huge criminal element. Offenses consisted of the occasional mischief maker or a cowboy burning off steam on Saturday night who overdid it on whiskey. The good folks of Spirit Ridge didn't cotton to rowdiness and expected their marshal and deputy to ensure every evening brought peaceful slumber. Frank Tanner saw to that. Men even checked their guns before getting a drink at Mrs. Bonifay's boarding house, the largest building in town. Trouble usually meant nothing more than breaking up a fistfight—at least, until McLaren and the others arrived.

Sam sat at the desk and riffled through the stack of wanted posters. Most had only names and descriptions, sketches were rare. He hadn't noticed before, but several general alerts in the Territory mentioned dark-shirted riders spotted near the scenes of recent train robberies. Railroad employees had been killed. The outlaws even ambushed and murdered a posse. Was McLaren responsible? Sam shook his head. The attacks were close together in time, but the distances too far apart for responsibility to fall solely with McLaren, Gates, and the Suttons.

He drummed his fingers atop the pile of papers with an uneasy feeling. The marauders' actions were vicious and cold-blooded as if they wanted no witnesses. Their violence sure made the railroad nervous. Burlington Northern Santa Fe posted a large reward for their capture. The inhabitants of Spirit Ridge pressed for an extension of the rail line from Prescott, not likely if railroad officials saw trouble in the area.

Sam walked to the telegraph and sent a wire to the territorial governor's office in Prescott alerting them of the deaths of the Sutton brothers and Gates. He spent the remainder of the morning sweeping up and handling other chores around the jail. His grandfather expected a tidy workplace on his return or Sam's ears would burn.

At noon, Sam ambled over to Bonifay's Boarding House for a meal. He considered returning home to see his grandfather, but might miss the stage. Then he debated skipping food altogether. The gunfight with the McLaren gang stirred the populace more than anything else in recent months, and Mrs. Bonifay was always eager for gossip. If he didn't show up to eat, she'd accost him in the marshal's office.

In his straightforward, matter-of-fact style, Sam related to the boarders the details of the shootout with full understanding that whatever he said didn't matter. The facts would be twisted into fable from one end of town to the other by nightfall, embroidered with the ebullient Mrs. Bonifay's colorful narrative.

"We were so worried when you chased after McLaren's gang," she gushed, "especially my Martha." Martha cleared dishes from the table. She stopped to glare at her mother and then flounced from the room.

Sam glowered at his plate and stifled a groan. Upon Martha Bonifay's eighteenth birthday last year, her widowed mother decided the time had come for her to wed Sam. Both his and Martha's individual desires were of no account.

"Martha was all fluttery, Sam, to hear how you set yourself in danger. Her heart palpitations were fierce. Why, I almost went to call on Mrs. Tanner for a calming potion, but Martha was set against it. The poor girl insisted she was perfectly well."

Because the palpitations were nothing but your fancies. Martha knew my grandmother would slap you silly and then order you to stop throwing your daughter at me as if she were a Kansas City whore.

Sam quickly finished eating and returned to the marshal's office. Mrs. Bonifay's aggressive approach to her daughter's matrimony made him downright aggravated in the woman's presence. Not that Martha had anything wrong with her other than an overbearing mother. She was a nice enough gal as were the few single women in town and the others on the farms and ranches in the county. Plenty made it plain they weren't averse to attention from Deputy Sam Tanner, but none caught more than his passing fancy.

Leaning back in the chair, Sam propped his feet up on the desk and clasped his hands behind his head. It's not that he was against marriage. His parents had a brief, but loving union. Frank and Lenna Tanner also had a fierce bond. He couldn't imagine being that way with any of the women around here. A spark of yearning lit inside for someone of his own, surprising him by its intensity. Lately, he spent more nights in town, thinking about building his own place at the glen. He had saved enough money. Maybe it was time to settle down, except nowhere in Spirit Ridge was a coyote whose eyes held sparks of gold.

Sam jerked upright, slamming his feet to the floor, and nearly upsetting the chair. "What the hell kind of thoughts got in your head. A coyote?" He blew out a disgusted snort. "You're a damn fool, Sam Tanner." He checked the hour on his pocket watch. Close to two o'clock. The stage would arrive at any time.

He ambled to the depot. Thirty minutes later, a cloud of dust from the stage kicked up on the horizon. The driver pulled the team to a halt in front of him.

"I'm expecting arrivals," Sam called. "Anyone on board?"

"Nope. Nothing but mail today." He tossed him a sack and then slapped the reins against the horses' rumps.

Sam's irritation rose. The hunt for McLaren was delayed again. The mysterious passengers proved to be nothing but trouble.

Chapter Four

The stage hit a rut, and Daisy groaned. "Lordy, my nethers ache from this jostling."

Nell patted her arm. "Try to rest. We'll be in Spirit Ridge in a few hours."

In truth, after many days of hard travel, her nethers also screamed in distress. Nell shifted to find a comfortable positon. Daisy was right. The habit was a miserable contraption.

Her thoughts drifted to her early days at *The Dispatch*, detailing the lives of the downtrodden. She took to wearing a nun's habit and calling herself Sister Regina. Most criminals respected the cloth, and the disguise allowed her to move safely in the roughest parts of town. The hidden pocket with the derringer was an extra precaution that served her well on several occasions.

As Sister Regina, she befriended prostitutes in San Francisco's red light district, offering a free meal and a sympathetic ear. In return, she listened to their woeful tales. Among those fallen women, she first heard the name The Mick whispered in fear. Nell pieced together scraps of information to outline his web of corruption.

Rumors linked the crime lord's activities with Colin Doyle, a respectable businessman, whose deep pockets opened wide for influential men. Doyle's path even crossed once with Nell on a trip to the opera with

Aunt Agatha. She at once categorized Doyle as a person who made social connections only to curry favor. Nell made a point to avoid his attention. Fortunately, he had no interest in a woman who refused to cling decoratively to his arm.

Nell's investigation progressed. The trail of Doyle's money and The Mick's criminal activities so entwined, she became convinced the two men were the same. Recently, Doyle's interest focused on the Arizona Territory. Men of the Burlington Northern Santa Fe Railroad which ran track through the area were frequent visitors to his home. If Doyle's sights turned southeast, then The Mick's had, too. All Nell lacked was proof. She unearthed the name of Daisy Tremaine. If anyone had evidence of Doyle and The Mick's connection, it was The Mick's newest mistress.

Daisy confirmed Nell's suspicions—Colin Doyle was The Mick. What Nell hadn't suspected, until hearing Daisy's story, was how far his treachery extended and how many innocents would die if they failed to reach Fort Braddock in time.

The stage slowed. "Spirit Ridge!" yelled the driver.

At last. Nell heaved a sigh. Another few hours, and they'd be behind the walls of Fort Braddock.

****

Sam paced in front of the depot, his mood as dark as the heavy clouds scudding across the sky. He pulled his collar tight as the wind whipped down the street. Scattered drops pattered to the ground sending passersby scurrying for cover. He'd met every stage for days, but none carried the mysterious passengers. Meanwhile, Reese McLaren slipped farther away. Sam glowered as a cloud of dust along the trail signaled the approach of Wells Fargo.

"Two for Spirit Ridge," the driver called as he reined in the team of horses.

The stage rolled to a stop. The drawn shades on the windows hid a view of the occupants. Sam opened the door and offered his hand. He gaped in astonishment as a girl in a black nun's habit with a carpet bag clambered to the street. She arched her back and groaned, "Sweet Jesus, my arse is sore."

"Sister Mary!" A sharp rebuke came from inside.

The nun flushed. "Begging your pardon. I-I meant, lordy, what a smarting ride."

Movement stirred within the stage. Sam offered another hand. "Allow me."

"Thank you." Strong soft fingers rested in his callused palm. A second nun with a satchel jumped lightly to the ground and dusted off her habit. She lifted her gaze. From beneath the veil, two brown eyes with flecks of gold peered into Sam's stunned face.

Suspicion instantly colored the nun's expression. She yanked her hand from his and shoved it into a pocket as if searching for something. "You're not Frank Tanner," she said in a decisive tone. "You're much too young to have served with Arthur Hollingsworth in the Yucatan. Who are you?"

Sam gawked at her, drawn in by the spark in her eyes. *How could it be?* "Pardon me, ma'am." He swallowed hard and tipped his hat. "My name is Sam Tanner. Frank is my grandfather. He's recovering from wounds. I'm acting marshal." He showed her the telegram. "I promised to meet the stage and get you settled."

The nun relaxed. "I see." Her hand came out of the

pocket.

"Giddup!"

From above came the clipped command from the driver and the flick of the reins. The stagecoach rolled out leaving the two women with Sam.

"We can't stay, Marshal. I am Sister Regina. Sister Mary and I must leave now for Fort Braddock. I expected your grandfather to guide us. I assume you can do the same."

Sam eyed her in disbelief. "Sister, you're talking a good thirty miles over rough country, and the weather don't bode well." He motioned to the two carpetbags at their feet. "Not to mention daylight is failing, and you ain't exactly packed for a hard ride."

"Thirty miles?" she murmured. "I didn't realize the distance was so considerable."

"A rail spur will shorten the trip," drawled Sam, "but until the railroad has a mind to build us one, we've nothing but trails between here and Fort Braddock."

Sister Mary pulled on her sleeve. "Please Ne—I mean, Sister Regina. Can't we rest for a spell? I'm plum wore out."

"You know that's not possible," she said firmly. "Marshal, how far can we go in the daylight left?"

He eyed her aghast. "You can't walk to Fort Braddock."

"Of course not. Do you have a livery? We'll obtain horses." Beside her, Sister Mary groaned.

"Mateo Perez is the blacksmith. He keeps horses to hire out, but—"

"Excellent. Take us there."

His irritation rose. Didn't she understand? "Ma'am, you can't—"

She picked up one of the carpetbags at her feet. "Now, if you please. Come, Sister."

Sam planted himself in her path. "Why the all-fire hurry to reach Fort Braddock?"

"Church business."

"Church business with the cavalry?" He gave a disbelieving snort. "There ain't a mission at Fort Braddock. Want to tell me what you're really doing here?"

"I can only say it's imperative Sister Mary and I reach Fort Braddock. I'm not at liberty to discuss the situation until then."

"Sister, I need more than that or you won't go anywhere. The country around here ain't easy on folks such as you. I gave my word to my grandpa and have a responsibility for your safety."

Sister Regina peered at him, studying his face as if to judge his character. The fire in the golden brown eyes dimmed. Undisguised sympathy took its place. "Forgive my brusqueness, Marshal Tanner. I understand the heavy burden of responsibility. I must hand deliver an important package to the commander at Fort Braddock. We have to leave quickly and not draw attention."

"You're in trouble."

"Yes. That's all I can say. Will you help me?" She didn't blink or drop her gaze. "Please."

Help me, It'sa.

The coyote's plea rang in his ears. The wind kicked up swirls of dust along the street. Thunder rumbled overhead. Fort Braddock was impossible today, but no point arguing in the rain. Mat would back him up. Sam snatched the satchels from the two sisters. "We can't make plans here. I'll take you to the livery." Her relieved smile sent a rush of unforeseen warmth.

"Come, Sister Mary," she said.

"I'm coming, I'm coming," Sister Mary grumbled, hitching up her tunic to trot alongside.

The two nuns scampered to keep up with his long legs. Sister Regina cleared her throat. "Forgive me for being so short, Marshal. Travel has worn on both Sister Mary and me. I should have asked after your grandfather's condition. How is he?"

"He'll mend, thanks," he said gruffly.

"May I ask who shot him?"

Sam pulled up short and stared at her. "I didn't tell you that. I said he was wounded."

"For a marshal, wounds imply gunshots. Otherwise, you would have been more specific as to the nature of his injuries."

Sister Mary broke out in a giggle. "She's a slick one, Marshal. Can't pull nothing over her. Not even Bart—" She clapped her lips shut and flushed.

Sister Regina shot her companion a hard look. "Sister Mary, I believe it is time for your period of silent contemplation. Forgive her exuberance, Marshal. She is young and new to the veil. You were saying about your grandfather…"

"We were in a posse trailing Reese McLaren and three others and had an exchange of gunfire."

"McLaren? I saw the name on a wanted poster when we entered the Territory. He has a fearful reputation as a gun for hire. What happened to the outlaws?"

"All dead, except for McLaren."

To his surprise, she nodded approval. "My

respects, Marshal. Surviving such a confrontation with no casualties is an accomplishment."

Sam arched his brow. "That's mighty generous praise for a woman of the cloth."

Sister Regina's composure appeared to slip and then she flashed a beneficent smile. "Psalm 106:3—blessed are they who maintain justice; who constantly do what is right…so Marshal, what of McLaren?"

"He got away and headed north. I aimed to pick up his trail again, but…" He glanced at her carpetbag. "I got sidetracked."

"My apologies for causing a delay in your duties. Perhaps the law will catch up with McLaren and save you the trouble."

"I hope not, ma'am." A fierce light shone in his eye. "His bullet wounded my grandpa. We got a score."

"Then I shouldn't wish to be in Reese McLaren's boots when you find him. Not one bit."

The little coyote had a bite. Sam's lips twitched in a grin at the passionate intensity of her words. The rain turned into a steady downpour, and they jogged the last few steps to Mateo's barn.

"*Hola*, Mat," Sam called.

The blacksmith stepped from behind a wagon with a missing wheel. "Back so soon, I—" He stopped short, gaping at the trio. "*Hermanas?*" Surprise switched to amusement. "What trouble did you get into, my friend, to need the help of not one, but two spiritual guides?"

Sister Mary giggled and eyed Mateo's bulging muscles with undisguised approval. "Nothing you couldn't handle, I reckon."

"That will do, Sister Mary," Sister Regina hissed. Sister Mary lowered her gaze to her shoes and blushed.

Sam made introductions. "The sisters just came off the stage and need to secure rides to Fort Braddock."

Mateo's obvious astonishment amused him. "Today? Impossible. The sun is nearly gone, and the weather isn't fit for travel."

"We must leave town," insisted Sister Regina. "We can spend the night outdoors."

"Sam, please tell me you play a joke on your friend."

"No joke. Sister Regina insists they must get to Fort Braddock with due haste. I promised an escort, and explained the impossibility of going today, but she's fixed in her intent. Perhaps, you can talk sense to her."

Mateo shot him a helpless look. "Other than Rio, the only horses I have to lend at the moment are my own and one that belonged to a Sutton. Both are spirited."

"I prefer a spirited mount," announced Sister Regina without a shred of concern.

Sister Mary showed less enthusiasm. She pulled on her companion's sleeve with an air of distress. "I can't ride a horse."

"You can't?"

For a moment, Sam held the irrational notion Sister Regina wished to let loose with an impious expletive.

"No, and my rump—" Sister Mary flushed. "That is to say, my lower parts are still mighty tormented from the jostling in the stagecoach."

Mateo motioned to the wagon missing a wheel. "I won't finish the repairs for several hours. You can leave in the morning."

A flash of lightning lit the barn. "That settles it," said Sam. "It's too dangerous to head out now. By tomorrow, the storm will pass. Rest up tonight, and we'll leave at first light with the wagon."

Mateo smiled at Sister Mary. "I am happy to escort you to Bonifay's Boarding House."

The two nuns exchanged nervous glances. "We mustn't be seen—" said Sister Regina.

"Yoo-hoo, Marshal." A strident call came from outside.

Sam glowered. "Mrs. Bonifay must have heard rumor of new arrivals. Nothing much in town gets by her."

Sister Regina's pleading eyes sought his. "We don't wish to answer questions."

Sam raised an eyebrow. What tricks was coyote up to? He turned to Mateo. "They need to hide."

With a puzzled expression, Mateo gestured toward the rear of the barn. "The stall next to Rio is empty."

Sam grabbed the carpetbags and hustled away the two women. They crouched in the straw.

Footsteps scuffled across the entrance. "Where is Sam?"

"*Buenos tardes,* Señora Bonifay. *Lo siento,* but I haven't seen him since early today."

"I happened to peer out my window this afternoon," came the pointed retort, "and noticed Sam at the depot. He appeared to await the stage. I swear I saw the feet of a woman disembark, but the view was obstructed. Martha called me away, so I can't be sure."

Sister Regina leaned toward Sam and whispered lightly, "Does this Martha approve of Mrs. Bonifay spying on the neighbors?"

"No one cottons to it," Sam whispered back, "but try telling that to Mrs. Bonifay."

"I went to the marshal's office," continued Mrs. Bonifay. "If a new arrival requires lodging, then I certainly need to know." The tenor of her voice dripped disapproval. "The door was locked. I pounded heartily and shouted, but no one answered."

"Is that a fact?" Mateo's tone was indifferent. "Then I suspect he wasn't there."

She drew herself up with indignation. "It's hardly proper for Sam to entertain a female guest in his quarters. I have my daughter's reputation to protect." A loud clap of thunder interrupted her protest.

"I reckon God just put in his two cents," murmured Sister Mary.

"Storm is breaking," said Mateo. "Best hurry home before you get drenched."

"When you see Sam, send him to me." Mrs. Bonifay's voice faded away. "I'll get to the bottom of this."

Mateo shut the large barn door behind her. "She's gone. You can come out."

Sister Mary chuckled. "You sure that door is strong enough to keep out the vermin?" Mateo flashed a grin.

Sister Regina's expression filled with sympathy. "Marshal Tanner, if Mrs. Bonifay is your future mother-in-law may God go with you, my son."

"Amen," giggled Sister Mary.

A flush crept up Sam's neck. "I have no designs on Martha," he spit out between gritted teeth, "despite her mother's notion to the contrary."

Mateo's grin broadened. "Mrs. Bonifay's disapproval of Marshal Tanner's bachelorhood is a constant source of amusement."

"For you," growled Sam.

"Since the boarding house is not a good choice," Mateo said, "where will you put your guests for the night?"

Sam rubbed his chin. "It's too far to ride in this storm to my grandparents' place. They can have my room behind the jail."

"Across from the boarding house?"

"Where Mrs. Bonifay has one eye out the window watching for your arrival," said Sister Regina. "We're safer here and will sleep in the stable."

Sister Mary wore a look of undisguised horror. "Nel—I mean Sister Regina, I reckon we can make it to the marshal's quarters without being seen."

"We can't take the chance. We won't be the first to sleep in a manger."

The nun wrinkled her brow in a puzzled frown. "A what?"

"Manger…stable…" She cleared her throat. "Like our good Lord…at Christmas."

"Oh, yes. The baby Jesus." Sister Mary crossed herself and lowered her eyes.

"I can't allow that, sisters," said Mateo. "My cabin is across the yard. You stay there. I'll sleep in the barn."

Sister Mary flashed a grateful smile. "That's right kind of you, Mr. Perez." Her voice betrayed a hint of melancholy. "Such courtesy is rare where I hail from."

They dashed through the rain as lightning crackled across the sky. The cabin sat next to a vegetable garden. Beyond was a chicken coop. Mateo's tidy one room house held a bed, table and chairs, and a woodstove for cooking and heating. He shuffled his feet. "My apologies, sisters. I wish I could offer better."

"It's right nice," burst out Sister Mary in protest,

"Cozy like." She eyed the shelves around the stove stacked with basics such as cornmeal and coffee, a few battered pots and pans and chipped enamelware. Her face took on a wistful expression. "I can't imagine anything finer than a place to call your own." Sister Regina gave her arm a comforting squeeze.

Sam motioned to Mateo. "We'll let the sisters get settled. I'll help with the wagon." The marshal paused at the threshold. For an instant, his gaze locked with Sister Regina's. Her brown eyes beckoned to him.

She's a nun. Get the hell out of here before you say something you'll regret.

He tipped his hat. "Ma'am." The door shut behind them.

Chapter Five

Mateo pulled at Sam's sleeve as they entered the barn. "Now, tell me what the hell is going on."

"I showed you the telegram days ago. That's everything I know."

He raised a disbelieving eyebrow. "These two nuns are the mysterious passengers Frank asked you to help? You aren't acquainted with Sister Regina? Your demeanor says you've met before today."

Sam shrugged, uncomfortable with Mateo's questions. The last thing he wished to discuss was the nun. "No. She must seem familiar, somehow."

Mateo opened his eyes wide with understanding. "You had another vision."

Sam stifled a groan. After Mateo was orphaned, he lived with the Tanners before striking out on his own. They became as close as brothers, and other than his grandparents, he was the one person Sam confided in about the visions. Mateo professed more faith in them than he ever did.

"It weren't nothing," Sam protested. "Only a dream of a coyote with brown eyes."

"That's all?"

His boot scuffed the dirt. "She may have had a woman's voice and asked for help."

"Visions aren't nothing," he scolded. "They're sent for a reason."

"What do you know? You ain't Apache."

Mateo shrugged. "Apache or Christian, what does it matter? God is God. In Christianity, God sends visions to saints. They're a gift meant to help guide others."

"I ain't no saint," Sam said dryly.

"With that, I won't argue." He rubbed his chin. "The spirits sent you a message to help this woman. What did your grandmother say?"

"She's already planning the wedding." Sam chuckled ruefully. "I look forward to the sight of her face when I explain a woman who took a vow of celibacy left the stage."

"Ah…you're distressed by her religious calling."

"No."

"You're a dreadful poor liar, *amigo*. You hoped your grandmother was right and greatly wished to see the coyote-woman with the brown eyes. They are most fetching, don't you think?" Mateo scratched his head. "The little one…Sister Mary…she doesn't speak as a woman of the cloth. She also crossed herself wrong."

"What do you mean?"

"The sign of the cross is always up-down-left-right. She made it down-right-left-up."

Sam raised an eyebrow. "Is there a difference?"

"Not to you, but as a young child I remember being severely chastised by a nun at the mission when I incorrectly made the sign."

"You sure she didn't reprimand you for something else?" joshed Sam. "You were quite the scurrilous ragamuffin when we met. As I recollect, you tried to steal my horse. Weren't there any to steal in Mexico?"

"*Es posible*, but I was no longer in Mexico. When I

54

tired of being a starving orphan begging for scraps in the streets of Nogales, I decided to head north and become a wealthy desperado instead."

"A twelve-year-old desperado?"

"Everyone must start somewhere, and even then I saw the horse was a fine animal and would fetch a good price. Fortunately, your grandparents caught me and amended my disreputable nature to leave only my innate charm." Mateo's expression turned serious. "All I'm saying is Sister Mary's actions are strange."

Sam peered through the rain to the little cabin. "They're hiding something, that's for sure. Why the damn rush to deliver a package to Fort Braddock?"

Mat followed his gaze. "Why the secrecy?"

"The answer is plain. They're on the run."

"Who wishes harm to nuns?"

"I've no idea."

Mateo clapped him on the shoulder. "You won't find the answers staring into the rain. Why don't you talk to Sister Regina again? Find out who or what is behind this."

"Wheedle a confession from her?" he scoffed. "Not with that one." One glimpse into those eyes had led Sam to a core of rock-hard stubbornness—the same as all the other Tanner women. Sam gritted his teeth, wanting to kick himself for thinking such a thing. She could never be a Tanner woman. "I'll help you with the wagon, instead. It'll take my mind off things."

"Like a pair of brown eyes?" Mateo flashed an impish grin. "God will not judge you kindly for lusting after one of his handmaidens."

"Now is a good time for you to take a vow of silence."

Sam shoved Sister Regina from his mind. For a while, work proved a distraction until his gaze strayed once more toward Mateo's cabin. Unbidden, the vision of the coyote rose to mind.

Confident, smart, clever. One who fights if need be, but prefers to use wiles instead of fang and claw. An animal easily killed by one bullet from a well-aimed gun. Then the eyes shut forever. The vision ended in death as the others.

Icy cold rippled through Sam, near stealing his breath. Not while he had life left in him. He made a promise to those eyes. No matter Sister Regina had no place in his life, he vowed to see her safely to Fort Braddock. God help any man who stood in his way.

****

When Nell and the marshal's gazes met on the doorstep, unbidden warmth rushed to her cheeks. She shut the door behind the two men, leaned against the wall, and slowly exhaled. His demeanor created the most intensely pleasant sensation that continued to linger in her middle.

Daisy ran a finger between her neck and the edge of the wimple. "Can I take this thing off now? My head itches something fierce."

Nell chuckled. "Mine, too."

Daisy unpinned the veil, and Nell helped remove the scapular and unfasten the wimple. Golden locks tumbled past Daisy's shoulders. Nell discarded her own headpiece and shook wavy brown tresses free. Both women gave a good scratch and then together heaved a sigh of relief.

"I don't understand how nuns can wear such contraptions all day long," Daisy grumped.

Nell winked. "Priests invented them to keep the sisters in line."

"I reckon you're right. Men delight in making life a misery for women."

Unconsciously, Nell's attention drifted toward the door. "Not all."

Daisy followed her gaze. "They sure were gentlemanly. You fixing to tell the marshal the truth? I do believe he's a good man and can be trusted."

"You seem convinced."

"He's got a look when talking to you, Nell—a queer look as if the marshal knows you already. I think he likes what he sees even though you're practically swaddled as a newborn babe in that getup." Daisy stared at the ceiling with an innocent expression on her face. She rocked back and forth on her heels. "I think you like what you see in him, too," she said in a sing-song voice.

"Really, Daisy," Nell scolded, "you've spent too much of your young life in bad company and talk too freely."

"That don't mean I'm wrong. I know bad men. I knew Colin Doyle was plumb evil as soon as we met, but when you're drowning and a man throws you a rope, you don't let go just because it's covered in shit." She cleared her throat. "Beg pardon."

Nell's lips twitched in a smile. "Nevertheless, for the moment the mission must be kept to ourselves. You understand what's at stake. We have no clue where the true loyalties of Marshal Tanner or Mr. Perez lie. Don't forget, Doyle offered five thousand dollars for your head. You must promise not to breathe a word to either one, no matter how kindly they speak."

Daisy's expression clouded over. "You're right about that. Money can make even good folk do unspeakable things."

Nell glanced at the stove. "I could do with a cup of coffee."

"Me, too. I'll get the fire going." As the coffee brewed, Daisy looked through the foodstuffs on the shelves. "Why don't we fix dinner? It's the least we can do for the trouble caused. Ma always said I was a right fine cook."

"That's an excellent idea. I see beans and bacon." Nell hefted a sack of cornmeal. "I'll make cornbread."

"I declare," Daisy teased. "A rich city gal who gets her hands dirty?"

"I haven't lived my whole life in San Francisco. When I was a child, my father took a teaching position near San Diego. My parents and I spent several years on a small spread where I learned to ride and shoot. According to Aunt Agatha, those rough years ruined any hope of turning me into a proper young lady of society."

"What are those?" Daisy pointed to a long string of green peppers hanging from a nail on the wall.

Nell's eyes lit up. "Jalapeños!" She pulled one off the string and handed it to Daisy. "The peppers are popular in Mexican dishes. Our housekeeper, Señora Suarez, was an exceptional cook and often used them. I loved to help her in the kitchen. She gave me her recipes when I left. She mixed roasted jalapeños into the cornbread. They add a pleasant bite."

Before Nell stopped her, Daisy bit off the tip and chewed. Her eyes widened to the size of saucers. She stuck out her tongue and fanned it in a frenzy. "My mouf's on fire."

Nell chuckled. "It'll pass. I said the peppers had a bite."

"You're going to put that in the cornbread? That's more punishment than recipe."

"Once I remove the seeds, the heat is less intense. Don't get the juice on an open cut or in your eyes though. You'll never erase the memory."

Daisy wiped the sweat from her brow. "I'll start on the bacon and beans. They won't try to kill me."

"You sound like Aunt Agatha. I once took her to dine at my favorite Chinese restaurant in San Francisco where I was particularly partial to the hot and sour soup. After Aunt Agatha sampled a spoonful, she appeared to speak in tongues, and then bounded from her chair, and drained the water glasses of several astonished patrons." Nell sighed. "It was a most unpleasant evening."

****

As darkness fell, the men headed to the cabin. Mateo inhaled and arched his eyebrows in surprise. "Something smells good." As they wiped their boots on the scraper, the door opened. Sister Mary had a basket hooked over one arm. "The eggs got used in the cornbread, so I'm fetching more. If that's agreeable with you, Mr. Perez?" She smiled shyly. Her headpiece was gone. Could anyone have guessed lustrous golden curls hid underneath it?

Clearly not Mateo.

"You look like an angel," he blurted. Sister Mary blushed. "I-I mean, forgive me, Sister," he fumbled and then took the basket from her arm. "Allow me to fetch them for you."

"Sister, wait!" Sister Regina hurried outside with the wimple. "We didn't expect you to return so soon."

Her headpiece was also discarded. Sam drew in a breath at the sight of brown locks with a glint of gold. He imagined fingers running through their silky perfection before mortification stopped him. *She's a nun, for pity's sake.*

"Please excuse us while we prepare," said Sister Regina to her companion. Sister Mary continued to smile at Mateo and did not appear inclined to move.

"Ahem," said Sister Regina sharply. Color rising to her cheeks, Sister Mary backed away and shut the door.

Mateo let out a long slow breath. "She's so young and beautiful. I swear no more than eighteen. Why does such perfection become a nun?" He shook his head and muttered, "I shouldn't have such impure thoughts."

Sam elbowed him in the side and whispered, "Now who's going to hell?"

"Both of us, my friend, if we aren't careful."

Sam stood on the porch while Mateo fetched the eggs. By the time he returned, the two sisters had secured their wimples. Sam experienced irrational anger at the headpiece. He wanted to tear it from Sister Regina and free her tresses from wrongful imprisonment.

"Will you stay for dinner, Marshal?" she asked.

Her gaze froze the words in his throat. Heat rose in his loins. Damn it…why did this unattainable woman cause such a sinful reaction? "That's kind of you, ma'am," he said in a rush, "but I best go to the office. I'll be here before first light so we can get an early start."

"I'll see you tomorrow, then. Goodnight, Marshal,

and thank you again for your help."

Sam tipped his hat. "Ma'am." He strode from the cabin before all common sense deserted him. He drew deep breaths, striving to bury lustful desire for Sister Regina. Tomorrow, he'd escort the two nuns to Fort Braddock, and they'd be gone from his life forever.

Forever. A dull malaise settled on Sam's shoulders.

As soon as he entered the marshal's office, Mrs. Bonifay hustled over with an invitation to supper. Sam declined, and she proceeded to grill him on his afternoon whereabouts. "I've kept an eye peeled. You were gone a long time without so much as a sign on the door."

Sam explained with a straight face he checked on his grandfather and denied meeting anyone at the stage. He showed Mrs. Bonifay to the door, but the gossipy harridan didn't appear satisfied. He half-expected her to demand to search his quarters. Sam locked the door behind her, relieved the sisters hadn't agreed to spend the night in his room. No doubt Mrs. Bonifay would perch at the window of the boarding house until dawn to keep a suspicious eye on him. The quicker the nuns were gone, the better.

Didn't he mean, the quicker Sister Regina left town, the better?

Strangely depressed, Sam sat at the desk and ate a can of cold beans before retiring to his room. He didn't bother to light the kerosene lamp, but stripped off his clothes, and lay on the bed. With hands clasped behind his head, Sam stared mindlessly at the ceiling. He closed his eyes and easily envisioned Sister Regina and her wavy brown hair.

He sighed. Sleep would not come easily this

evening.

****

It'sa stretched his wings, riding the updraft. The sun's rays beat upon his feathers as he reveled in unfettered freedom. To the west was Spirit Ridge. Razor-sharp eyes combed the deserted countryside around the town. No…not quite empty. Far below, a subtle movement brought his instantaneous attention. A hare poked its nose from a burrow. Ears twitching, it sniffed the air, but the scent of the eagle was too distant to warn of danger. It hopped into the open.

Hunger ignited the craving for blood. Wings back, It'sa dove—noiseless death from the sky. A shrill scream from the hare pierced the silence, and then talons and beak tore effortlessly through flesh. As meat ripped from bone, he gave thanks to the Great Spirit for the gift of the animal's life. In due time, nothing remained. It'sa groomed the blood from his feathers and then spread his wings to once again take to his solitary rule of the heavens.

"Help me, It'sa."

From the top of a hill, a coyote peered into the distance. She let loose with a mournful howl, demanding attention. "They are coming."

It'sa screeched in anger, flapping his wings. The coyote was an intruder, distracting him from the beckoning skies. He ignored her call and launched into the heavens while her brown eyes tracked his path. It'sa paid her no mind and circled higher and higher until the coyote was a solitary dot on the landscape. The eagle caught and held an updraft. As he banked toward the rising sun, a disturbance on the horizon captured his notice.

Although not a single cloud marred the sky's azure perfection, a shadowy curtain crept over the hills. The eagle's instincts screamed an alert as the blot spread across the range. Trees wilted and died. Flowers crumbled to ash. It'sa watched as the shadow approached the coyote. Feral rage at the dark menace coursed through his blood. He screeched a warning. She jumped down the slope and bounded away, but the shadow moved with lightning speed. It'sa dove toward the earth.

Too late.

The shadow rose in a wave and crested, blotting out the sun. It engulfed the coyote. Her head broke the oily black surface. She flailed her paws, struggling to stay afloat.

"Hurry!" the coyote cried. "They found us!"

Chapter Six

Sam bolted upright in bed, gasping for breath. Drenched to the skin, his heart drummed a wild rhythm against his ribs. He stared at his hands with fingers splayed apart, half-expecting talons and feathers to sprout from nails and skin. Stumbling from bed, Sam staggered to a dry sink that held a basin and pitcher. With shaking hands, he splashed cool water on his face. Never had a dream been so real. Even when his mother lay dying, he merely wakened with a sense of grief and impeding death.

But this…Sam steadied himself against the dry sink. He still felt the breeze brushing his cheek, the sun beating on his back. He straightened up. His fingers balled into fists. The shadow was a putrid canker on the land, the embodiment of death. Unchecked, its power would grow like a fierce wind, strong enough to batter down doorways and rip loved ones apart. He glanced out the window with a burning desire to seek his grandmother's council, but urgency weighed heavy on his shoulders. The coyote's cry echoed in his ears.

Hurry! They found us. The desperate plea had come with Sister Regina's voice.

Sam donned his clothes and bolted to the marshal's office. He tucked one revolver in each holster and stuffed the remaining cartridges into a saddlebag. The scant number of bullets served double duty for both the revolvers and the Winchester. He penned a quick note and left it on the desk for his grandfather.

The skies cleared overnight. The moon hung low in the sky. Dawn's arrival was only a short time away. Sam went directly to Mateo's barn and threw a blanket and saddle on Rio's back.

Mateo stretched across several bales of hay. He opened a sleepy eye, sat up, and yawned. "You woke early, *amigo*. It's not yet dawn. Where are you going?"

Sam tightened the saddle cinch. "To the ridge. Rouse the sisters."

"Trouble?" He rose to his feet. "Hold on, I'll fetch my rifle."

"Just need to check the trail." How could he explain the horror of the shadow? Sam slipped on the bridle and then swung into the saddle.

Mateo grabbed the reins. "Another vision?"

"Can't say for sure. See to the sisters. I'll return straightaway."

Mateo released his grip. Sam nudged Rio's sides, fighting the urge to press to a gallop. No matter how well known the route, racing with only moonlight to guide the way was too risky for both horse and rider. Instead, they trotted to where the trail paralleled the high point of the ridge.

Sam dismounted and then scrambled up the rocky slope, murmuring a quick prayer the vision had only been a nightmare. The height offered an unobstructed view to the east. Gray morning light gave way to tinted streaks of amber and rose across the sky. At any minute, the sun's full brilliance would wash over the horizon.

Movement below drew his immediate attention. A

dozen well-armed men in dark clothing rode along the trail. Sam let out a curse. He skidded down the hillside slick with last night's rain and hopped onto Rio's saddle. "No easy trot this time, boy." He dug in his heels, and they galloped to Spirit Ridge. Mateo and the sisters waited in the barn. He had already hitched the horse to the buckboard.

Sam jumped off Rio. "A dozen armed men to the east of us headed this way. I'd set store by an honest answer, Sister Regina. Are they looking for you?"

Sister Mary's faced paled. Sister Regina draped an arm around the girl. "No," she said. "They're looking for her, and they'll kill anyone who gets in the way."

"Why?" he demanded.

"Remember I told you I had to deliver a package to Fort Braddock? Sister Mary is the package. I'm sorry, but we can't waste time with further explanations, Marshal. We must leave without delay."

"How close are they?" said Mateo with concern.

"Near on the ridge by now. Once at a gallop, won't take but minutes for them to reach town."

"Ride north and cut across to the trail."

"That's rough country. We won't get far in the buckboard. The trail through the ridge is the quickest way out of town, but we can't make it past them without being spotted." Sam pictured the route in his mind. "Fast riders have a chance if they circle into the woods and then head through the break."

Mateo let out a protest. "The buckboard won't pass through there, either."

"I-I don't know if I can outrun them on horseback," stammered Sister Mary. "I-I ain't never done any riding other than our old mule around the farm."

Sister Regina's face set in grim determination. "Mr. Perez, I need your fastest horse."

Mateo raised an eyebrow. "Sister?"

"If they've tracked us this far, then they are surely on the lookout for a woman in a nun's habit. I'll lead them through the woods, buying enough time for the wagon to escape."

"You look nothing like me," cried Sister Mary in protest.

"People see what they expect to see. A woman in a nun's habit makes a break for freedom; ergo, the men will assume I'm the woman they seek. Do not fret. I can ride as if the devil himself chased me. Marshal, I'm counting on you to escort Sister Mary to safety at Fort Braddock…Mr. Perez, I need that horse."

Sam grabbed her arm, eyeing her in horror. "Are you loco?" he shouted. "You don't know any of the trails. It's easy to get turned around and lost. Beyond the woods is the wash. It ain't more than a stream, but last night's storm held a chance of high water off the mountains. Granted, it's more than likely cleared by now, but you don't want to be anywhere near when a torrent rushes down. We can hide Sister Mary in town and make a stand here."

"Time has run out to organize a resistance, Marshal. Sister Mary has a price of five thousand gold on her head—and those men don't seek her alive."

"Damnation." His eyes blazed. "You are full of surprises today, Sister. Don't you think I should have been made aware before this?"

"I give you permission to chastise me later. Now, either shoot me or stand aside for you won't stop me."

Sam glared at her. The steadfast expression in her golden brown eyes brooked no discussion. "We go together…Mat?"

"I'll get Sister Mary safely to Fort Braddock. I swear it."

Sister Mary clasped her companion's hand. Her lower lip trembled. "You know what will happen if they catch you."

"Then we won't be caught." She hugged her tight. "Godspeed."

Her response came as a choked whisper. "And you."

While Mateo helped Sister Mary into the wagon, Sam grabbed a bridle off the hook next to the stall of a big bay. "He's fast. The horse belonged to a Sutton, and he could ride hellbent for leather."

"As can I, but…" Sister Regina examined her habit with an expression of distaste.

Sam's tension eased. Mateo had no sidesaddle, and riding was difficult in those cumbersome skirts. She saw her folly. He'd talk reason to her and go alone.

Sister Regina grabbed a knife off the workbench. His eyes widened as she slit the habit past the knee.

"Don't gawk, Marshal. The time for niceties is over. Speed is of the essence now." She tucked the knife into her boot.

Sam saddled the bay. He glimpsed a shapely leg as Sister Regina swung herself with ease over the horse's back. He mounted Rio. "Sister, after this is over, you and me will have a long hard talk."

She flashed a brilliant smile. "Your determination that we'll come through this adventure unscathed does nothing but bolster my confidence."

"Damnation." He didn't offer an apology for the rough language, nor did she ask for one.

"The second the riders take off after us," Sam said to Mateo, "make a break for it." Mateo gave a terse nod and held tight to the reins. Sister Mary tensed beside him, her face pale.

Sam and Sister Regina galloped through town. Sam cast a cautious eye in the nun's direction, relieved to note she didn't exaggerate her skill in the saddle. Her experienced grip effortlessly controlled the big bay. She shifted position, freeing her leg even farther from the confines of the habit. The stocking had ripped, exposing more smooth pale skin. He experienced a sudden urge to tear off the rest.

Damnation, control your thoughts, man!

The morning sun etched long shadows across the land. A cloud of dust from cantering horses kicked up no more than a quarter mile away. All the riders wore black. An image surfaced from his dream—the poisonous shadow spreading across the landscape.

Sam shuddered as if a cold chill swept through him. "Dark riders," he murmured. "Got reports of them robbing trains. They ain't squeamish about killing."

"How do we make our approach?"

"We'll ride toward them as if we have no suspicions. If the men are after Sister Mary, they'll make a move. When they do, head for that rise. The other side is thick woods. I know the land well. Stay close. We can play a good game of hide-and-seek through the switchbacks long enough for Mat and Sister Mary to sneak by."

They cantered toward the oncoming riders. Sam rested his hand lightly on the holster. At two hundred yards, one of the men pointed at them. Almost as one, the troop pulled black bandanas up to their eyes and spurred their mounts.

"They made their intentions plain," he growled. "Ready, Sister?"

"Ready, Marshal."

They swung off the trail, dug heels into their mounts, and then bolted toward the rise. From behind came the crack of a rifle shot. They urged the horses faster. Bullets pinged off a boulder as they raced past.

"Someone behind us is a good shot," shouted Sister Regina above the pounding of the horses' hooves.

"Let's not make it easy for him, Sister."

"You read my thoughts to perfection."

Both horses strained forward, progress slowed considerably by the effort of the climb. Sam hazarded a glance to the rear. The dark riders quickly closed the gap.

More shots rang out as Sam and Sister Regina reached the top and then headed downslope. Here, the trees grew thick, blocking the line of sight of their pursuers, but slowing their escape.

"Take care, Sister," Sam warned. "Rough ground makes it easy for a horse to stumble and throw a rider." He led them into a copse, momentarily muting the sound of pursuit.

"Have we lost them?" she whispered.

"Not yet."

Sister Regina's body tensed in the saddle. The horse picked up on her nerves and danced a skittering sidestep. She tightened the reins and gave the bay's neck a firm pat. "Steady on."

Sam eyed her with approval. She had grit, no

doubt. A horse whinnied nearby. Something heavy crashed through the brush less than thirty yards away. Sam glowered, marking the pursuers' location. The outlaws split up and aimed to trap them in the middle.

Sam offered a revolver. "Can you shoot?" Sister Regina took the gun without hesitation. They moved deeper into the woods, edging by a rocky outcrop. Every few minutes, Sam paused to get a bearing on the outlaws.

"I hoped they'd give up the chase," he whispered, "but they aim to pen us in the middle. Our best bet is a notch in the rock ahead. Tight quarters so we ride single file. They will, too. Good place for an ambush. Let's hope they reckon the same and don't press hard on our tails."

A voice shouted. Hooves pounded in their direction. "They saw our tracks," yelled Sam. "Make a run for it."

Sister Regina cocked the pistol and charged toward the rocks. Sam galloped right behind her. A rider burst from the brush. Sam fired. The rider jerked in the saddle and tumbled to the ground. After the explosive retort of Sister Regina's gun, another rider landed in the dirt. Men on horseback wove between the trees. Sam and Sister Regina fired repeatedly, sending the outlaws to cover.

The break was in sight. "Go!" Sam shouted.

The narrow opening was barely four feet wide. Sister Regina's horse balked at the close quarters. Two more riders thundered past the trees. Sam fired off several rounds. One outlaw's mount reared and stumbled into the other as the second masked man pulled the trigger. The shot aimed at Sam went wide and ricocheted into a rock.

Sam slapped the rump of Sister Regina's horse. The bay jumped forward and entered the switchback. One swift kick to Rio's side, and the palomino followed. Sam twisted in the saddle, firing behind to discourage immediate pursuit. The notch continued for several yards and then opened into a ravine with a steep incline.

"Where to, Marshal?" asked Sister Regina.

"We can hold them off here. Only one rider can edge through at a time. They may see the hunt as futile, but my instincts say that ain't likely. The outlaws can always choose to climb over the top and dry gulch us."

"You have another plan?"

"Follow the ravine to the creek. The water will mask our tracks. It's longer to Fort Braddock, but I know this country and plenty of places to hide. They don't. I warn you, the trail is rough."

"I don't believe they'll give up, either. Waiting for trouble doesn't sit well with me."

"Agreed. Let's ride."

Sam took the lead. They had bought time, but how much? As they neared the bottom of the ravine a horse's whinny cut the silence. Riders made it through the break.

Ahead came a muffled roar. "Hell and damnation," muttered Sam.

"What's wrong, Marshal?"

"I reckon this ride will get a bit more interesting, Sister."

Sam guided their horses through dense brush into a clearing. The meandering creek he had hoped to see was now a raging torrent.

Chapter Seven

Nell eyed the churning water with dismay. "You have an optimistic notion of what constitutes a little creek, Marshal."

His expression registered shock. "The storm last night must have been fiercer than usual in higher elevations. I expected the water to have receded long before now."

Nell's heart pounded. No way back, no way forward.

The marshal scanned the raging waters. His jaw tightened. "We're in a fix. It won't be long before the dark riders figure how we disappeared. I'll hold them off. Ride downstream. Once you find a safe crossing, go east. It's a hard trail, but with luck you'll make Fort Braddock before sundown. I'll buy as much time for you as I can."

"No!" The horrified protest exploded from her lips. "No matter how good a marksman, meeting them alone is suicide."

A fierce light burned in his eyes. "I swore to keep you safe. I don't know what troubles embroil you and Sister Mary, but I can say for a fact death results if those men catch us."

Nell fought a wave of despair. She had known Marshal Sam Tanner for less than a day, but to consider this the last meeting brought agonizing pain.

"Come with me," she pleaded.

He moved his horse so close to Nell, their knees brushed against each other. The marshal grabbed her hand. "Tell me I'm wrong. Assure me they'll show mercy."

Nell sought in desperation to craft another lie. For once, her tongue failed when his eyes demanded truth. "I-I can't."

"I won't see you harmed for all the world. Oh, hell…" An internal conflict played rapidly across his face. "God made your beauty; surely he won't judge me harshly." Without warning, he pulled Nell toward him and kissed her.

Nell had been kissed before, but never with lips that left a burning imprint. Her heart pounded against her ribs as surprise gave way to assent.

Sam pulled away. The release left her empty. "Go now," he commanded, turning to face the coming marauders. "Don't look back."

Her hands shook as she eyed the swollen waters. "How many miles until a safe crossing?"

"A ways. Don't figure on crossing until the level drops. I'll keep them pinned as long as I can."

Until a bullet ends him. Nell had faced danger before and fought impossible odds, but a final parting with her marshal carved a pit of heavy dread in her heart.

Her marshal?

No—she had no right to claim him. Even so, he was a good brave man whose death wouldn't be on her conscience. An idea formed—a lunatic's idea, but when one was in desperate straits, experience taught her not to be overly particular.

"What are you waiting for?" he barked. "They're coming."

"I have another plan. We cross the water together right here."

The marshal gaped in stunned amazement. "Has all sense deserted you?"

"Those riders are sure to look upon the water as we have. They won't dare a crossing nor believe we had either."

"High water drags a horse and rider right under. No way in hell will I allow you to cross. Now get a move on."

"I was afraid I'd have difficulty convincing you," Nell stated with calm assurance. "So you must simply follow me. H'yah!"

Nell read horror in the marshal's eyes as she wheeled her horse toward the torrent. He made a desperate grab for the reins, but she smacked him in nose, and he pulled up with a start. "I do apologize," she called over her shoulder.

The horse stumbled into the roiling water. The current snatched at them with deadly force. Nell dug her heels viciously into the bay's ribs. The horse whinnied in terror, ears pulled back, eyes near rolled into the sockets. As she forced him forward, muddy water thick with rocks and branches overlapped her boots. A swell crashed into them, knocking the stallion off balance. Hooves flailed wildly seeking solid ground.

There was none.

The horse strained at the reins, swimming in a frantic effort to keep his head above water.

"That's it," Nell urged. "Keep going. You can do it."

They battled in the center of the floodwaters as the current pushed them at a terrifying pace. Clumps of detritus bobbed on the surface. Nell's heart lodged in her throat as the horse's head sagged lower. Fighting against the current, the bay made little headway toward the opposite shore. Nell's legs gripped tight against the heaving flanks as exhaustion threatened to overwhelm the animal. Around them, debris-clogged waters swirled and churned. Then, came a thump followed by a slight steadying to the rough ride. Her spirits soared. Hooves met solid ground once more.

"Come on…just a little farther."

A broken sapling as thick around as Nell's thigh pitched through the water. She caught a glimpse just before it hit and jerked the reins to the side in an attempt to steer the horse out of its path. The evasion came too late. The log slammed into them with a sickening thud, knocking the horse off balance. He went under, dragging Nell with him.

Nell inhaled a lungful of water. Kicking her feet free from the stirrups, she swam upward. Crazed with fear, the horse flailed, colliding into her. She went under again, dragged down by heavy skirts. Her head broke the surface long enough to cough up muddy water and suck in a mouthful of clean air. She futilely splashed against the rushing current.

Panic threatened to swallow her whole as water washed over Nell's head. She shut her mouth, lungs near to bursting. One hand strained to reach above the flood. She choked back another gush of water as the torrent engulfed her.

A firm hand took hold, fingers laced tight as steel bands encircled Nell's wrist. One hard yank and her head emerged. "Got you!" The marshal's face strained with the effort to hold her above the flood.

Nell grabbed for him with leaden arms. He reached with his other hand and snatched a handful of cloth. Seams parted with a rip as he hauled her to the saddle. Nell doubled over vomiting water.

"Easy, now." Strong arms held tight around her. "I've got you. I won't let go."

Nell closed her eyes and pressed tight against his chest, gasping for breath as she coughed up the last bit of water. She sagged against him. The pounding of his heart filled her with relief. He was alive. He was safe. Her arms encircled his waist, holding tight.

The palomino moved with a steady gait. Nell opened her eyes and nearly cried with relief. They had reached the opposite shore and dry ground at last. The horse scrambled up the bank, blowing hard.

"Sister?" said the marshal. "Sister, I have to dismount. Can you hold on?"

Numbly, she nodded. The comforting pressure of his arms released as he slid from the saddle. Nell bit her lip, wanting to cry out for him to return and hold her again. Her face flushed. She was safe now. No need to cower like a frightened child.

As the marshal led the palomino into the thicket, the sounds of rushing water faded away. "Stay here. I'll spy on our pursuers. You hear gunfire, you run. Don't come look for me."

"Marshal—"

"Damn it, woman! Must you always argue? Do you know what fear you brought to my heart when I saw you go under?"

His outburst brought a weary smile. "I was only

going to say be careful…and thank you."

Judging by the surprise in his expression, he expected a frosty retort. Their eyes met. Nell filled with unexpected warmth. "Forgive my actions, Marshal. I couldn't bear to see you fall by their hands."

"I'll be back directly," he responded gruffly.

The marshal took off his coat and wrapped it around her shoulders. Dampness made the shirt cling to every hard line of his muscles. He melted into the brush, moving with the grace of one of the forest creatures. Neither the crackle of a leaf nor the snap of a twig marked his progress.

Nell's hand went to her lips. She still felt the kiss and the yearning it evoked. How would it feel to have her true name whispered from those same lips as he wrapped his arms around her again? Nell thrust the thought aside. Their moment of passion had been a brash response to a highly-charged emotional situation. The marshal had a man's interest in her face and figure, but surely frowned on the life she chose.

A pang of regret dove straight through Nell's heart. She had no wish to see his expression fill with censure as had so many others. The nun's disguise was fortuitous. The habit by its nature warded off further advances. When they reached Fort Braddock and she admitted the truth, his interest will surely cool. The marshal would return to Spirit Ridge never to cross her path again.

The flood of fear produced by the crossing abated, but with the stilling of her pounding heart came the cold. Nell shivered. Sodden clothing leached heat from her body. She lost the veil in the floodwaters, but tugged at the wimple clinging to her face.

"Damnation, Daisy was right. A man surely designed this headpiece."

The ties were wet and knotted, but Mateo's knife was miraculously still tucked in her boot. Nell sliced off the fastenings. Discarding the wimple, she shook her hair free.

Nell blew on her fingers to instill warmth, but to no avail. She slid off the saddle and wrung as much water out of the habit as she could. Her feet were cold and miserable. The soaked petticoats clung to her freezing legs. She used the knife to cut through and discard the underskirts. They were nothing but a hindrance.

"Ahem."

The brush had parted silently. The marshal stood behind her, staring at the display of leg. Flustered, she dropped the tunic. "Did you see the dark riders?"

"They came through the break, but none dared a crossing. The marauders are gifted with more sense than others I might name," he noted dryly. "They rode downstream, no doubt to seek low water."

"My horse?"

"No sign. I fear it drowned."

"That's unfortunate." Nell patted Rio's neck. "This poor creature served us well, but is too weak to carry us farther without rest. We'll have to walk until he recovers, slowing our progress."

"The other horse's death may work to our advantage," he mused. "A washed up body might lead them to believe the same end for us, and they'll drop the hunt altogether." He gave her a penetrating look. "Will they?"

Nell took a deep breath. "I won't lie. I doubt anything will dissuade them from the bounty. They work for a man with deep pockets who rewards success and doesn't forgive failure. He wants Sister Mary dead very badly."

"And they think you're Sister Mary." He swore under his breath and grabbed the palomino's reins. "We keep moving, then." He buttoned the jacket around her shoulders. "It will help keep in the warmth." His fingers gently brushed a sodden lock from her cheek.

Despite the chilly air, a fiery ember flared within Nell. She sought out his eyes. Would he kiss her? Nell dropped her gaze, acutely aware of her appearance—sleeves torn off, the seam of her skirts indecently ripped exposing even more skin. *Damnation, this won't do.* A physical attraction was expected when rescued by a handsome man, but acting as a wanton was beyond reproach. Propriety must be maintained especially when she didn't fit into the marshal's life, nor he in hers.

"Thank you." Nell clutched the coat tight around her. "I'm grateful for everything you've done."

"It's your turn to talk now, Sister," he demanded. "I'll have the truth of those men."

The marshal had not only saved her life, but also risked his own. Nell's intention to keep the mission secret until Fort Braddock wavered. Her identity must stay hidden, but he deserved to know the nature of the danger on their trail. "Have you ever heard of a man named Colin Doyle?"

"Can't say as I have."

"Dig deep enough and you'll find Doyle sitting atop a pile of foul corruption. If one wishes to purchase opium, a whore, or a politician in San Francisco, The Mick can name a price." Nell described his criminal enterprises.

The marshal raised an eyebrow. "How does a nun come by such information?"

His skeptical look made Nell uncomfortable. She mustered every drop of sincerity. "Not all of us live in cloisters. My mission of service often took me to less reputable parts of the city. I heard whispers about Doyle and investigated on my own. People confide tales to a nun they won't tell others."

"What's this to do with Sister Mary?"

"Doyle's ambition reaches farther than San Francisco. Sister Mary discovered Doyle purchased property outside Prescott in the Arizona Territory. Ostensibly, he decided to expand his business enterprises by becoming a gentleman rancher, but instead plans an attack nearby. Men, women, and children will die."

Sam's eyes widened. "For what purpose?"

"Unfortunately, I don't know. That's why we journey to Fort Braddock, to warn the cavalry and convince them to hunt Doyle's army before the assault commences."

He eyed her with doubt. "Sister, Doyle can't recruit men for an army and not have any folk nary the wiser."

"I considered that. It seems illogical, but I've noticed the wanted posters since entering the Territory. Many outlaws vanished without a trace. What if Doyle hires those on the run?"

"I'll grant you plenty of desperados will gladly offer their talents for a price. It ain't hard for a man to disappear in the Territory if he's of a mind." The marshal rubbed his chin. "We've had reports of dark riders like those following us. They've robbed trains and killed with abandon. Chills me to think their acts ain't random, and they follow orders."

"Doyle has the money and resources to buy their loyalty," said Nell. "If he isn't stopped, his evil will spread like…like…"

"A dark shadow across the land?" His voice dropped. He peered into the distance as if striving to see the future unfold.

"Rather poetic, Marshal," Nell admitted with a slight smile, "but yes. You voiced my ultimate fear. That's why it's imperative Sister Mary gets to Fort Braddock with her information. We must convince the commander to act against Doyle."

"The Army is stretched mighty thin around here, Sister."

"We had no choice. Doyle bought too many political favors. No one will listen in San Francisco. His plan begins soon. Any delay only allows his strength to grow."

He let out a long breath. "I find your notion chilling, Sister."

Nell heaved a sigh. The past days had been wearing. She was exhausted and now aching with cold. "Sister Mary and I barely escaped San Francisco. Until now, we stayed one step ahead of Doyle's men. Any person who ever stood in The Mick's way conveniently disappeared, the body never found. I have no intention of allowing the same fate to befall Sister Mary."

Impulsively, Nell grabbed the marshal's arm, halting him in his tracks. A rush of sudden emotion brought a pink flush to her cheeks. She must keep him at her side. "I've seen the ruthlessness firsthand of Colin Doyle. He'll kill man, woman, and child to reach his goal. If no one prevents his evil plot, innocent blood will drench the land. Do you believe me?"

****

Was the story true? Sam interpreted his vision as danger in Sister Regina's future, but could the warning be for everyone in Spirit Ridge? For each inhabitant of the Territory? How much faith should be put in dreams? A desire built within him to reach out and embrace the call to action.

Once the gift is accepted, It'sa, there is no going back.

Did acceptance of the challenge mean only more images of death? Sister Regina still lived, but they were hardly safe. Death could be but moments away for both. Was his fate to save her life just to see it end? Or could the visions hold more? Was he ready to fully embrace the gift?

Not yet.

He pushed thoughts of visions aside and turned his attention to Sister Regina. "I believe you, *Baya.*"

Sister Regina regarded him with a puzzled expression. "What did you call me?"

Lips twitched in a smile at the slip of his tongue. "Coyote—in the language of my Apache grandmother. Coyote was smart and brave, but a trouble-maker, nonetheless."

Sister Regina laughed, a musical sound to his ears. "I can't argue such an apt description." They walked in silence for a while until she said, "Your grandmother is Apache?"

Sam stiffened, regretting the earlier admission. He hadn't meant to bring up his mixed blood. Outsiders' reactions invariably included narrow-minded disapproval. "Yes. My grandfather was a cavalry scout.

Once married, they settled in Spirit Ridge where he became marshal. They have a spread outside town. My grandmother is an Apache healer," he added with pride. "The town doesn't have a doctor. Folks come from miles around for her help." Sam braced for a condescending remark on his grandmother's skills. Brown-eyed beauty or not, he wouldn't allow Sister Regina to insult Lenna Tanner.

"How fascinating," she said, to his stunned amazement. "I'd very much like to meet your grandmother."

"I reckon she'd have a heap to say to you, too," he muttered, dryly. "If you don't mind my saying, Sister, you don't talk much like a nun. What's your story? You never had a hankering for a husband, children, and a home of your own?"

She appeared reluctant to speak. "There isn't much to say, Marshal. I-I decided on a life of service instead."

"That's the whole story? Where'd you learn to fire a gun and ride a horse?"

"I wasn't born a nun," she said lightly. "As a child, I had my own horse, and my father taught me to shoot. What of you? Did your parents approve when you followed in your grandfather's footsteps?"

"My pa joined the Army when he came of age and married my mother back East. He died when I was little, and Ma brought me to live with my grandparents. She passed soon after. I'm thankful she decided to come."

"Have you lived nowhere else?"

"When I was younger, I itched to head out on my own. For a time, I left Spirit Ridge for a stint in the Army as a scout." Unknowingly, his voice tightened.

"During those years, I first ran into Reese McLaren."

"The man who shot your grandfather?"

"He was attached as a scout to another company. Damn good, but I never much liked him. He had a rough way of talking about women I didn't cotton to. McLaren lit out after killing a prostitute. Found out later, she wasn't the first. After my time with the Army ended, my heart called me home. Once I set foot again in the Territory, I knew I'd not live anywhere else. I work with my grandpa on the ranch and as deputy. I've enough saved to get my own herd come spring."

"The land has a wild beauty that beckons."

As do you, Baya. She shivered, and Sam pulled the jacket close to her neck. "I'm sorry," he said. "We dare not stop to light a fire."

"I know. I-I'll warm up if we continue to walk. Tell me more of my coyote."

He blinked in surprise. "Your coyote?"

"My namesake, then."

Sam was still for a moment. "I can pass on a yarn from my grandmother that tells how coyote found a husband. *Baya* spotted a young Apache warrior sitting by a campfire roasting his kill. She was taken with his handsome features and prowess as a hunter and decided he'd make a fine mate. She came to him as Coyote Woman and expressed her desire."

"Coyote Woman sounds very sensible," said Sister Regina with a twinkle in her eye. "No dilly-dallying. I approve of her forthrightness. Go on."

"The warrior didn't want Coyote Woman for a wife as she had the reputation of a clever trickster."

"Not because she was part coyote?"

He grinned. "No. By every account, she was a

rather fine-looking woman."

"That is generally characteristic of the male," she teased. "Prizing the female's appearance, but unwilling to accept her as an intellectual equal. I suppose Coyote Woman was outspoken, too."

"No doubt. After all, she was a coyote. They ain't shy about voicing likes and dislikes."

"So she'd never be the silent, dutiful wife. I'll bet the hunter didn't take to that aspect one bit."

"I reckon not because he turned her down. Coyote Woman was angry. 'You wish only for obedience in a wife. What use is that? We will hunt together. You will never go hungry. At night, I will lie at your side. You will never grow cold. I will bear fang and claw to those who wish you harm. My wiles will keep you safe. I will make a good wife and love you as no other. I only ask in return to accept my coyote nature. Don't bind me tight, but allow me the freedom to run where I choose.' "

"Well," Sister Regina huffed, "only a fool refuses such a sensible proposition."

"The hunter was intrigued, right enough, and drawn more and more to Coyote Woman. Still, doubts lingered. They were two different beings. She was a trickster. How could the hunter trust the coyote's nature and be sure of her feelings? *Baya* offered a test. 'Plunge your knife into my chest,' she told him. 'My love for you is so strong even death cannot part us.'"

Sister Regina arched an eyebrow. "He agreed? I must say, that sounds unduly harsh."

"The warrior did as requested. He stabbed Coyote Woman, and she fell dead at his feet. He commenced weeping, realizing he loved her."

"Finally, albeit, a trifle late. Please tell me the story doesn't end there. I was rooting for them."

Sam's eyes gleamed. "You never struck me as the sentimental type, Sister, but be assured the tale continues. The hunter stared in amazement when *Baya* opened her eyes. She explained that to protect her heart, she removed it long ago. Now, she handed it to him. 'I see your tears and know you love me. It is yours to keep.' Her cleverness impressed him. The hunter placed her heart inside his own chest to keep it safe and from then on their two hearts beat as one."

Sister Regina wore an amused expression. "That's romantic and at the same time appalling. I most certainly would have found a less painful way for him to prove his affections. Not to mention, his complete willingness to stab his true love in the chest bodes poorly for future outcomes of any disagreements."

Sam chuckled. "Now you truly sound like my grandmother. She was convinced Coyote Woman eventually killed her husband after he ignored her good advice one too many times. My grandfather often teases her and says that's why he makes sure she wins every argument."

As they continued to walk, Sam told her more stories, but as the hours dragged on Sister Regina became less talkative. She panted heavily, her once brisk pace slowed. Sam watched with mounting concern. They only had one canteen, and the water was nearly gone. "Are you all right, Sister?"

Sister Regina waved away his concern. "Please don't worry on my account."

"Hold on." He stopped and reached into the saddle pack.

Her teeth chattered. "W-We must keep going."

Sam removed jerky wrapped in oilcloth. "We can rest a few minutes. Eat a bit to keep up your strength." He tore off a piece of jerky and pressed it into her icy fingers. "You're freezing," he cried in alarm. "You must get warm."

"We have no time to spare. Those men are still on our trail. They may have reached low water by now and crossed to the other side."

Sam patted Rio's neck. "I reckon he's rested enough to carry us." He eyed Sister Regina warily. His next offer was bound to raise an eyebrow. "We huddle together and the cold won't cut so sharp." She pulled the jacket tighter as if uncomfortable with the suggestion. "No arguments, Sister." He motioned toward the sky. "The sun is headed behind the hills. You need to warm before nightfall." At her hesitation, his anger rose. "Surely, you can admit to some weakness."

She stiffened. "No, I can't."

His tone gentled. "I won't think less of you. If anything, I admire your gumption. You got it in spades."

Her tense posture relaxed. "I accept your offer and apologize for my shortness. Taking help is difficult for a woman in my position. Acceptance implies fragility. Once viewed by others as frail, no one values your intellect."

Sam raised an eyebrow. "Ma'am, I can't imagine anyone envisioning you as delicate. You must be acquainted with mighty peculiar priests."

Sister Regina's lips twitched in a smile. Sam helped her into the saddle and then settled behind her.

One hand clutched the reins, the other wrapped around her waist. Her clothing was icy cold against his palm. A quick jab with a boot heel and Rio took off at a steady gait. With a sigh, Sister Regina leaned into his chest, her body conforming to his as if two halves melded to make one whole. Sam held her tight.

"S-So cold," she whispered through chattering teeth.

"Rest, *Baya*," he murmured in her ear. "I won't let harm come to you."

"My Apache hunter," she chided gently. "Not trying to steal my heart are you? Fair warning, I removed it long ago."

I would find it for you. I wish to hear our two hearts beat as one. He brushed away a sense of regret. "You talk too much, *Baya*," he teased. "Like the coyote who howls for no purpose at the moon."

"I'm sure she has a very good a purpose," Sister Regina argued. "She simply keeps it hidden."

"Hush, *Baya*. Stop howling at the moon. We have far to go."

The sun dropped below the horizon. The wind picked up, bringing a chill to the night air. At first, the full moon lit the path, but then clouds scudded across the sky. Sam slowed Rio to a walk. Sister Regina's body shivered violently against him. He tried to engage her in conversation by telling more stories of Coyote Woman, but her voice became steadily weaker. Fear rose in Sam. If she didn't warm in due time, exposure would result, and they were still far from their goal.

Chapter Eight

"Sister, we can't keep riding," said Sam. "You're chilled to near freezing. I need to stop and build a fire."

"T-those m-men—" Words barely got past her chattering teeth.

Sam filled his words with false confidence. "The moon is hidden behind clouds, making travel perilous. They must make camp. So will we."

He reined in at a granite headland, high enough to give them shelter from the wind and block the fire's glow. Sam helped Sister Regina slide from Rio, supporting her weakened legs. He had no time to pack a bedroll, so instead removed the palomino's saddle blanket and wrapped it around her shoulders. From the bottom of the saddle bags, Sam dug out matches kept dry in a tin. The ground was mercifully laden with tinder. Within a few minutes, a cheery fire blazed. Sister Regina stretched out frozen fingers toward the flames.

Sam cleared his throat. "Sister…You need to remove the wet clothing or you won't warm. I'll wait over there."

He stood behind a tree. From nearby came the soft rustle of cloth. Unbidden, a picture rose to his mind of Sister Regina standing naked in the firelight, flickering beams of light lapping against her skin. He stifled a groan.

"I'm finished, Marshal." He turned around. She still wore his coat, with the horse blanket clutched tight. Her clothing scattered on the ground, including a lacy chemise decorated with pink bows. Sam forced his eyes away. Who suspected nuns hid such feminine delicacies under all that black? "I'll rig a line for your garments near the fire. They'll dry and help keep us sheltered from the wind."

Shivering, she nodded her thanks.

As he strung the rope, Sister Regina bent to retrieve the clothing. The blanket slid off one shoulder and the coat opened. He turned his back, pretending not to notice. In truth, he caught more than a glimpse of what the habit sheltered underneath. Sam stifled a curse. *What the hell were the gods thinking when they gifted a nun with two perfect breasts?*

"Did you say something, Marshal?"

"No, ma'am." He swallowed hard. "Let's sit by the fire." They settled by the granite boulders. Sam placed her boots at the edge of the flames to warm them and then slipped his gloves over her feet. Sister Regina flapped her toes up and down and rewarded him with an irreverent giggle. Then Sam made her eat more jerky and drink water even though Sister Regina protested with wry humor she had swallowed enough to spring her own internal lake.

After a time, Sam noted to his relief her shivering lessened in intensity. He rubbed his hands and moved them close to the flames, thankful their rough shelter cut the wind. If only he could so easily remove the knowledge of her naked body pressed next to his. The alcove was a snug fit for two people. Her weight shifted. Movement of her thigh against his brought a sudden rush of desire. He stifled another curse.

"Marshal?"

"I-I was just saying," he stammered, "it's a pretty night."

Sister Regina gazed overhead. The clouds had passed, and now the moon shone once more. Stars twinkled in the cloudless sky. "It is, indeed. I know it's impossible, but I swear there are more stars in the heavens here than in San Francisco. Between the fog and the gaslights, you barely see a glimmer." She sighed. "Despite the imminent danger, this is lovely country, Marshal."

"No argument from me, ma'am. I reckon I'd never care to live anywhere else."

"No, I don't suppose so, nor do I envision you content in another place."

Her voice held a wistfulness Sam didn't fathom. "Sister?"

"It's nothing."

"What about you?" said Sam. "Will you return to San Francisco after you complete your mission to Fort Braddock?" His heart dropped when she answered yes without hesitation.

She gazed into the flames with a pensive look. "My work is there. I suppose it will be the parting of the ways for us in the near future, Marshal. No annoying coyote nipping at your heels any longer. Much better for you. How long until we reach the fort?"

"Hard to say—sometime tomorrow. I don't want to push Rio too hard with him carrying both of us. Rest now while you can."

"Perhaps I'll close my eyes for a moment."

Sister Regina's weight relaxed against him.

Breathing slowed. Her head lolled onto his shoulder. A hand slid from her lap to touch his, and Sam started at the coolness of her skin. Despite the fire, she needed more warmth. He shifted to place an arm over her shoulders and then clasped both of her hands. She muttered sleepily and nestled close, a perfect fit against his chest. He leaned a cheek against her hair and stared into the flames. Why did such an unobtainable woman come into his life? He shouldn't allow himself this much contentment. She would depart in a short while leaving nothing, but a memory.

Sam inhaled deeply. Despite the rigors of their escape and a good dousing in the muddy river, her scent drew to mind fields of wildflowers blooming in the spring. *This moment is what I'll take of you. I'll never let the memory go.* He shut his eyes and dared to plant a soft kiss on the top of her head.

"Rest well, *Baya,*" he whispered.

****

It'sa soared high overhead scanning the earth. His beak opened, and he let loose with an angry shriek. Trees cluttered his view of the ground. Although the first chill of autumn tinted the landscape with red and gold, the leaves remained fixed on the branches hiding game from sight. Not good for the eagle's hunting, even with sharp eyes. He banked into the breeze as a coyote bounded to the top of a granite boulder.

His heart filled with unexpected gladness. "You returned, Baya. The dark did not swallow you."

"For now," she said. "What do you see from so high above, It'sa?"

He circled overhead. "An unwary coyote soon to be dinner."

Baya laughed, displaying no fear. "Not for you. A coyote won't cower in the dirt and welcome death. Does It'sa seek a dinner that will fight him with fangs and claws?"

The eagle flapped his great wings, annoyed at her impertinence. "Perhaps not."

"We should hunt together."

What nonsense did the coyote speak? "The eagle always hunts alone."

"As does the coyote, and yet we both hunger."

"Game may be scarce here, but I see the twitch of a fieldmouse's tail in the tall grass. I bring death from the skies. How can you help with paws tied to the earth?"

"Your eyes are keen, but cannot see everything. My ears hear a single scratch in the fieldmouse's burrow even buried under deep snow. My claws dig out prey. We each have different skills, It'sa."

The eagle considered the words of the coyote. Two different beings, yet together perhaps neither would hunger. "We will hunt."

"What nears, then, or is your vision less sharp than your boasts?"

Her teasing rankled. "Clearer than yours, Baya." A stirring in the distance attracted his attention. "Movement to the south."

Beating powerful wings, he banked and then sliced through the air like a hunter's arrow. Far below, a troop of ten riders galloped across the range. Their long black shadows intertwined to create an ugly black scar slashing through the landscape. Screaming in defiance, the eagle circled once and then hastened to the coyote.

"Dark riders approach."

The coyote narrowed her eyes. "The hunting will be good."

****

Nell stirred, warm and content. Feeling seeped again into aching limbs. The chill had sunk so deep as to make her believe warmth would only ever be a distant memory. The near collapse was entirely her fault, of course. A plunge into icy water always risked exposure, but she stubbornly fought the consequences, convinced pigheadedness alone could prevail against bodily weakness. She sighed; thankful Arthur hadn't witnessed her foolishness. He'd have her head and rightly so. If the marshal hadn't insisted they stop, she'd have walked until dropping in her tracks. What good was that?

Yawning, Nell puzzled at the unusual sensation of weight around her shoulders. Her eyelids fluttered open. She drew in a quick breath with the realization her body nestled tight against the marshal's chest, hands clasped firmly in his. Her first instinct was to draw away, but she hesitated. His eyes were closed. He must be resting. If she stirred, he'd rouse, and his exertions had been as severe as hers. The more reasonable and compassionate solution was to stay in this position.

Nell rested her head against his chest, listening to his thrumming heart. Contentment seeped into her. Unconsciously, she counted the beats, *one…two…three…*slow and steady. Did he dream? What visions invaded the sleep of such a man? Hunting perhaps? Riding the range in perfect freedom? The notion suited her image of Sam Tanner. No doubt, his dreams weren't of a nun—not even a near-naked one. A pink flush crept into her cheeks. She must rouse and dress, but not yet. The marshal might awaken, and he needed rest. Nell closed her eyes again, glad to have discovered a perfectly sensible excuse to stay pressed to his side.

What would it be like to wake to the thrum of his heartbeat every morning? To have his smile greet her when she opened her eyes? The marshal didn't smile often, but maybe he only needed a reason. *Some woman will give it to him, but not you.* The contentment evaporated.

Without warning, his heartbeat soared to an alarming level. He murmured a few unintelligible words. Nell opened her eyes. She sat up and regarded him with concern. His face twisted in a scowl. She gently shook his shoulder. "Marshal?"

He jerked upright gasping for breath.

Nell touched him sympathetically on the arm. "Did you have a nightmare?"

"A vision," he stammered. "We must leave without delay." He sprang to his feet and gathered her clothes off the line, tossing them to her. "Get dressed." He turned his back.

"Vision?" Nell asked, slipping on the chemise. "What do you mean?"

"No time to explain." He reached his hand to her and averted his eyes. "Hand me the blanket. I'll saddle Rio."

As he snuffed out the embers of the campfire, Nell dressed, thankful her clothing was dry. "How long until dawn?" she asked as he helped her onto Rio.

"Less than an hour. Moon's still up. There's

enough light to ride. We must be well past the woods before the sun is high."

Nell refused his coat, insisting she was no longer chilled. He appeared loath to waste time in argument, so left it unbuttoned and then mounted, pulling the flaps around her. Nell's mouth opened to protest, but no words came out. After last night, the marshal had proven himself a gentleman. He now offered an efficient method to keep them both warm. Denying him the chance to offer a small relief from the hardships of the trail was inexcusably rude, and she was quite content with his arms around her.

After a nudge to the palomino's sides, they were away. Nell tried not to dwell on the unexpected sense of comfort, but found it difficult as his body swayed against hers. Conversation, Nell decided, could supply a needed distraction. "You said you had a vision," she asked. "What did you mean?"

The marshal shifted in the saddle, sending another interesting sensation along her thighs. "Nothing you'd make sense of," he said brusquely.

"Please tell me," Nell insisted. "I'll try to understand."

The words came slow and deliberate. "The visions are similar to dreams. My grandmother's father was an Apache medicine man. He knew how to walk with the spirits. I reckon some of his power passed to me."

"Spirits warned of danger?" she said in fascination.

"It ain't always that simple," he stammered. "*It'sa* came to me—the word means eagle in my grandmother's tongue. According to her, he is my spirit guide."

Her lips twitched in a smile. "An eagle suits

you…what did he say?"

"Not to me—he spoke with *Baya*." The harshness of his tone eased. "She seems to always appear when trouble looms. Why is that?"

Nell was inexplicably pleased Coyote Woman entered his dreams. "Pure coincidence. What did he tell her?"

"Riders approach from the south. Then I awakened. I don't expect you to believe me," he added gruffly.

"On the contrary," she rushed to assure him. "I'm not one to discard such happenings as a matter of course. If your spirit guide issued a warning, heeding it is sensible."

The tension left his body. "I never reckoned a nun to have such an accepting attitude."

Nell bit her lip. She said too much, not sounding at all as a woman bound to strict religious dogma. Her ruse couldn't continue indefinitely, but her mental composure needed him to believe she was unable to form romantic entanglements. "I'll speak honestly, Marshal. Despite wearing the habit, I claim no expertise in all spiritual matters. I don't understand the truth of your dreams and can't determine whether they are sacred in nature or just innate warnings resulting from instincts and experience. Either way, I trust your judgment."

"Thank you, Sister." He sounded grateful.

"What else did *It'sa* discover?" At his hesitation, she insisted. "Please don't spare me the truth. If trouble heads in our direction, I need to know."

"Riders crossed the low water. They left the dead behind, for I counted ten instead of twelve. They push their horses hard and close the gap with due haste. We have little time before they are upon us."

Nell shivered with a sudden chill, but not from wet clothing. No matter where the marshal's warning originated, the danger was real and drew closer with every passing minute. They pressed forward, stopping only once to water the horse from a small spring. Once the trees thinned into scrubby grassland, the marshal urged Rio to a trot. Nell's spirits lifted. They'd seen no sign of the riders and Fort Braddock neared.

As midday approached, they reached a well-trod path through a wide gully. Rocks peppered the steep sides. Thousands of years of wind and water carved them into irregular shapes. Some almost seemed to sport human features; eyes wide and mouths open as if to urge them to quicken the pace. An uneasy sensation of being watched quivered down Nell's spine. She fidgeted in the saddle and forced her gaze away.

"This is an old Indian trail," said the marshal. "Fort Braddock is no more than a few miles now."

Nell closed her eyes and enjoyed the warmth of the sun on her face. Soon they'd be safely ensconced behind a wooden palisade and beyond the reach of the dark riders. If luck held, Mateo and Daisy had already arrived. If not, she would insist the commander immediately dispatch a search party. No doubt he'd comply. When need be, she was extremely stubborn and persuasive.

The marshal's body twisted in the saddle, and he peered behind them. His muscles tensed against her, and Nell's heart quickened in alarm. "Trouble?"

"Not yet, but…" He reined in the horse. "I'm going to higher ground. Wait here." He dismounted. Nell opened her mouth to offer a vehement protest, but before a word escaped her lips, he made a wry face and offered his hand. "I don't reckon you'll stay without an argument, so come with me."

With a grin, she dismounted. They scrambled up rocks and boulders. At the top, the marshal dropped to one knee and scanned the terrain. Nell crouched next to him. She followed his gaze to a dust cloud rising in the distance. Indistinct shapes became men and horses. *One...two...three...*ten black riders on the trail. She swallowed hard, trying to still her rising fear. "It appears your vision was correct."

The marshal glowered. "They're riding hard. We have a few minutes—no more. Come." They slid down the incline. He removed his rifle and fished a handful of bullets from the saddlebags. They lost one revolver in the river. He reloaded the other and pressed it into her hand. "Keep to the trail and you'll reach Fort Braddock."

Nell gazed into his eyes. Something deep and powerful drew her in. No, not this. She froze in horror, unable to give voice to the obvious truth.

The marshal's expression held no trace of fear. "We've no chance to outrun them with both of us on Rio. I promised to see you to Fort Braddock, but that is a promise I can no longer keep. We part company here, and you go alone. I'll ambush them from atop the rocks. I can take out a few and keep the rest pinned until you're well away."

He said a final goodbye. The marshal planned to stand his ground, protecting her escape until killed by a bullet from a marauder's gun. The calm acceptance of his fate shook Nell to the core. "No!" she cried. "We must think of another other way. I can't leave you here to die. I-I won't."

His fingers gently brushed her face and tucked an errant strand of hair behind her ear. "Stubborn *Baya*, always with an argument, but this time in vain. We're outnumbered and outgunned. If we both die here, then no one will bring word of the dark riders to the cavalry. You must go to Fort Braddock alone."

Nell's body went cold. His life couldn't end here, not alone among these desolate rocks. Escape must be possible for both of them. Nell couldn't think. She couldn't breathe. What could she say to convince him to run?

Nothing.

His decision was made. No argument existed to stay his course of action. He'd remain behind. Her throat tightened. "Sam—"

"I will tie you to the saddle if need be." Strong arms wrapped around her waist and lifted her onto the palomino.

Nell took his hand, gripped by a fierce desire to hold onto him forever. "This isn't goodbye," she insisted with savage intensity. "You stay alive, Sam Tanner. I'll bring help from the fort." Rio pranced, picking up on Nell's wild emotions. "Or I swear to God, I shall drag down the pearly gates of heaven to find you and…and…then shoot you again myself."

He put her fingers to his lips. "Ride hard, *Baya.*"

The marshal dropped her hand. Nell dug her heels into the horse's sides, and they raced forward. She dared one glance over her shoulder, but he had already turned away to scale the incline. She leaned over Rio's neck urging the palomino faster. "Run as never before—until your heart bursts if need be. We won't let him die."

From behind came a shout and the sound of pounding hoofs. They spotted her. A rider spurred his horse and broke from the gang, closing in fast. Nell's mouth went dry as he raised his rifle. She took aim with the pistol knowing he had the range. A shot echoed among the rocks. The marauder jerked in the saddle and tumbled to the dirt, brought down by the marshal's bullet.

The dark riders wheeled their mounts toward the rocks and prepared to return fire.

Chapter Nine

Sam located a vantage point with adequate cover and a full view of the trail. From his position, the dark riders had to pass directly into his line of sight. His lips pressed together in a tight thin line. He'd not give up a single inch of ground to those bastards without a fight.

One rider pulled ahead of the charge. Using his legs to guide his mount, he dropped the reins and raised a carbine to his shoulder, muzzle pointed toward Sister Regina.

Sam held his breath. He slid his finger around the trigger of the Winchester, sighted down the barrel, mentally adjusting for speed and distance. Frank Tanner's training rung in his ears. *Steady, Sam. Stock firm to the shoulder. Lead the target. Gently squeeze, don't jerk.* Sam's finger tightened on the trigger. The blast echoed in the rocks. The dark rider's head snapped back, and then he fell from his horse.

A flurry of shouted orders came as the rest of the band scattered for cover. Sam pressed flat to the ground. They planned to flush him out now, and he had no intention of making the job easy. A clatter of loose pebbles drew his attention. An outlaw skulked beneath him. Sam's lips twisted in a grim smile. Dark clothing did nothing to conceal a hiding place among buff-colored rocks. He gripped the rifle, waiting for the black clad figure to move a fraction more…Another shot, and then one more of their number was cut down.

Bullets whistled around his head. The outlaws had clearly marked his location now and baited him to waste scarce ammunition before their final move. Sam eyed his stock of ammo. After loading Sister Regina's pistol and the rifle, only a handful of cartridges remained. He'd make them last as long as possible. Sam sat patiently with his back to the rocks. When every round must count, only a fool was drawn into aimless gunplay.

Time crept by. Gravel skittered to the right breaking the silence. Sam slid across the ground, cocking the lever and firing. A man cried out in pain. Not a kill shot, but the wound took the gunman from the fight. Another figure inched along the incline. Sam fired, but the man ducked, and the shot went wide. Two more men dashed to nearby boulders. They peppered the surrounding rocks with bullets. He hunkered down and returned fire sending them scurrying for cover.

With the last advance, the outlaws gained precious ground. They wouldn't hold from a charge much longer. A rider tried to make a break, but one shot from Sam's rifle convinced him the idea had been ill-advised. The outlaw didn't rise again.

Sam rechecked his ammunition. Six rounds left. The gunmen now changed tactics, easing into a circle while keeping behind the rocks. In a matter of minutes, they had Sam completely surrounded—seven well-armed killers against his rifle and six bullets. If luck held, he'd stop a few more before the fight ended.

He took wry comfort the visions had been right. They presaged death although, this time, the life lost would be his own. Sam had no regrets. At least his spilled blood wasn't in vain. He gave thanks to the spirits for the warning and didn't think to dicker for more time on earth. All that mattered was Sister Regina escaped, soon safe with the Army at Fort Braddock. The information Sister Mary carried would spur the cavalry to act and put an end to the shadow threatening to spread its poison across the land. Innocent lives saved. If the Army acted too slowly, then *Baya* would nip at their heels, baring teeth to urge them forward. Of that, Sam had no doubt.

No sound broke the silence. Even the wind stilled. An icy calm descended over him. The outlaws were positioned for the final charge. Sam readied to meet them.

As if privy to his unspoken thoughts, a hail of gunfire erupted. Shots resounded from all sides as the gunmen advanced. Sam fired, emptying the rifle. He placed his weapon on the ground.

Sam drew the hunting knife tucked inside a boot. Sunlight glinted off the polished blade, case-hardened steel from Spain, honed to razor-sharpness—a gift from Lenna Tanner on his thirteenth birthday. The knife had belonged to his Apache great-grandfather, and the edge tasted many an enemy's blood. The gunfire ceased. The dark riders surely suspected his ammunition had played out and he hid in the shadows of a crevice, cowering from death.

They were wrong.

Sam charged and caught the glimpse of a stunned face. One quick thrust of the knife into the outlaw's chest and a lifeless body dropped at Sam's feet. Just beyond, four others advanced up the ridge. Four barrels pointed at him, four fingers on the triggers. Sam let out an Apache war cry to honor his ancestors and raced to meet them.

The dark riders sighted on his heart. Gunfire exploded through the gully.

****

Gunshots rang out from the gully behind Nell as she raced along the trail. Blind rage threatened to overwhelm her. She had deserted Sam. Running from danger wasn't her way. Nell fought the urge to rein in and wheel the horse around. An unladylike curse escaped from her lips, and instead, she pressed Rio for greater speed. Sam was right. Bullets claimed them both if she returned now. His only chance was for her to find help. She voiced a silent prayer to both God and the Apache spirits.

Nell bent low over Rio's neck willing her own strength into the horse. How long could the stallion travel at top speed? How far ahead was Fort Braddock? She shook the questions from her mind. Whenever death dogged her footsteps, it was best to only focus on the trail ahead.

The sound of gunshots faded. Did the fight end already? An image of Sam lying in a pool of his own blood rose to mind. Her throat tightened. *No! Clear your thoughts. Don't see his death.*

Nell squinted, staring into the distance, as a dust cloud appeared on the horizon. Shapes took form—riders in dark clothing. She sat up in the saddle, eyes searching the vista, but the empty landscape didn't hold a single hiding place. Nell swallowed hard and gripped the pistol. She had but a full round of bullets, and the soaked derringer still secure in her hidden pocket was useless. The odds were most definitely not in her favor, but they wouldn't take her without a fight. *Forgive me, Sam. Death drew both our names from the hat today.*

A rider gripping a pennant on a pole led a troop of a dozen horsemen. Nell's heart gave a leap at the sight of the cavalry standard flapping in the breeze. Only one man wasn't dressed in regimental blue. Mateo Perez waved his hat in the air.

Both joy and relief flooded through Nell. "That way," she shouted, gesturing down the trail. "Sam is in trouble."

"Where is he?" Mateo called.

"Dark riders have him penned among the rocks. Hurry!"

An officer with a captain's insignia shouted to her. "Fort Braddock is ahead. Keep to the trail." Without pausing for an answer, he spurred his horse to a gallop. The rest of the soldiers, including Mateo, thundered after him. Nell watched them gallop away, torn by the raging desire to follow. She reluctantly turned Rio to the trail.

"No matter how convincingly you argue the point," she murmured in exasperation, "the cavalry won't allow a woman to lead the charge."

Rio whinnied. He put his heart into a hard ride, but now blew heavy breaths. She patted his neck. "I know. You want to go after him, too, but you need both food and rest. Our fight is over at the present. We can only wait for their return." She glared back at the trail, the cavalry now no more than a distant dust cloud. "I despise waiting." Rio nickered as if in sympathetic agreement.

As they rode toward the fort, a sick knot of fear formed in Nell's stomach. She dragged Sam into her trouble, and he had offered his life to protect her. All she furnished in return was a weak thank you. Had that desperate parting been their last? Nell repeatedly peered behind with the fervent hope for a sign of the cavalry's return—of Sam's safe return. Within minutes, even the dust cloud from the horses' hooves settled. Nothing but a stretch of barren landscape met her eyes.

She swallowed a lump in her throat. "*It'sa*, Sam told me you were his spirit guide. Please keep him safe."

After several miles, the trail jogged around a series of limestone boulders. In the distance loomed a cluster of wooden buildings. Nell gaped in surprise. Fort Braddock was more outpost than palisade. Not even a fence guarded the perimeter. Instead, a manned watchtower sat at the end of the trail. Underneath, a woman waved a frantic greeting.

"Daisy!" Nell shouted in elation.

With an excited yell, Daisy hitched up her skirts and ran to meet her. No longer dressed as a nun, she wore the flowered cotton frock Nell last saw on her in San Francisco.

"I was so worried," said Daisy. "What happened? Where's the marshal?"

Had exhaustion finally claimed her? The near-death experience taken its toll? Or was it merely the memory of the final sight of Sam Tanner bravely climbing the rocks to near certain death. Nell slid from the palomino's saddle. Her throat tightened. "Oh, Daisy, he's in terrible trouble…and…and…I can't help him."

Daisy gathered Nell, holding her tight. "There, now. Tell me everything."

They walked to the fort leading Rio, one of Daisy's arms draped around Nell's shoulders. The story of their desperate escape spilled out. "I feel so helpless, Daisy. I left him alone. If I hadn't talked Sam into escorting us to Fort Braddock—"

"We'd both be dead," stated Daisy firmly. "Don't fret now. You can't rescue everyone yourself, Nell. You have to leave something for the cavalry to do."

Nell chuckled. She drew herself up. Daisy was right. Wallowing in self-pity was pointless. "You have a way with words, Sister Mary, or rather, Miss Tremaine. I see the religious life wasn't agreeable."

"I durn near chucked the habit before the wagon came to a full stop. Wouldn't that have taken those soldiers in the fort by surprise? Let me tell you, I was a rare sight when we arrived, although not as bedraggled as you are now. I've seen people struck with consumption more robust."

"Again, I'm so thankful for your brutal honesty. Tell me what happened to you and Mr. Perez."

"We avoided the riders," said Daisy, "but the trip took longer by the back trails. When Mateo and I reached the fort and realized you two hadn't shown up, we demanded a search party dispatched at once. Mateo was sure you ran into trouble." Daisy shifted on her feet. "I used words not entirely clerical to urge Captain Abernathy to action. After they left, I determined no point remained for me to wear the habit any longer— not that I'll miss it."

"Captain Abernathy is the commander?"

"Yes. Everything happened so fast, there wasn't time to tell the whole story."

"A captain in charge?" murmured Nell. "I expected

a larger detachment of soldiers."

"His wife told me since the end of the Indian Wars only a small command is stationed at Fort Braddock. Nigh unto as many settlers as soldiers live here now." Daisy examined her with a critical eye. "What you need," she said firmly, "is food, a good wash-up, and sleep."

"I'd be obliged for the first two," said Nell, "but the third won't come until I know Sam is unharmed. He saved my life." Her voice hardened. "If the cavalry arrives too late, I'll never forgive myself."

"Weren't nothing more you could have done," said Daisy kindly. "Your feelings run deep for the marshal, don't they?"

"And must be kept locked inside, but a brave man doesn't deserve to die in that awful place."

Daisy's hugged her tight. "Don't give up hope. I have no doubt you'll see your marshal again."

Her marshal…Nell's spirits lifted. "For now, I'll see to Rio's comfort. It's the least I can do."

Daisy led her across the fort's grounds to the stables. Two children swung a rope as a third skipped to a singsong chant. "In fourteen hundred and ninety-two, Columbus sailed the ocean blue…" A little girl clutching a rag doll stood nearby to watch. As the women passed, she looked up and waved hello with a gap-toothed grin.

"I hadn't realized so many families called the outpost home," said Nell.

"Over fifteen women and children including those of the settlers," said Daisy. "The captain's wife has been dreadful kind. She asked me to call her Eliza and offered to put you and me up in their quarters. After the men left, I explained I wasn't a real nun, and we were in disguise. She's eager to hear our tale, but I wasn't up to talking until you arrived." Daisy flushed. "I-I didn't let on about my life in San Francisco."

Nell squeezed her hand. "Nor will I."

A blacksmith offered help in the barn with Rio. He promised to give him a good rub-down and see to his needs. Nell made certain the palomino had plenty of water and feed and gave him a grateful pat before leaving.

Eliza Abernathy welcomed Nell warmly and led her to a room with a bed to share with Daisy. A basin of hot water was at the ready. "When you're done washing come downstairs for something to eat. Do you need assistance?"

"Daisy will stay with me." Nell suddenly realized she wasn't the only one with worries. "I can't thank you enough for your kindness. I know you're concerned for your husband's safe return."

"Think nothing of it. In times of trouble, women must stick together." She promised to send word as soon as the watchtower reported the return of the company.

Nell cleaned up and changed clothes. She removed the derringer from the habit's hidden pocket, thankful to see it appeared unharmed. A good cleaning should return the weapon to service.

Daisy filled her in on the details of their escape. "The road was something fearful, parts washed clean away. Mateo became worried and suspected you hit high water. Hearing that got my stomach all twisty."

"I note he is Mateo to you now and no longer Mr. Perez," she teased.

Daisy's cheeks flushed. "H-he asked me to call him that."

"Did you tell him you weren't a nun?"

"No, I was careful not to say anything, seeing as how we traveled alone, but he may have garnered a few doubts." Pink colored her cheeks. "A time or two when we hit a bump, I may have accidently resorted to an inappropriate description of my painful nether regions."

The flush deepened. "Mateo is an orphan same as me. He was left on his own when his folks died. Life could have taken a wrong turn. Frank Tanner caught him stealing, but instead of arrest, he and his missus took him in. Mateo is much beholden as they treated him as family. Now, he's working hard to make the blacksmith and livery a success."

"He's a good man. Perhaps…?"

Daisy looked away. "Before long, he'll know how I lived and with what manner of people. Even a good man won't overlook such an unhappy past."

Nell grabbed her by the shoulders. "Any man who rejects you is a damn fool, and you needn't have more to do with him. I don't apologize for my rough language and mean every word. You are the bravest person I've ever met." Her tone softened. "No one has to know the truth. When I tell my story, I'll say you were a servant in Colin Doyle's house. You do the same."

"Lie?"

"Not exactly. You were in his house and served him."

"Oh, Nell," she chuckled, "that's a wild tale even for you." Daisy eyed her with a knowing expression. "What about your marshal. Is he a fool, too?"

Nell wore a wistful smile. "Most men are when it comes to women who don't conform to society's expectations. I imagine he'll be glad my safety is no longer his responsibility." Despite her swift assurance to Daisy, Nell found it difficult to imagine Sam Tanner angry when he learned the truth. All she heard was his gently teasing voice. *Baya, as I suspected. You are a trickster. I must guard my heart from you.*

"You say that easily," said Daisy, "but are drawn to him, too, I think. Ain't nothing wrong with admitting it. Any man will also be lucky to have you."

"Thank you, Daisy, but Sam Tanner and I are from two different worlds—the eagle and the coyote."

Daisy frowned. "What's that now?"

"A legend Sam told me of two Apache spirits. His grandmother said his spirit guide was *It'sa*, the eagle."

Daisy grinned. "You are the coyote rousing trouble? That's a right fine team."

"Perhaps, but the eagle rules from the skies, and the coyote's home is the land. Soon, I must go back to mine and Sam to his—" Her voice broke off. If he returned.

"I can't stop the worry either, Nell. Mateo is no soldier, but told the captain he refused to stay behind. The marshal is a blood brother to him." Daisy lowered her gaze. "Everyone treads dangerous ground because of me."

"No," Nell admonished brusquely. "Never forget peril exists only due to the actions of Colin Doyle. I swear to you if either man is harmed, we will rain fury upon Doyle's head as he never imagined."

Mateo had brought their carpet bags on the wagon. Nell changed into fresh clothing, and like Daisy, delighted in freedom from the restrictive nun's habit. Although, in her case, nothing resembling religious garb remained. She examined the tattered habit with an amused expression. Sister Regina lay in eternal rest at last, and quite the worse for wear.

Eliza called them downstairs. The children were napping. She prepared a small repast. Worry kept Nell and Daisy from generating interest in food, but they gladly related their escape.

Eliza listened with rapt attention. "Here I believed shooting an occasional rattlesnake enough adventure for a lifetime."

"Is the name Colin Doyle mentioned in these parts?" said Nell.

"No, but Micah has orders from headquarters to be on the lookout for men dressed in black as you described. They were involved in several deadly train robberies. In the most recent, they took nothing from the passengers, but killed the engineer, conductor, and soldiers guarding a boxcar."

"How awful," cried Daisy.

Eliza shuddered. "I never heard the like."

"What was in the boxcar?" asked Nell.

"I don't know the details, but at least some of the stolen supplies were for Fort Braddock and other Army installations. Micah is concerned because our stock of ammunition runs low. Another supply train has yet to be sent."

Nell and Daisy returned to their room to wait. Hours passed as the sun made a slow descent toward the horizon. Nell tried lying on the bed and then sitting. Finally, she paced the floor. No coyote took kindly to a cage.

"I can't abide another minute of inactivity." Nell's outburst caused Daisy to jump. "I'm going outside to walk. At least I won't wear the finish off the planks in here." She brightened. "I'll send a telegram to Arthur and let him know we arrived."

"I'll come with you," said Daisy. "I swear these four walls are closer by the second."

Nell frowned in thought on the way to the telegraph office, composing a message in her head. Discretion was wise as Doyle's informants no doubt watched the wires. "To Arthur Hollingsworth," she told the operator, "care of *The San Francisco Dispatch*, San Francisco, California. Package arrived safely. Regards, Eleanora."

After Nell sent the telegram, neither woman expressed a desire to return to the confines of the room. They strolled the grounds, passing barracks and the few homes. Wives removed washing from the lines as small children clung to their skirts. Eliza waved as she tended a vegetable garden. From the stables, came the loud clang of a hammer hitting an anvil. One man sat on a porch cleaning his rifle—a tranquil scene overarched by order and military discipline.

As shadows lengthened, so did Nell's alarm. "Night will be upon us within an hour. If they don't return directly, the cavalry will have to camp overnight."

Daisy bit her lip. "That won't do for any wounded."

"Where are they?" Nell burst out in frustration. "Why haven't they returned or at least sent a man ahead with news?"

"Riders approaching!" shouted the guard in the

watchtower.

Nell hitched up her dress and took off at a run. She grasped a rung of the watchtower's ladder, and without a moment's hesitation, began to climb.

The soldier peered over the side with an expression of horror. "Ma'am, you can't come up here—"

Daisy called cheerfully from the ground. "Save your breath, darlin'. You'll have to wrestle her to the ground, and I lay my money on her to best you."

Nell reached the platform and demanded the soldier's spyglass. The flabbergasted man handed it over without protest. She placed it to her eye and focused on the horizon. Barely discernable in the distance were men on horseback. A rider with a pennant led the way—the cavalry returned. Straining in the dim light, she tried to identify the faces of individuals, but to no avail. Instead, strange cargo tied on the saddles of horses without riders drew her attention. The blood rushed out of her face as the truth became evident. The bundles were bodies of the dead wrapped in blankets.

Chapter Ten

Nell steeled her emotions. With polite thanks, she returned the spyglass to the still dumbfounded soldier and clambered down the ladder to Daisy. "They're coming, but I can't make out faces."

Word spread fast through the compound. Wives and children spilled from their front doors. Time slowed to a crawl. Nell was vaguely aware Eliza joined them. The captain's wife balanced her baby son on one hip while a little girl about three years old with deep blue eyes clung to her apron.

Eliza squinted in the near light. "This is the worst part, hoping to see if all returned—" Her face creased in a smile. "Micah rides at the front." She dandled the baby and drew the little girl close. "Papa shall be home soon, my little loves."

Daisy swallowed hard. "Nell, I see horses without riders, but on the saddles…"

Nell grasped her hand. "Bodies of the dark riders," she whispered. "They must be." Nell had no memory of inhaling, but breath blew out in a rush when two figures riding in the rear of the troop drew close enough to recognize.

"It's them," Daisy squealed. She gave a little hop on her toes. "They're alive."

Sam was alive. Nell rubbed a trembling hand down to smooth her skirt and added a quick pat to her hair.

The horses trotted into the grounds. Several of the cavalrymen wore makeshift bandages. Sam dismounted in front of her. Lines of exhaustion etched his face. Nell wanted to throw herself into his arms, but instead only chided, "You're late. You kept me marking time for quite a while."

The weariness left his eyes. His smile filled her with pleasant tingling warmth. "I apologize, ma'am. I was unexpectedly detained."

Nell returned the smile. "I forgive you." Her gaze fell to a dark blotch on his shirt. "You're hurt," she gasped. She placed a hand on his chest. "We must get you attention."

"Blood's not mine." Sam covered her hand with his. "Captain Abernathy showed up before the marauders took their revenge though they put up a stubborn fight. Two wounded hightailed it out of there. We would have given chase, but had wounded of our own and headed back to Fort Braddock for supplies. The troop will start out at first light. From the amount of blood they left behind, I don't reckon the outlaws can get far."

Sam gazed into her eyes. His two hands clasped hers in a gentle grip. The warmth inside Nell built to a flame. "Mat told me you were safe," he said, "but I had to see for myself. You caused me much worry, *Baya*," he chided with tenderness and then took in her appearance with a puzzled expression. "What tricks are you up to now? You stole another's clothing."

Oh, dear. Nell flushed and drew back her hand. "Yes…well…about that…actually, this is my own dress, made by a skilled seamstress. The style is all the fashion in San Francisco."

He frowned. "Your dress? I figured nuns only wore the habit."

She cleared her throat. "They do, but during our recent adventure I neglected to detail every circumstance of our departure from San Francisco—"

"Pardon me." The captain had been in whispered conference with his wife. He now touched the brim of his hat to Nell. "Eliza tells me your name is Miss Bishop. I don't wish to ask, but will you examine the faces of the riders to see if you recognize any of them? I understand if the task is too distressing." Eight rough bundles now stretched on the ground.

"Nonsense," she replied smartly, much to the captain's obvious surprise. "The request is sensible. Daisy will look as well."

"I will?" she said weakly.

"Yes, you will."

"Miss Bishop?" said Sam with a confused expression.

"Daisy?" murmured Mateo with an equally puzzled look.

Nell's flush deepened. "I'll explain in a moment."

Two privates untied the ropes and threw off the blankets covering the marauders. Nell grimaced. Dead men were never pleasant to gaze upon, those who died in a gun battle even less so, especially if sporting bullet holes to the head. She forced back the queasiness in her stomach, refusing to make a spectacle of herself by vomiting over a row of corpses. "Can't say as I recognize any of them. Daisy?"

The girl paled, but gave each a searching look. "No. They're not any of Doyle's crew from San Francisco." Daisy pointed to a corpse. "What's that gray mark on his shirt? Funny kind of decoration."

"It's a chevron, ma'am," said a corporal. "I ain't never seen it on a shirt other than Army issue."

Nell turned to Captain Abernathy. "Perhaps it marked him as their leader."

"My thoughts, too, but unfortunately, they are all beyond questioning now."

Sam stared at the man wearing the chevron. "He matches the description of Curtis Hobbs. We got a flyer on him six months ago. Hobbs is wanted for train robbery in Utah. Report came he might be headed our way bound for Mexico. Can't say for sure though. The description didn't note a bullet hole in his head to mess up his fine features. Not that I'll voice a complaint on your shooting skill, Mat. His next shot would have messed up my fine features for sure. Better him than me."

The captain ordered the dead searched. The corporal searched through their pockets. Each one carried one hundred dollars in gold coins. "Newly minted, sir. Someone paid them for their trouble."

"Miss Bishop," said Captain Abernathy. "Several of my soldiers are injured because the dark riders tried to prevent you and Miss Tremaine from reaching Fort Braddock. I need an explanation."

Sam's frown deepened. "So do I, Miss Bishop."

"Yes…you see…that is, to say." Nell cleared her throat again. "Daisy and I aren't nuns."

"*Qué*?" said Mateo. "What's that?"

"Could we go somewhere to talk?" said Nell sheepishly. "It's a long story."

Captain Abernathy offered his office. As they walked to the headquarters building, Sam strode to

Nell's side. "Who are you, really?" he muttered harshly.

"My name is Nell Bishop. I'm a reporter for *The San Francisco Dispatch* newspaper."

Mateo turned to Daisy. "And you? Are you a reporter, too?"

"No." Color rose to her cheeks, and she turned her face away.

Captain Abernathy led them inside and motioned to a long table with several chairs. "Please have a seat, Miss Bishop, Miss Tremaine. Now, kindly tell me your story from the beginning." As Nell detailed her investigations of Colin Doyle, Captain Abernathy's astonishment was plain. "You took an extraordinary risk, Miss Bishop."

"You sound like Arthur," Nell chided. "I adopted the disguise of Sister Regina and took every precaution to go undetected. No one was apt to accost a woman of the cloth."

"Except Bart," Daisy added helpfully, "so Nell shot him." The men's eyebrows all rose in unison.

"What's that you say?" sputtered the captain. "Shot whom?"

"One of Doyle's henchmen," answered Nell tartly. "He attacked Daisy. I couldn't stand by and do nothing, and lost no subsequent sleep over his death. I assure you, Captain, I'm not a fool. I know how to shoot and am fully prepared to defend myself in a dangerous situation."

"I can attest to that," said Sam wryly.

Nell glanced his way. The marshal's initial irritation over her deception appeared to have vanished. Her spirits rose.

Captain Abernathy shook his head in disbelief. "Miss Bishop, the story you tell is incredible. How can you be so certain this Doyle fellow plans an attack in the Territory? Where is your proof?"

"The dark riders—"

"Could simply be a gang of outlaws. Reports of such appeared recently. They are vicious, no doubt, but not an army."

"Doyle sent those men after us because Daisy discovered his intention. He must prevent us from sounding a warning to the authorities." Nell looked at Daisy, and her heart swelled with pity. She had grown fond of her, admiring the girl's pluck and courage, but the next few minutes would prove difficult. Nell reached out for Daisy's hand, sending a subtle message with a squeeze. *Lie about the past. They will never hear the truth from my lips.* "Tell them what you uncovered."

Daisy drew a shaky breath. "Doyle's office had a private entrance to the street. Guests came that way when he didn't want them seen. A man from the Arizona Territory visited several times over the last few months. Doyle always ordered me from his office when he arrived. After one such visit, I spied a deed on the desk to a parcel of land near Prescott, Arizona, in Doyle's name. It wasn't there before so I know the man left it."

"Can you describe him?" said Abernathy.

"No, I never saw his face nor heard his name. On his last visit, I wasn't supposed to be there, but forgot my shawl in the alcove behind the office. As I fetched it, I heard Doyle walk up the back stairwell talking with a man. There weren't time to leave, so I hid. Doyle asked the man if all was ready in Prescott. He said yes. They had plenty of ammunition. With men of their own, the Army no longer posed a threat. Doyle was pleased. He opened the safe and gave the man ten thousand dollars as promised, and then asked if he wanted to count it. The man declined and said, 'If you can't trust a partner who can you trust?' Doyle told him he'd bring more when he joined him for the attack."

Daisy shivered. "The man asked if the women and children were to die, too. Doyle said yes; a complete massacre brought the plan to fruition that much sooner. The pleasure of ordering the death of innocents filled both their voices. I was so afeared. The moment Doyle and the man left, I went to my room and threw a few things into a satchel. Doyle caught me leaving the building. When he saw the carpet bag, his face twisted in rage. He demanded to know what I heard and tried to force me inside." Daisy shuddered. "I knew death lay through that door, so I kicked him in his…" Her face reddened. "His necessaries. Doyle let go. I ran until Nell found me."

Captain Abernathy eyed Daisy with undiluted skepticism. "That's quite a tale, Miss Tremaine."

"This is not a young woman's flight of fancy," Nell protested. "Colin Doyle put a reward of five thousand in gold on her head. Why do that if he didn't fear the information she carried?"

"We only have your word on that, Miss Bishop." The captain eyed Daisy sharply. "What exactly was your position in Mr. Doyle's household?"

Nell jumped in. "She was a servant."

The captain ignored her. "You forgot a shawl in the back room of an office. What sort of services did you perform there for a man of such unscrupulous character?"

Mateo half-rose from his seat, scowling. "Captain, I don't like what you imply."

"I simply ask for the truth, Mr. Perez. If Miss Tremaine wishes me to throw the weight of the U.S. Army behind these extraordinary accusations, then I must be convinced of her character." He turned once again to Daisy. "What sort of business was it? What did you do for Colin Doyle?"

Don't, Nell pleaded silently. *Don't say it.*

Daisy's voice dropped to a near whisper. She cast her gaze on the tightly folded hands in her lap. "Whatever he desired."

****

Mateo sat back in his seat. "A prostitute?"

Daisy met his stricken expression. She straightened her shoulders and then turned to look Captain Abernathy in the eye. Her voice took on a new strength. "I hold no pride in my past. I did what was necessary to survive, but I'm not a fallen woman now, nor ever will be again. That life is gone forever. I'll die rather than return."

"Good God," snapped Captain Abernathy in disgust to Nell. "You expect me to take the word of a common strumpet who sells her favors. Why she probably made the whole thing up as revenge on a disgruntled lover."

Nell rose from the seat, heat rising to her cheeks. "How dare you! Do you think it easy for Daisy to come here, admit her past, and be subject to your condemning judgment? She could have lied about her circumstances, but chose to reveal the truth. She has more courage than all of us in this room put together. Death hangs over her head, but instead of cowering in fear or running away, she determined to come with me and tell the truth—no matter the consequences. At least show as much fortitude as Daisy, sir. People will die unless you release your prejudices and listen."

"What would you have me do, Miss Bishop?" barked Captain Abernathy.

"First off," Sam said, in a tone that brooked no argument. "I reckon you owe an apology to Miss Tremaine for your unkind words. She came in good faith. I haven't known either of these ladies long, but don't judge them as purveyors of fanciful tales."

"Strange notion coming from you," Captain Abernathy grumbled. "Didn't they lie about their identities from the beginning?"

"They had cause," said Mateo softly. "That's no reason to doubt them now." A faint pink color rose in Daisy's cheeks.

Sam squirmed in his seat at the memory of the stolen kiss. Even a habit hadn't prevented amorous thoughts. "Ain't easy for women traveling as they did. Can't fault them for taking on a disguise. Never know what kind of folk you meet on the road." Nell shot him a grateful look.

Captain Abernathy shifted in his seat. The harshness in his expression softened. "I apologize, Miss Tremaine. I spoke out of turn. I appreciate your admission was difficult, but even if I believed this wild story, you have no idea where or when the supposed attack occurs."

"Prescott must be warned," declared Nell.

"From an unspecified danger?" he sputtered. "Be

reasonable, Miss Bishop. I can't order troops away from Fort Braddock when I'm not convinced the situation is as dire as you contend. If a man gathered an army out here, surely we'd receive word."

"God help us if you're in error, Captain," said Sam.

He raised an eyebrow. "You give credence to this tale?"

"Have you been stationed in Fort Braddock long?"

"Six months."

"I've lived here near my entire life. This is a wide-open land where men can still hide, especially those who know the terrain. Consider the safety of your wife and children. Doyle scoffed at the Army. He's confident you can't mount a defense against his plans. Are you prepared to bet their lives the range won't run red with blood?"

"There must be something you can do," insisted Nell, "beyond ordering the cavalry to action. Can't you alert the territorial governor?"

"There is none. Governor Tritle resigned. His successor has yet to be appointed." Captain Abernathy gazed thoughtfully out the open window. From nearby came the sounds of children playing. "I'll telegraph Lt. Governor Morgan in Prescott and express my concerns. He can make inquiries concerning recent rail shipments or reports of strangers arriving in Prescott. We should get a response by morning." He pushed back from the table. "In the meantime, you are all invited to dine with my wife and family this evening at seven."

"Thank you, Captain," said Daisy. "Until then, I'll retire to my room. It's been a most tiring day." She stood. Sam and Mateo rose at once—a common courtesy for a lady, but not one obviously expected by

Daisy. Her expression filled with gratitude.

Flustered, Captain Abernathy got to his feet. The gruffness left his voice. "You are welcome in my home, Miss Tremaine. I see no need to inform anyone else at the fort as to the unfortunate circumstances of your past. As far as the U.S. Army is concerned, you were merely a servant in Doyle's household. I won't mention your name to Lt. Governor Morgan either."

Daisy swallowed hard as if overcome. Nell linked an arm with hers and led Daisy out the door. At the threshold, Nell paused. Her gaze locked with Sam's, and she smiled. It warmed him as the summer sun.

Sam turned to Captain Abernathy. "Request permission to ride along, sir, when you go after the dark riders. You are several men down. I know the Territory and used to scout for the Army."

"Don't you have a town to return to, Marshal?" said Mateo with a grin.

"I reckon they can do without me for a spell."

"Then, I also offer my services to the captain," said Mateo.

Sam raised an eyebrow. "Don't you have a business to run?"

"Jeb can mind things until I return. I'll send a wire. He owes me for new shoes on his horse and can work off the charge taking care of my place a few more days."

"I should send a wire, too," said Sam. "I reckon my grandparents wonder what's become of us. The note I left explained little."

"Thank you, both," said Abernathy. "As our scout was also wounded in today's encounter, I appreciate the assistance."

After Sam and Mateo sent the telegrams, the captain made arrangements for quarters. Both men kept to their thoughts on the way to the barracks. Sam shot a glance at Mateo. Should he bring up Daisy? Her admission stunned them, to be sure. How deeply could his friend's feelings run after a few days?

How deeply did his feelings run for Nell Bishop?

As they settled in, a corporal named Romero who fought with them against the outlaws entered bearing two cavalry shirts. "The captain sent them over as you're riding with us tomorrow and seeing as your own got bloodied in the skirmish."

"My appreciation to him, Romero," said Sam. "Good shooting today. I saw you drop one of the riders."

"Thank you, sir. I must say, for our quiet little outpost that was a month's worth of excitement packed into a few short hours. You reckon we're to see more?"

"I truly wish I could answer that."

Romero shut the door. Sam discarded his worn shirt. "That was gracious of the captain," he said, "but thanks might be due more to Mrs. Abernathy. She may not cotton to two such bedraggled men at her dinner table."

"True. Men tame a land, but women civilize it." Mateo's voice drifted away. "I never thought Sister— Miss Tremaine was a…" The strain on his face showed as he struggled to even say the word.

"She ain't anymore," said Sam kindly. "God knows what desperate circumstances drove her to such a life, but she can't have chosen with a light heart. She gave no hint as you traveled together?"

Mateo shook his head. "She mentioned a painful

past, so I did not press further. I assumed she overheard Doyle in church. Religious oath bound her not to repeat his words. That accounted for her inner turmoil and unwillingness to discuss how she gained such knowledge…*Estúpido*!" He smacked the side of his head. "A man like Doyle doesn't confess sins in church."

"Don't take it to heart," said Sam. "Miss Bishop had me buffaloed, too. They're a pair, all right."

Mateo walked to the window. He gazed toward the Abernathy's quarters. "On the road to Fort Braddock, I told her of my years living with your grandparents, and my livery and life in Spirit Ridge. I pointed out trees and plants along the way and gave their names. Having always lived near San Francisco, the beauty of this country charmed her." He turned to Sam. "For one bred to city life, Miss Tremaine is strong. The rigors of the journey wore hard, but her only concern was for the safety of you, Miss Bishop, and me. I admit I was shocked to learn she wasn't a real nun, then pleased. Now…" He shot Sam an agonized look. "What do I say to her?"

"What's in your heart?"

"Truly," he stammered. "I-I don't know. I can't seem to think straight."

Sam clapped him on the shoulder. "Once you see her alone, the right words will come."

"What happens when you and your little nun are alone?" Mateo said. "Will the words come easily then? She seemed most relieved when you returned." He regarded him with suspicion. "What happened between the two of you on the range?"

Sam shifted on his feet. "I kissed her."

Mateo's eyes widened. "You kissed a woman you believed a nun? I had impure thoughts about Sister Mary, but you will surely burn in hell, my friend."

"I expected to die," grumbled Sam. "I didn't want to pass over to the other side wondering what her kiss was like…so I did."

"Don't leave me wondering," Mateo scolded. "What happened? Did she return your affections?"

"I took her by surprise," he admitted with a sly look, "but it was right nice. Can't say as I felt any guilt."

Mateo chuckled. "What now? Do you still have strong feelings for Nell Bishop? Ah…I see the answer written on your face. Will you confess your heart?"

Sam tossed Mateo a shirt, but didn't reply.

****

They ate a pleasant, but subdued, dinner at the Abernathy's home. The demands of the day wearied them all and put a damper on animated conversation. Mrs. Abernathy placed Sam across from Nell. The position made it difficult to avoid casting glances in her direction. Not that he made more than a half-hearted attempt. Even in the room's kerosene lantern light, her brown hair shone with streaks of gold, mimicking the coyote in his dreams.

The desire built to soak up the very sight of Nell and burn her image into his heart. No longer in a shapeless nun's habit, free of the dust and grime of the trail, he furtively regarded every delicate feature. A face so lovely, and yet at times capable of emitting unexpected ferocity. Sam recalled the sudden sting of her fist and then her fearless gallop into the churning waters—a last mad effort to prevent him from sacrificing his life. Nothing much stopped *Baya*. A slight smile twitched his lips.

The cut of her modern dress emphasized a woman's figure. Sam imagined her again wrapped in the blanket by the fire, the glimpse of her naked body. He stabbed at a piece of meat. He had no call to think such things. She may already be promised to another, but damnation, her beauty and spirit took his breath away. *No, Baya, I don't regret that kiss at all.*

He looked up from his plate and, for an instant, locked gazes with Nell. She flushed and turned to Mrs. Abernathy. "Are you from the West?" she asked in a rush.

"Heavens, no," she laughed. "I'm from New York and had never been more than a few miles from home until I met Micah. We married there and then moved to Fort Hamilton where both children were born. I admit to nervousness when Micah received orders to Fort Braddock. I heard such frightening tales about the difficulties of life without the modern conveniences of a city, not to mention the danger and isolation of a station in the Arizona Territory. I was struck numb with terror at the first sight of a rattlesnake. That is," she chuckled, "until Micah taught me to shoot."

"Indeed," her husband said with a teasing smile. "I often come home to find her in the yard blasting away for the sheer pleasure of it, and terrifying the neighbors."

"Don't believe a word of it," Eliza chided. "Although, I must confess a new sense of pride in overcoming the hardships of this place. Young ladies flirting during the cotillions at home would be horrified to hear I can slaughter a poisonous reptile without batting an eye.

"The truth is," she continued, "the children and I have grown to love it here. The air is sweet and clean, the land displays wild beauty, and we are not so cut off from civilization. A stage passes through from Prescott twice a week, but in the future Fort Braddock may not be so isolated. Rumors fly concerning the addition of a rail spur, perhaps all the way to Spirit Ridge and then to Tucson."

"You don't say?" said Sam. "That's news to me." Mateo echoed his surprise.

"The newspaper comes from Prescott," said Captain Abernathy. "A delegation of railroad men will arrive any day to announce the new spur. The guess is fifty-fifty whether it will be to Fort Braddock in the east or a more western line. The territorial government has pushed to bring more settlers to our area. Right now, Fort Braddock is little more than an outpost, but the Army is considering the transfer of troops into the region for a cavalry training command. If they do, that gives the railroad one more incentive to extend the tracks. Although, I understand such decisions are as much about politics as profit."

After supper, Captain Abernathy requested Sam return with him to his office to review maps of the area and plot their course of action for tomorrow. Sam bade a polite good evening to the women. He exchanged no more than a few words with Nell since his arrival at Fort Braddock. Her relief had shown plain when he rode into camp, but what were the depths of those feelings? Sam burned with frustration. With action always preferable to speeches, he was at a loss how to proceed with such a woman. Perhaps, Nell expected courting phrases men used in cities. Sam vainly tried to recall one, but his mind drew a blank. Damnation, women complicated life.

For a while, he brushed aside thoughts of Nell and discussed the next day's expedition with Captain Abernathy. With plans complete, Sam bade him good evening. Instead of heading to the barracks, he shoved his hands in his pockets and wandered aimlessly across the grounds. Nell occupied too much of his mind to sleep.

Sam's path led to the stables. Earlier, he checked on Rio, pleased to note the horse had received attentive care and recovered from his hard ride. He decided to look in on him one last time.

From the barn came the soft glow of lantern light and a whispered voice. Sam recognized Rio's whicker and then heard the *crunch-munch* of teeth chewing. He took a step inside and then pulled up short. Nell stood at the horse's stall. A lantern on a pile of wooden crates emitted gentle illumination. Rio chewed with contentment and then nudged her impatiently.

Nell scratched his nose. "You're a good boy, aren't you?" She laid the last bit of carrot in her palm. With a delicate nuzzle, Rio's lips worked the treat into his mouth.

For a moment, speech failed him as Sam drank in the sight of Nell's beauty washed by lantern light. Flecks of gold danced in her hair. "Spoiling my horse, Miss Bishop?"

Nell startled at the sound of his voice and flashed a guilty grin. "Forgive me. I couldn't sleep so came out here. I should have asked permission, but decided a few carrots did no harm. Rio deserved a reward after his labors. Will you ride him tomorrow?"

"No. Captain Abernathy offered me an Army mount. Rio earned more than a half-day of rest."

"We asked much of him, and he delivered without complaint."

Sam strode up to the stall and rubbed the horse's nose with affection. "Yup. He is full of surprises—as are you."

Nell flushed. "I deeply apologize for the deception, but you now know my reasons."

"I can't say you were wrong, Miss Bishop. It's a mighty dangerous path you wander. It ain't easy to trust a stranger."

His words seemed to please her. "Call me Nell. I hope we are no longer strangers, but friends."

"If you call me Sam. Are you done with secrets now?" he teased.

She chuckled. "I have one more left. My full name in Eleanora, but if you wish to stay friends, never use it."

Brown eyes captured his gaze. "It pleases me to believe we're more than friends." Nell's breath quickened as his own heart beat a wild thrumming. "Nell Bishop is as strange on my tongue as Sister Regina. You'll always be *Baya* to me."

The confession triggered a smile. "The coyote continues to nip at your heels." At once, she lost her cheerful manner. "I won't be with you tomorrow when you hunt the dark riders. You must promise to take care."

"I will." Despite the evening chill, warmth steadily increased in the barn.

"I must also thank you for your actions toward

Daisy," Nell continued in a rush. The pink in her cheeks deepened in color as if they, too, gained inner heat. "The truth about her previous life must have shocked everyone."

"We've all made mistakes. I reckon we all have the right to fix them."

"Does Mr. Perez feel the same way?"

"I can't speak for Mat, other than to say he is a good man, and not one given to harsh judgment. He overcame hardship in life as well and understands the struggles people face to break with the past."

A stray lock fell across her face. Sam gently tucked it behind her ear. The dull illumination in the barn caught more of the deepening color in her cheeks. He smoothed down her hair.

"Sam…" The light in her eyes shone bright. "I-I was so glad to see you safely returned. I want to offer thanks for everything you've done for me."

Two hands callused by years of rough work and hard riding cradled her face. "I don't need your thanks," he whispered. "I've known you but a few days and never believed any woman could affect me so deeply in such short a time. When you disappeared beneath the water, my heart slipped away with you."

Nell's breath seemed to catch in her throat. "Y-You were simply concerned for my safety, having taken on the mission to Fort Braddock as your responsibility."

"Not, so, *Baya.*" His thoughts emptied. All words became meaningless. Sam bent down and kissed her. Lips, welcoming and warm, pressed against his. A fire reached deep within his soul and grabbed hold. His arms slid to Nell's shoulders and across her back, pulling her close against his body. Nothing existed anymore—not the stalls, not the horses, not the fort itself. Only the growing desire to lose himself in this woman and never let her go.

His lips went to her face and neck, delighting in the touch of her skin. She sighed in pleasure, adding fuel to his fire. Here was a woman whose passions ran deep. "You fill my heart, *Baya*," Sam murmured in her ear. "My life has been yours since the moment you stepped off the stage at Spirit Ridge. I've never felt such desire for any other woman." He kissed her again, long and slow, reveling in the sweet taste of her lips. "All the love I have to give is for you alone."

Nell stiffened beneath his touch and then pulled away. "Sam…w-we can't."

"Forgive me, *Baya*," he stammered, shamed by his lack of self-control. "I shouldn't have taken such liberties without permission."

Her hands trembled. "No…I…it's not that."

She spoke with such regret an awful notion seared his heart. "Another man stakes his claim on you in San Francisco." A simple "yes" from her lips would extinguish the light from his world forever.

"No, Sam. I have no one."

Relief flooded him. "I understand. I ain't a man who knows how to say other than what's in his heart. I pushed for this too quickly. A barn in the middle of the night is neither the time nor place to discuss such sentiments. I'll wait until the trouble with Colin Doyle is over. When you are ready, *Baya,* I'll come to you then."

"Oh, Sam." Tears filled her eyes. "Don't you see we have no future? I can't start something that will end in heartbreak for us both. My life is in San Francisco, while yours is here."

Sam issued a vehement protest. "Then I'll make a new life in San Francisco."

"No, you belong here. I sensed that from the first time we met. You draw your strength from the land. Your soul will die in the city."

He ran his fingers through her hair. "It dies without you, *Bay*a."

"You say that now, but it's not so." Nell's voice was unsteady. "You'll find a woman suited to this life to stay home, tend to your needs, and not be drawn away by mad pursuits. She'll follow respectable activities and bring no shame or embarrassment to the Tanner name. You'll have the life you deserve."

"I'll be satisfied with no other," he said. "In my heart, I knew that after my first dream. The spirits warned me you were coming and charged me to save you. They already knew what I didn't—we are bound as Coyote Woman and her hunter."

"You don't understand, Sam." Her voice broke. "The work I do is important. My life was so empty of purpose, but now it is filled with meaning."

"Can't you find purpose and meaning here? I'll never ask your spirit to change."

"You say that now…"

"If the coyote's spirit is transformed, then so is the coyote. I want you as you are—fire and fierce determination, stubbornness to drive a man wild. Others in the Territory need a coyote to nip at their heels and herd them in the right direction."

"I-I can't." Nell stepped back. "I must finish what I started. Please don't ask more." Her breath came as a regretful sigh. "Don't give your love to me."

"It's already done," Sam whispered. "You could sooner ask me not to breathe." The pain in her eyes cut right through him, sharper than his great-grandfather's blade.

"Please go." She begged.

"Rest now, *Baya*. I'll trouble you no more this evening." Sam took her hand and pressed her open palm to his lips, savoring the last sweet taste. He stepped away from her and then without a backward glance strode from the barn.

I understand, Baya. You spoke without words. Coyote Woman buried her heart from the hunter, but I'll find it. Even if I must search forever.

****

Nell leaned against the stall, seeking support for trembling legs. Her eyes followed the tall figure of Sam Tanner as he left the barn. Heat still emanated from where his lips pressed against her palm. She stared at her hand. A thumb stroked the patch of skin sending more warmth shooting up her arm, filling her with a yearning ache.

Call him back. Don't let him go.

Her arms dropped limply to her sides. Then what? Her place was in San Francisco. She built a life of purpose there—everything she ever wanted. How could Nell explain to a man from the Arizona Territory to give that up meant becoming less than a whole person? How could he understand her existence as a woman in a man's world where everyone expected her to decorate a husband's arm, keep his house clean, bear his children—and, above all, never act contrary to societal expectations. Could she now bury herself among the piñon trees and find contentment as a marshal's wife?

Nell hung her head. With a man like Sam Tanner, for a time, but eventually her restless spirit and unguarded words would take flight. She had lived without a voice and then one day found words—she'd never go back to obedient silence. If they married, people would judge Sam harshly by the actions and eccentricities of his wife. The love and desire in his eyes would turn to regret and, finally, the bitter cold of resentment. Nell couldn't bear the idea of bringing him pain.

She pushed herself away from the stall and picked up the lantern. "You're a fool. You should never have kissed him. Why didn't you merely offer thanks and leave the barn? If you showed no interest, his affections would have died. How could you encourage him and let a casual encounter go so far?"

Why did the words of this man affect her so? They were from different worlds. How did he move her so deeply? When their lips met, it felt as if her heart opened for the first time. A troubling notion occurred. What if it had?

"No," she said bitterly. "I can't let it, for his sake as well as mine."

Nell walked across the quiet grounds. Her body ached with the desire for his hands on her again, rough and callused, but filled with the promise of gentle caresses. With leaden steps, she returned to the Abernathys' quarters. The feelings awakened for Sam Tanner on the desperate ride to Fort Braddock wouldn't swiftly be put to rest. Common sense dictated romantic inclinations be swept aside at once. Delaying the inevitable only brought grief.

She sighed. Simple words, not so easily

accomplished. Not one of those rich polished gentlemen from Aunt Agatha's parties in San Francisco ever brought such yearning for an embrace. Had any other man ever sparked the same desire as Marshal Sam Tanner when he murmured *Baya*?

The night sky freckled with millions of stars, in the near future chased away by the fiery brilliance of the sun. The eagle would soar again, riding the updrafts, ruler of the sky. While far below, no more than a tiny speck on the landscape, the coyote prowled the wild places alone. Mournful sorrow as resonant as the coyote's howl gripped Nell's heart. Eagle and coyote may hunt together for a time, but never share a home.

Daisy was asleep by the time Nell returned to their room. She was glad, afraid her mental agitation would prompt questions she had no wish to address at the moment. She crawled under the quilt and shut her eyes, willing sleep to come. Her body surrendered to both physical and mental exhaustion.

Nell awoke just before dawn to the sound of a bugler's call. A tattered snatch of dream about an eagle evaporated, leaving a faint uneasy impression of a duty left undone. She bolted upright in bed. Sam was leaving.

Stay where you are, every sensible thought screamed out. *Forget last night ever happened.*

Do shut up!

Nell slipped from the covers, trying not to disturb Daisy as she hurriedly dressed in the dark. Dashing to the stables, Nell spied the men outside loading their horses. She watched as Sam saddled a cavalry mount, discreetly admiring his well-muscled form and the sturdy confidence of his movements. Even from a distance, he radiated quiet strength.

Sam turned and caught her gaze. The heat rose in Nell's cheeks as he led the horse over to her. Surely the flush wasn't visible in the dim light. "I came to say goodbye before you left."

Sam grinned. "You're out of breath. I don't usually have that effect on womenfolk."

"Do they swoon at your feet instead?" she teased.

Deep brown eyes met hers. "I've left no woman behind in Spirit Ridge, *Baya*. It pleases me to know you'll think of me after I've gone."

The flush deepened. "I will. I expect you to take care and return in one piece. You have a way of getting into predicaments," she scolded, "and you won't have my help to pull yourself out."

"Seems I recollect," he said in a gently chiding tone, "the predicaments were mostly your doing."

Nell chuckled. "I suppose they were." Her tone turned serious. "Will you promise to use due caution?"

"I'll keep a sharp eye. And you? Will you promise to stay out of trouble until I return?"

Nell wore an impish expression. "I promise to try."

"I ask no more of Coyote Woman." His smile sent a flutter to her heart.

"Mount up!" The terse order cut through the chilled morning air.

"I must go." Sam swung into the saddle with easy grace.

Nell's heart dropped. It was wrong to give him false hope. They were from two different worlds. A life together was impossible. Tell him now.

Words of rejection died on her lips.

"I'll return directly, *Baya*." Sam nudged the horse's

sides and got in line with the others.

Mateo sat stiffly in the saddle as Sam and Nell spoke. Now he turned to Nell and touched the brim of his hat. "*Adios.*" His voice softened. "Please tell Daisy I said goodbye."

"Move out!" As the first light of dawn broke over the horizon, the troop galloped away.

Nell watched until they disappeared from view. "Come back to me, Sam Tanner," she whispered. "You must."

Then what? Will you refuse him?

Her gaze drifted over the empty landscape. "Ridiculous. You can't fall in love with a man you just met…can you?" She shivered in the dawn chill and walked to the house for her shawl.

Daisy opened a sleepy eye and yawned. "Lordy, they make an unholy racket early around here. I thought the country was supposed to be quiet."

"The cavalry just rode out."

Both eyes opened. She sat up. "You saw the marshal."

Nell wrapped the shawl around her shoulders. "Only to say goodbye and wish him well. Nothing more. I owe him thanks for everything he's done."

"I don't reckon he needs your thanks. I seen the way he looks at you." Daisy reached out and grasped Nell's hand. "I ain't the brightest person, but one thing I know is the deception of men's words when they aim to coax their way into a bed. Most women don't recognize such slickness, but if you're around enough men, their lies scream out. Understand, it ain't just the voice. You can read it in their eyes and their stance. Their very touch is a lie. They are hungry dogs, and a woman nothing but a piece of meat, bought and paid for to fulfill desires." She shuddered as if recalling a painful memory. "It ain't that way with the marshal. He carries no falsehood in him when he looks at you."

Nell sighed. "It doesn't make the illogic of my situation any easier to confront."

"Could be you think too much, Nell Bishop," Daisy chided. "Might be it's time to let go the logical reasons you shouldn't do something and hang onto the one reason you should—because you care for the man. I'm talking dead plain, Nell. You done so much for me. I want to see you happy."

Nell hid her amusement at Daisy's fierce insistence. "I want to see you happy, too. Mateo glanced at you often during dinner. His gaze held kindness and understanding rather than harsh judgment." Her tone softened. "This morning he asked me to tell you goodbye. Sam believes Mateo isn't the condemning type. Nor do I."

Daisy lowered her gaze. "Perhaps not, but as he's gone with the cavalry, neither of us can know for sure."

Nell squeezed her arm. "I'll consider your sage advice, Miss Tremaine, but for now put matters of the heart aside. I could do with breakfast."

Daisy threw off the covers. "Now that's the first sensible thing you've said."

Eliza bustled about the cast iron stove. "I try to stay strong for Micah, but it's always so hard to part. The company carried full packs, so we might not see them for several days." She reached into her apron pocket and handed a telegram to Nell. "No reply yet from your editor, but Micah asked me to give you this."

The sympathetic expression on Eliza's face told

Nell everything. "Morgan reports nothing amiss in Prescott."

"I'm sorry," said Eliza. "Perhaps the men will discover evidence to convince him after they apprehend the dark riders, but I must warn you Morgan is not a man easily persuaded."

"You don't find him agreeable," said Nell.

Eliza laughed. "It is so obvious? No, I don't. Thaddeus Morgan lords his position over others. I've heard talk he's from a family in the East with more social position than money. It's no secret he hoped to receive the commission as governor. It must grate on him knowing he soon must offer welcoming words to another." A sound of a baby crying drew her attention. "Jamie is awake. If you'll excuse me…" She wiped her hands on the apron and hurried off.

Daisy nudged Nell. "Read it."

Nell unfolded the paper. "Message received. No unrest in Prescott. No unusual shipments at depot. Threat from Doyle or dark riders is fabrication."

"Fabrication!" Nell crumpled the telegram into a tight wad. "He so much as called us liars."

"Can't rightly say I'm surprised," said Daisy with a sigh. "We told a peculiar tale."

"Which doesn't mean it should be dismissed…Come, help me set the table and lay out breakfast for all of us. If I don't do something constructive, I'll go mad."

They finished breakfast preparations. Eliza returned with Sally and James in tow, and they sat down to eat. As Eliza fed the baby, she said, "I don't believe either of you made up tales—not that my opinion counts with Lt. Governor Morgan. If it is any consolation, Micah won't dismiss your accusations as lightly as Morgan. He was eager to question the dark riders."

"I'm pleased to hear it." Nell bristled. "I don't take kindly to being called a liar by anyone."

Eliza snorted in disgust. "Morgan's opinion and mine often are at odds."

"Indeed. Such as?"

"Well, I shouldn't say…"

"Nothing will get to Morgan's ears," she hastily assured her. "I know little things can affect a young officer's career."

Eliza chuckled. "Such as a wife who refuses to hold her tongue? Trust me when I say, I've held it plenty around him. Fortunately, our paths don't cross often. Although he can be gracious and charming to those with whom he curries favor, Morgan maintains a superior attitude over Micah, as if talking with such a lowly army officer is beneath him. Well, he won't be in Prescott long," she stated with satisfaction. "The new governor will appoint his own man and boot Morgan out the door."

"When will that be?" said Daisy.

"Directly, I hope. The different parties must finish squabbling. Politicians fight for influence. The railroads desire someone to look with approval on their own business practices. Settlers only require a person committed to keeping law and order in the Territory."

Once breakfast finished, Nell and Daisy insisted on helping Eliza with the chores and children. Eventually, Nell excused herself to sneak a few more carrots to Rio. The horse whinnied a greeting as she entered.

"Yes," she murmured wistfully, patting his neck. "I

miss Sam, too, but it will be our little secret."

Nell broke off a piece of carrot. "Sam spoke of his visions. The admission must have been difficult. I'm certain he doesn't broadly disclose his gift, especially with white women in religious garb not known for respect of Indian ways." Rio nuzzled her hand, and she fed him the last piece. "I never expected to find my heart in the Arizona Territory. I don't know what to do. Any suggestions?" He nickered as if in sympathy for her dilemma.

Returning from the stables, she met Daisy crossing the grounds. "The children are napping. They're sweet little things, aren't they?"

"They are, indeed."

Daisy shifted on her feet. "Eliza spoke with great kindness to me. She must suspect I wasn't a servant in Doyle's household."

"Do you suppose her husband told her?"

"No, but Eliza is smart as a tack. She told me out here a woman can turn her life around. In the East, folks considered her shy and delicate. Tough to reckon, ain't it?"

"Not really," said Nell with a smile. "I was once considered fragile."

Daisy chuckled. "Now that's as hard to swallow as a horseshoe."

"It's true. After a prolonged illness as a child, I suffered debilitating weakness. Against doctors' orders and much to Aunt Agatha's horror, my parents decided the way to combat frailty was more physical and mental activity, not less. Within a short time, all signs of weakness disappeared although I continue ever since to horrify Aunt Agatha." Nell gave Daisy's arm an affectionate squeeze. "Change in one's fortune is possible."

A soldier walked from the telegraph office with a paper in his hand. "Miss Bishop, a wire just came for you from a Mr. Hollingsworth in San Francisco."

Nell grasped it eagerly. "Arthur must have understood my cryptic message."

"What does it say?" said Daisy.

"Pleased package arrived safely," she read. "Hope contents prove useful. Our mutual friend left. No date of return given." Nell looked up from the paper with an anxious expression. "Dash it all."

"Mutual friend?" asked Daisy. "What does he mean?"

"Nothing good, I'm afraid. Arthur promised to keep watch on The Mick. This message means he's no longer in San Francisco."

Daisy gasped. "Doyle told his partner he planned to arrive when the attack was fixin' to begin."

Nell stared into the horizon. "Blood spills soon, Daisy, and we still have no idea how to stop it."

Chapter Eleven

Sam crouched to examine the faint hoofprint in the dirt. "One of the riders slowed even more." He pointed to brown speckles on the leaves of a nearby creosote bush. "His wound opened again, and he's bleeding freely."

Captain Abernathy wore a look of admiration as he peered down from the saddle. "Damn, you have good eyes, Marshal. That's a fact. We couldn't have tracked either of the gunmen half this distance." He glanced at the sky. "How far ahead, do you suppose? Not much daylight left."

"They're close. The trail is fresh. I'd say less than an hour ago. Judging from the amount of blood, one won't get much farther. We need to hightail it out of here if we want answers before his demise."

"You still accept Miss Bishop's tale even after the telegram from Morgan? You read it, sir. None of it supported her wild accusations."

Sam mentioned nothing to Nell that morning, but his concerns had grown since the wire arrived. He expected some of the contents to support her, but the news of all quiet from Prescott brought no sense of relief. The shadow's poisonous fingers continued to inch forward. Of that, he was certain.

"Morgan's wire was plain," Sam murmured gruffly, "and left no doubt as to his beliefs. Let me ask you, Captain—how sure are you he conducted a thorough investigation? His reply came through mighty fast." Captain Abernathy appeared reluctant to answer, and Sam raised an eyebrow. "You noted it, too. Something funny about this business with the dark riders. Don't tell me you can't feel it."

"I admit Morgan's quick response weighs heavily," he said with chagrin. "Miss Bishop was quite impassioned in her beliefs. I've no doubt ordinary bandits didn't chase you, but those wishing personal harm. The way the dark riders fought, one might think they had military training—most unusual for run-of-the-mill desperados." He stared at the ground and shifted in his saddle. "Let's be on our way, Marshal. I'm anxious to question the wounded men and determine their true purpose in the Territory."

"You stirred up a hornet's nest, *Baya*," Sam murmured, as he swung onto the horse's back. The memory of Nell at Fort Braddock brought a smile to his lips and lightness to his soul. She had arrived out of breath to say goodbye, concern for his safety evident on her features.

He started at a sudden jab in the ribs. "Mind on the job, cowboy," said Mateo with a cheeky grin, "and not a pretty girl."

"Saw you daydreaming a time or two. Wasn't by chance about a little blonde slip of a girl with bright blue eyes?" Mateo stared straight ahead without answering.

The blood trail led to a wooded area bordered by thick scrubby vegetation. Sam tensed in his seat. His hunter's eyes scrutinized the rough terrain searching for any sign of the quarry. Every boulder, every tree served as a hiding place for an ambush.

"We're close," muttered Mateo with a cautious glance around.

"Yup, they ain't far ahead. Open wounds slowed them to a walk. Right now, one is cursing your name with each bounce of his horse."

Mateo snorted. "Had I arrived a second earlier, he wouldn't speak at all."

"I'm thankful," said Sam with gratitude. "I never expected to see another sunrise."

Mateo winked. "Thank your grandfather. He taught me to shoot."

Sam removed his hat and wiped his brow. "I feel the dark riders nearby. Hell, I can practically smell 'em."

"Do they believe we gave up pursuit? They don't hide their tracks any longer." Mateo motioned to hoofprints in the sandy soil and shook his head. "A scout isn't needed to follow such an obvious trail. Why aim for here? It makes more sense to turn south to Mexico. The cavalry won't ride past the border."

"Can't say what was in their heads, but you're right. Their route makes no sense." A disturbed area on the ground drew Sam's attention. He held up his hand to bring the troop to a halt.

Captain Abernathy reined in beside him. "What is it, Marshal?"

A distant whinny broke the silence. "Hear that?" Sam whispered. "Keep your voice low, Captain, and your men and horses quiet. See the new hoofprint? We got more company. Another rider picked up our friends' trail and joined them. I reckon the three are well past that gully by now, and into the hills." He squinted. "No lookouts. They ain't spotted us, yet. Might not even know we're right behind."

The captain pulled out a spyglass and made a quick scan of the landscape. "Let's not give them any time to discover our arrival. I don't like the idea of a fresh newcomer, but the odds are still in our favor." He gave the signal to dismount. "We split up and pen them in the middle."

"They won't come quiet," warned Sam. "Do that and we'll have to kill them before we get answers."

"You have a plan, Marshal?"

"Mat and I circle to the rear and cut off their retreat. With luck, they'll be too occupied with your troops to note our approach. With the cavalry to the front and our guns behind, they may come to their senses and drop their weapons."

"Agreed, Marshal. My men and I will set up crossfire to prevent escape on horseback. Watch yourselves," he cautioned. "We're far from Fort Braddock, and I've no desire to carry bodies with us."

Sam and Mateo grabbed their Winchesters and darted to the rocks. Sam motioned Mateo to a flanking position. "I'll move in close," he whispered. "Keep an eye out for anyone trying to slip past us." Mateo gave a terse nod. Sam silently edged around a stand of alders. The brush rustled. Sam froze in place, pressed flat against a tree.

"You shouldn't have come," growled a voice.

Heart pounding, Sam expected the click of a trigger followed by an explosion of gunfire. He relaxed when a second man, weak and strained, answered. "What the hell you expect us to do? Weren't no place else to go. Trent and me couldn't get to Mexico. Not shot up like we is. We barely made it this far. As 'tis, Trent is near the end."

"That trail of blood left behind," said the first speaker, "is plain enough even for a tenderfoot to follow."

The man's voice brought a frown to Sam. Something in the tone rang familiar.

"Orders were to head straight to the border if you ran into trouble," the man continued. "You could have wired Prescott from Mexico and still got paid. Weren't smart thinking to come this ways. Now your horses are spent with the cavalry hot on your trail."

The voice continued to tug impatiently at a memory in Sam that stubbornly refused to surface.

"I didn't see no one dogging us," the wounded man growled.

"I did. They'll be upon you right enough."

"Then we ride out," he answered with a wheezing cough. "We ain't far from camp. We'll lead them into a trap."

"The three of us are outnumbered, and you're closer to life than death. I've no desire to be taken prisoner."

"Trent and me ain't dead, yet, and we won't talk. We shown our loyalty."

"True, but it's a wonder how even the most ardent vows of loyalty disappear when faced with the reality of a hanging. Moreover, the death of an entire cavalry troop will surely arouse unwanted interest in this part of the Territory."

The wounded man coughed again. "What do you reckon we do?"

"Well now, a thought just occurred to me. Ever

hear tell the meaning of a loose end?"

The tone was as hard and cold as mid-winter ice. Sam's finger tightened on the trigger. What was it about that voice?

"You mean on a lasso?" the outlaw answered, obviously confused.

"Yep, on a lasso. What happens if the end is loosened?"

"The knot slips and the lasso ain't good for shit."

"That's a fact. So it's best to take care of a loose end directly. A second stumper now occurs to me. What is more useless than one loose end?"

"What the hell kind of game is this?" the outlaw barked, fear tinging his voice. "What are you doing?"

"The answer is two loose ends."

Sam started as two gunshots came in rapid succession. Rifle to his shoulder, he bolted around the tree, and then crept forward. After twenty feet, he reached a clearing and pulled up short at the awful sight. Two men in black shirts lay dead on the ground, bullet holes in the center of their foreheads. One man's hand still rested on his holstered gun as if cut down reaching for the weapon.

Sam took off after the sound of hoofbeats. Rounding a boulder, he glimpsed a black-shirted rider on a roan with two white fetlocks before he galloped out of sight.

"Sam!" Mateo shouted.

"Here. I'm all right." He jogged to the clearing.

Mateo stood over the bodies, his mouth agape. "What the hell happened?"

Before Sam answered, Captain Abernathy hailed them. "No need to hurry," Sam yelled. "They ain't going nowhere."

Captain Abernathy and the rest of the troops crashed through the underbrush. "Why did you fire?"

"I didn't. One of their own killed them." Sam described the conversation.

Captain Abernathy gaped at the corpses. "This person murdered his own men to prevent their capture?"

"He was afraid they'd talk."

"I've never heard of such callous disregard for life even among the most desperate outlaws. Oh, they turn on each other soon enough in a squabble over money, property, a woman, or believed insult, but this…"

Sam eyed the grim scene with disgust. "The information the killer feared they'd impart must have all-fired importance."

Abernathy's expression hardened. "Something peculiar is going on in these hills. Marshal, I need to know where our mysterious friend rode to in such haste and what forces are at his disposal."

"The killer didn't talk as if he came a fair lick." Sam peered at the sky. "We have a few hours of daylight left. I can make good time alone."

"Not alone," insisted Mateo.

"Very well, gentlemen," said Captain Abernathy. "We'll remain here. I'll count on a report before dark."

Sam and Mateo retrieved their horses and took off in pursuit. The trail wove in and out and often disappeared altogether. Now and then, Sam dismounted to give the ground a thorough inspection when tracks seemed to vanish from sight.

Mateo let out a low whistle. "He's good. Lucky you were along."

Sam smirked. "The dark rider knows the country, that's for sure, but, I know it better." He examined an impression in the dirt. "This is an old Indian trail, but used recently by others. We've come a roundabout ways since leaving Fort Braddock. I don't reckon we're more than twenty miles from Prescott."

Mateo glanced at the sky. "Not much sun left. Captain Abernathy expects us directly."

"Got a funny feeling we're not far from our quarry." Sam pointed toward the rocks. "That way the trail narrows and then bends around a switchback into a notch in the hills. We'd be spotted easy by any lookouts. I say we tie up the horses and follow the high ground for a spell. If we don't see anything, we head back."

They secured the horses, then crept up the incline using scrubby brush and rocks for cover. As they approached the summit, the hair rose on the back of Sam's neck. He grabbed Mateo's arm and made a motion to get down. They crouched in the dirt behind a creosote bush, straining to hear.

Every one of Sam's instincts screamed a warning. Someone was out there...

A glint of sunlight flashed off a metallic surface. Sam tapped his friend's shoulder and gestured. Mateo's eyes followed Sam's gaze to the entrance of the notch. Two black-shirted men armed with carbines guarded the trail.

He drew his head close to Sam's ear and whispered, "Only two. We could take them easy."

"Best not till we know what they're protecting. Follow me. We'll move to the other side of those trees. From there, we can sneak to the top of the rise and get a look-see at what they're so eager to keep secret."

Bellies flat to the ground, they inched away from the trail and out of the gunmen's line of sight. The wind now brought the sound of men's voices and the scent of horses. Finally, they reached the crest and spied over the rim.

Sam sucked in a breath. "What the hell?"

Both men gaped with astonishment. Encamped below them were dozens of men and horses.

****

Daisy paled. "The Mick is in the Territory. We're too late."

Nell's expression was grim. "Not yet, but the authorities in Prescott must be warned."

"That won't do no good. We already received Morgan's answer. He put no stock in our tale."

"Then he must be persuaded in person."

"Unless you fetch further proof, he don't strike me as a man to listen. Only capture of the dark riders will alter his position."

Nell glowered. "That could take days. When did Eliza say the next stage arrived for Prescott?"

"The day after tomorrow."

"Not soon enough. I must ride to Prescott now."

Daisy gasped. "Nell, you ain't serious."

"Completely. If Morgan needs proof of Colin Doyle's activities, then I'll bring it to him. He couldn't have done a thorough investigation in such a short time, but merely dismissed our accusations out of hand. I'll find evidence of Doyle's activities and convince him to act."

"Shouldn't we bide our time here for the marshal? He'll return with the dark riders in custody."

"We've no guarantee of their success. Without doubt, Sam can track the villains, but they were wounded and may already be beyond questioning. Dead riders won't support our story."

Daisy raised an eyebrow. "He ain't going to be happy you left."

Nell managed a slight smile. "I only promised to try and stay out of trouble. I can't sit here and waste precious time when danger is imminent. If Morgan refuses to act without proof, then I intend to find it."

"How?"

Nell considered several options before seizing the most logical. "The depot master at the train station. If Morgan even bothered to contact him at all, he gave no more than a cursory glance at the shipping manifests and noted nothing out of the ordinary. By God, that man shall not dismiss me so lightly."

"Dismiss us, you mean. If you're set on going, so am I."

"It's too dangerous. Need I remind you, Doyle is either in Prescott or nearby?"

"Which is why it's safe," Daisy argued. "He'll never expect to find me on his doorstep. Besides, I know The Mick's men and you don't. If they're in town, I'll spot them first." At Nell's hesitation, she added. "If you don't let me tag along, I'll tell Eliza what you plan and she'll throw a conniption."

Nell's eyes twinkled. "Dear me. Blackmail, Miss Tremaine?"

"I prefer to think of it as firm persuasion. When do we head out?"

"As soon as Mateo's wagon is hitched. If anyone asks our destination, I'll say we're restless and decided on a short ride. The trail to Prescott is well marked, and the weather is fine. We'll arrive in a few hours."

Daisy sighed. "I'll scare up Sister Mary's habit."

"Don't bother," said Nell much to Daisy's obvious relief. "That disguise has run its course, and anyone at the fort who catches sight of you dressed as a nun will ask questions."

Daisy frowned. "I hate to cause Eliza worry. She's been so kind."

"I'll leave a note in our room explaining the real reason for our departure. By the time she opens it, we'll be too far along to stop."

As they gathered their belongings, Nell fingered the derringer. She had given it a good cleaning since the drenching in the river, it was sensible to be prepared. She loaded a bullet in the chamber and dropped the weapon into her pocket.

Fortune favored their exit. Eliza and the children were in the garden and didn't notice them enter the stables. Nell tossed their bags in the wagon bed. She covered them with an old blanket Mateo brought for Daisy's comfort during the ride from Spirit Ridge.

Nell flashed a charming smile at the blacksmith, explaining their intention to take a short ride around the perimeter.

"The cavalry left this horse behind because he has a shoe loose," said the blacksmith. "Won't take long to fix if you care to sit tight."

Nell chaffed at a delay. If they didn't leave now, they'd lose light before arriving in Prescott. Her eyes lit on Rio. "Please, hitch the other one. We'll take him instead."

The blacksmith obliged, and they rode out of the

fort. Nell held her breath, but no one paid them any undue interest. As they lost sight of Fort Braddock, Daisy nudged Nell playfully in the side. "The marshal won't be pleased you stole his horse."

"I hope to have Rio secure in his stall by the time Sam returns."

"And if he's not?"

With a sigh, Nell tied her bonnet's ribbons under her chin. "I'll add horse thievery to the list of my other sins."

They traveled slowly, not wishing to overexert Rio, and stopped once to down water and leftover biscuits from breakfast that Nell packed. By the time they arrived on the outskirts of Prescott, morning had become afternoon. They found a livery and made arrangements to board Rio.

Daisy dismounted with a groan. "Lordy, I've been bouncing on that seat like a nervous cat. I've no regrets leaving San Francisco except one—comfortable padded carriage rides."

Nell straightened up and stretched the kinks from her back. "It's been a hard day even for a person used to strenuous activity, but you've done well, Daisy. I didn't expect half so much. I'm proud of you." The girl flashed a pleased smile and reached for her carpetbag. "Leave it," Nell said. "We'll find a boarding house later and send for them."

"Where first? The train station?"

"Not yet. We'll try the land office." Nell got directions from the liveryman. As they walked the street, she cautiously eyed the other pedestrians. "Notice anyone with a familiar face?" she whispered.

"No, but I confess to a nervous flutter in my

innards. Must be all these people."

Nell regarded her with surprise. "Why, I barely count twenty townsfolk."

Daisy chuckled. "This is the most crowded street I been on since San Francisco. I must be growing fond of clean air and wide open spaces. Heading to city life again will be hard."

"Why must you go? As Eliza said, opportunities abound to change one's fortune here."

Her voice softened. "I believe the more distance I put between myself, the West, and certain people, the better for me."

"You speak of Mateo?"

"I fear to see condemnation or pity in his eyes." Abruptly, the wistfulness left Daisy's expression. She linked her arm with Nell's. "No matter how this turns out, I don't regret a minute of our adventure. I'm glad we went to Spirit Ridge."

For an instant, Nell felt Sam's lips pressed against hers. "So am I."

The clerk at the land office was most obliging to Nell's cordial smile and polite inquiry. A man named Doyle did, indeed, buy a large tract of land outside town. "Well, that went smooth as glass," Daisy said as they left. "Do we have enough to take to Morgan?"

"No. We proved Doyle's interest in the area, but he broke no law. I had hoped he used underhanded means, but the land office legally recorded the purchase. Blast the man, he even paid more than a fair price—probably to allay any suspicions."

"Where to next?"

"The train depot. Recruiting men isn't enough to build an army. You need supplies and equipment. I hope to unearth evidence they arrived by rail."

As they approached the depot, Daisy's steps slowed. With a haunted expression, she stared at the sign in front for the Burlington Northern Santa Fe Railroad. Nell gave her a consoling pat on the arm. Railroad men were known frequenters of Doyle's establishments. How many had he forced Daisy to entertain?

"Linger outside," Nell said, kindly. "I can do this alone."

She shook her head. "No. I ain't gonna be bound in misery to my past."

The only person in the depot was a man outside on the platform writing arrival and departures times on a chalkboard. He wore a hat with the company logo.

"We need to see the stationmaster, please," said Nell.

The man motioned inside. Next to the ticket counter was a door with Stationmaster stenciled on the front. "Sorry, ma'am. He's not here right now and won't return until tomorrow."

Nell proffered her friendliest smile. "Could you help us, then? We have a few questions on recent shipping invoices."

"Invoices are the concern of the stationmaster. They're kept locked in his office, and I don't have the key. You'll need to come back."

Nell stifled her disappointment and left the station with Daisy. "Another day of delay is inconceivable," she burst out in frustration. "A few inquiries to other businesses may unearth more details on Doyle's activities."

"The more questions you ask in town, the greater

the chance word gets to Doyle of someone poking into his business."

"I see no other way around it."

Daisy glanced at the depot. "Can you pick a lock?"

Nell flashed an impish grin. "Aunt Agatha sent me to one of the most exclusive women's colleges in the east. The dormitory enacted a most unreasonable curfew. Of course, I can pick a lock. Whatever is on your mind, Miss Tremaine?"

"I'll distract the clerk long enough for you to slip into the office." Daisy chuckled at Nell's raised eyebrow. "Don't worry. I ain't planning to seduce him on the tracks. I've given up that sinful life, but I still got enough proper charms left to draw attention from the door."

Nell squeezed her arm with affection. "I didn't believe you'd fall back on your old ways for a moment. My concern is for your well-being. If we're caught, neither the railroad nor the authorities will view our actions kindly."

"Then I reckon," she said pertly, "we shouldn't get caught."

"I agree. I need two hairpins."

"Here, take mine." Daisy removed two pins and handed them to Nell. "How long do you need?"

"At school, I garnered renown among my fellow coeds for unlocking the front door of the dormitory in under a minute."

They returned to the station. Nell pressed flat against the wall near the office out of sight of the clerk and nodded. Daisy winked and walked to the platform. "I'm so sorry to trouble you again. I must have lost my necklace out here. Could you possibly help me search?"

Her voice trembled convincingly. "It was a parting gift from my dear aunt, Eleanora. She is a saintly woman who gave it to me when she took holy orders…"

Daisy led him from the window, prattling about dear sainted Aunt Eleanora. Nell crouched in front of the lock and deftly inserted the hat pins. With a pull and twist came a subtle click, and she slipped inside the stationmaster's office. The small room contained a rolltop desk, chair, and several filing cabinets, one of which held drawers conveniently labeled Shipping Invoices.

Nell riffled through the paperwork. The forms were separated by incoming/outgoing, then by date and name. She yanked any paper with Colin Doyle at the top and set it aside. By the time she reached the end of the last drawer, a significant stack had accumulated.

Daisy's voice approached. "Then Aunt Eleanora wrote to say she had an audience with the Pope. Isn't that thrilling? I reckon they'll have plenty to jaw about. While I'm here may I trouble you to see the train schedule?"

"It's posted outside," said the clerk in obvious bewilderment. "We stood talking right in front of it for the last few minutes."

"Oh, yes, of course, how silly of me. Please show me again. My, you have such nice handwriting…"

Nell bundled up the papers, tucked them inside her waistband, and then buttoned her jacket. She listened at the door to make sure Daisy and the man were gone and then slipped outside again. A few twists of the hairpins, and the lock reengaged. The stationmaster would be none the wiser on his return.

"There you are," Nell called out cheerfully, striding

to the platform. "I've been looking all over for you."

Daisy answered meekly. "My necklace is missing. This kind gentleman has been helping me search."

"No need to worry your little head. I found it outside on the street."

Daisy clutched her heart and heaved a dramatic sigh. "I'm so relieved." She smiled at the clerk. "Thank you ever so much for your kindness."

"Now if you will direct us to the territorial governor's office," said Nell with a sweet smile, "we'd be obliged."

As they walked, Nell thumbed through the sheaf of papers. Her eyes lit up at the inventory of items. She pulled those that appeared the most damning and handed the rest to Daisy. "Orders for ammunition spaced out over several months. More than any gentleman rancher ever needed. Here's one for tents. This receipt alone is for a dozen. Others list cots and blankets. I see nothing for livestock, no farm implements." She snorted in disgust. "Morgan never approached the stationmaster, but surely these will convince him to investigate."

"What of the rest?" Daisy flipped through her stack of forms. "They're mostly household goods: coffee, beans, and such."

"You need more than one pot and pan to feed an army. Keep hold of them for now. If Morgan needs further convincing, we'll throw them in his face."

Without warning, Daisy grabbed Nell's arm and pulled her into a doorway. Nell followed her horrified gaze down the street. Colin Doyle stood in front of the territorial government offices casually smoking a cigar.

Chapter Twelve

Mateo studied the encampment. "I count close to fifty men in dark shirts. No telling how many in the tents. What are they doing here? Are they all outlaws?"

"You ask fine questions, *amigo*," Sam murmured. "I got no answers, but they've been here a while judging by how the ground is trampled. There are enough tents erected to house them plus supplies for both men and horses."

Mateo let out a snort. "They'll be mighty uncomfortable once winter is upon them."

"I don't reckon they plan to stay that long." He motioned to a tent with two armed men. "I wonder what they're keeping in there. It's the only one with sentries."

A wagon pulled in front of the tent. The driver jumped down and spoke to the guards. All three went inside. They returned struggling with a heavy wooden crate. As they lifted it to the wagon bed, a man in the rear lost his grip, and the back end of the box slammed to the ground. The cover jarred loose giving a view of the contents. Sam drew a breath at the row of neatly stacked carbine rifles.

"Those are Army issue," Mateo muttered. "How'd they get hold of them?"

Sam scowled. "The train robberies. They were after weapons."

The men shoved the crate into the wagon then loaded two more on top along with several boxes, the size used for ammunition. One of the men stopped to take off his hat and wipe his brow. An ugly scar ran along the side of his face from hairline to cheek.

Sam nudged Mateo. "We got a flyer not long ago on an outlaw named Orrin Wilkes with a scar to match that description. He's out of Texas wanted for train robbery and murder, but was spotted crossing the New Mexico border a few months ago. Ain't been seen since."

"Instead, he headed here," murmured Mateo. "An unusual army Doyle recruited."

Another man rode to the group loading the wagon. Sam's eyes narrowed. "Roan with two white fetlocks—that's the rider we tracked." The man barked a command for the men to hurry. Then he wheeled his horse around, his face now plainly visible. Sam's jaw tightened. "Reese McLaren."

"I advise caution, my friend," whispered Mateo. "You can't march over there and arrest him now."

Sam grunted. "Don't aim to arrest him. I aim to shoot him."

"You can't do either with dozens of gunmen milling about."

Sam's gaze went to the now fully loaded wagon. The driver flicked the reins. McLaren followed as the wagon rolled away. "I itch to know where he's going."

Mateo grinned. "Why don't you stroll down there and ask them? I'm certain they'll be happy to tell you."

"Maybe I'll do that."

"*Qué?*"

"I have an idea, but we need to report our findings

to Abernathy first."

Mateo eyed him askance. "I don't like that look. It's a look that says the idea is dangerous, and your grandmother would surely disapprove."

He smirked. "You're right. Come on, I'll explain on the way."

Once more, Sam and Mateo edged past the lookouts. They retrieved the horses and then hurried along the trail to rejoin the soldiers. The cavalry had begun to settle down for the night. Two soldiers were in the process of digging graves for the corpses. Another knelt on the ground, preparing to start a fire. "Hold up on that, Romero," Sam cautioned. "We got trouble ahead and don't want to give away our position." He described the discovery at the dark riders' camp.

Captain Abernathy clenched his fists. "Miss Bishop and Miss Tremaine are due an apology. Their story is no longer outlandish. Those men are militia, and we are outnumbered and outgunned. I'll return to Fort Braddock and wire for reinforcements. Let's hope they don't move on Prescott before then." He scowled. "Someone in the city must have noticed that many men and supplies traveling through the area."

"Señor Morgan has very bad eyesight," said Mateo dryly.

The captain's face flushed with anger. "Miss Bishop and Miss Tremaine deserve a second apology. Morgan's investigation was superficial—if that." He ordered the men to break camp.

"Just a second, Captain," said Sam. "I have a way to scare up more information and need a black shirt."

Captain Abernathy raised an eyebrow. "Marshal?"

"I plan to slip into the camp after night sets in and

join the riders."

"Don't look at me," said Mateo wryly. "I told him he was loco."

"Sir, I admire your courage," said the captain, "but I must agree with Mr. Perez. Did you not just say you knew McLaren?" He motioned to the dead bodies. "Remember what he did to two of his own men? He won't show any mercy if you're discovered."

"He left with the wagon and ain't in camp."

"That doesn't mean he won't make a prompt return."

"I'm fixing to stay out of McLaren's way. The rest won't give me trouble. I recognize a few from descriptions on wanted posters, but none is apt to know me." His lips twitched in a smile. "Miss Bishop fooled a heap of people with a simple disguise not so long ago dressed mostly in black. If people only see what they expect to see, I aim to prove she's right. All I need is the shirt."

"Surely someone will notice a new man among them."

"Not unless they take a headcount. I'll wear my hat low and draw no attention."

The captain eyed him with doubt. "You take quite a risk, Marshal."

"It's worth it to get a handle on their plans. Mat will stay behind and keep hidden. I'll pass along a message if I hear anything noteworthy. He can deliver it to you at Fort Braddock."

"Very well, then." The captain offered a handshake with Sam and Mateo. "Gentlemen, may fortune grant her favor. I hope to see you both again in the near future…" He paused and shot a glance at the bodies.

"Alive and well, that is." He mounted his horse and gave the signal for the cavalry to follow.

Mateo looked at the sky. "We have an hour of daylight left. Sure I can't talk you out of this?"

"Nope," said Sam with a grin, "but you can help me strip a shirt off a dead man."

He sighed in resignation. "As you wish. I suggest the one with the less obvious bullet holes."

****

Nell drew in a breath. "It appears as if Doyle is in no hurry. You must leave this instant, Daisy. I'll join you at the livery."

Daisy issued a vehement protest. "He knows you by sight, too, Nell."

"We only met once and briefly."

"That don't mean Doyle won't recognize you. He surely received word by now I traveled with another woman."

"Dressed as a nun. Features are hardly visible beneath a habit. Even the dark riders had no clear idea of my appearance. They merely saw a nun and gave chase. I won't back down now because of the risk. I came here to speak to Morgan and won't leave until I do." She squeezed Daisy's hand. "It's imperative you get off the street. We don't know how many men traveled with Doyle from San Francisco. They may be nearby and recognize you. We've come so far, Daisy. I won't have you hurt for all the world."

Daisy was unconvinced. "I'll fetch the town marshal."

"To do what? Arrest Doyle for smoking a cigar in public? For legally purchasing land outside Prescott? His conduct has done nothing to call for intervention.

169

With an attack imminent, I must press our case directly to Morgan. Only he can order the law to act." Nell peered from the doorway at Doyle. "Light is fading. His back is to the entrance. The bonnet will obscure my face. With my head turned away, I can easily slip by unnoticed. Please, go. I promise to return with all due haste."

Daisy appeared to wrestle with her mental turmoil before giving Nell a quick hug. "Very well," she grumbled, "but be careful."

Nell watched as Daisy turned the corner. None of the pedestrians on the street followed or even glanced in her direction. Convinced of Daisy's safety, Nell walked to the building. Her eyes focused on the door. Despite earlier brave words, Nell's heart pounded. She fought a nearly irresistible urge to peer at Doyle.

As Nell crossed the street, Doyle tossed the stub of the cigar. She turned her head and scampered up the steps. Once inside, she dared to peek out a window facing the street. Doyle was gone. A clerk directed Nell to Morgan's harried aide. She politely requested an immediate meeting with the lieutenant governor.

"Mr. Morgan is a very busy man," he said in a clipped tone. "He won't see anyone without an appointment."

Nell paused to consider the best way to get an audience. Eliza Abernathy had stated Thaddeus Morgan belonged to a socially prominent family. Members of socially prominent families often sported large egos that responded well to regular feedings. She flashed her most charming smile. "Please inform him Miss Nell Bishop from *The San Francisco Dispatch* newspaper requests an interview."

The aide agreed to pass on the message. He returned shortly to say Mr. Morgan granted a few minutes of his valuable time. Nell stifled a shout of triumph.

He ushered her to an office on the second floor. "I should warn you," he whispered nervously. "Mr. Morgan has not been in good humor since receiving word Washington will soon announce the new governor—not that he ever had a sanguine disposition."

"I heard he wished for the appointment himself." Nell shot him a sympathetic look. "A difficult man?"

The aide mopped his brow. "Mr. Morgan is most settled in his manner. When a situation is not to his liking, he is easily perturbed."

The lieutenant governor sat behind a large mahogany desk. As Nell entered, he rose from the chair and strode forward to greet her. She shot him an appraising glance. Thaddeus Morgan was ramrod straight with a neatly trimmed mustache. He wore boots polished to such a high gloss they reflected clear images of the room. More than likely, not a speck of trail dirt ever sullied the leather. The cut of his expensive tailored suit rivaled the skills of the best outfitter in San Francisco. *Where on Earth did he find their like out here?*

They shook hands. His nails were evenly filed. The skin on his palms was smooth and without a single callus. Morgan motioned Nell to a seat and then shot the aide one scathing look. The man quickly backed from the room and shut the door.

"Miss Bishop, I understand you asked for an interview. I'm afraid I can't give any details on the new governor as we have yet to receive a name. I'm happy to discuss my involvement in maintaining order in the Territory during the interim. Your readers will, no doubt, find it of interest."

My readers would, no doubt, be bored beyond belief.

Nell settled into her seat, irritation rising. She was tired and hungry. Dammit, couldn't the man even offer a sherry? She stifled her pique. "That's not why I'm here. I don't wish an interview, but have information on a danger to the populace of Prescott."

"Let me put your fancies to rest, Miss Bishop. If trouble existed, I'd know." His smile was so patronizing, Nell fought the urge to slap it off his face.

"They aren't fancies," she stated flatly. "My warning concerns a man from San Francisco who recently purchased property in the area. His name is Colin Doyle."

Morgan stiffened in his seat. His smooth self-possession displayed a crack. "You are the one spreading wild rumors. I received Captain Abernathy's wire concerning dark riders. This Doyle person supposedly poses a threat. I thoroughly investigated the matter and discovered nothing to it. He's a law abiding landowner." Smugness highlighted his features. "I'll have words with Captain Abernathy for listening to the rants of a hysterical female. Now, excuse me. I'm occupied with important government matters."

"I am neither ranting nor hysterical," she retorted, "nor am I one of your subordinates who can be dismissed with a wave of the hand. By God, sir, you'll listen for I refuse to step foot outside this door until you do."

Morgan clenched his teeth. "I won't have a woman

dictate to me."

She smiled sweetly. "I'm not dictating, merely offering options. Either allow me the courtesy of several minutes of your time or have me dragged from the room. That, sir, shall be quite a scene, one which will entertain all the good people in the lobby. Why, word may even reach to the new Territorial governor. I'm sure he'll be impressed when he hears you tossed me bodily into the street. He may decide to offer you a position in his cabinet on the spot."

The muscle in his jaw twitched. "I'll grant you two minutes."

Nell launched into an abbreviated version of the story, barely pausing for breath as she stressed the urgency of her mission. "Once informed of your wire to Captain Abernathy, I came straight from Fort Braddock to convince you of the seriousness of the situation."

"I'm at a loss as to your actions, Miss Bishop." He spoke with haughty disdain. "Nothing is amiss in Prescott. You say a *servant* gave you this information. I can hardly give credence to such a wild yarn." Morgan's imperious manner raised Nell's suspicions he discovered Daisy's true relationship to Doyle. Perhaps Captain Abernathy hadn't been as discreet in his wire as he professed.

"I assure you," Nell stated without hesitation. "This woman's social standing may not be high, but her word is beyond question." No wonder Eliza Abernathy distained him so. His arrogant smugness was beyond belief.

Morgan rose from his seat. "You have the fine makings of a tawdry dime novel, Miss Bishop, and little else. Now, if you'll excuse me, I have important matters that require my personal attention."

"The riders—"

"Mere desperados. The law will eventually catch up with them." Morgan strode from behind the desk. The expression on his face hinted his patience at an end, and he prepared to force her out the door. "Mr. Doyle is no threat to the Territory. Good day, Miss Bishop."

"They why has he received large shipments of guns and ammunition?"

Morgan's eyes went wide. "What's that you say?"

Nell spread the invoices across his desk. "As you can see, he has been stockpiling for months. He also ordered tents and enough supplies to feed and house an army. These are hardly the receipts of a gentleman rancher."

Morgan stared in shock at the papers. "Where did you get these?"

"They are real, have no doubt. The stationmaster will confirm the shipments."

On occasion, necessity called for the use of a little white lie. Nell stood. "I am on my way to meet with the marshal right now. I can convince him to take action if you refuse."

Morgan stiffened. "That won't be necessary, Miss Bishop. These invoices change everything. I'll make immediate inquiries into Mr. Doyle's business and discover the truth."

"I expect due haste. Doyle's arrival signals the onset of his plan. We have no time to waste."

"I hardly think—"

No, you hardly think at all. "At the very least the marshal must be alerted, and the Army notified so more troops can be ordered to Fort Braddock. They are severely undermanned."

"Madam, the safety of people in the Arizona Territory is my primary concern." Unexpectedly, he smiled and took her by the elbow. "I apologize for my brusqueness. Be assured, I'll leave at once to discuss this situation with the marshal in person."

Nell shook off his grip. His soothing tones were as irksome as his earlier condescension. "I'll come with you. I began this investigation and have every intention of holding fast until it's resolved."

His face turned red. "Very well, I see you'll have it no other way." Morgan ushered her downstairs to the rear exit. "The marshal's office is at the end of the alleyway."

The lobby was busy. Nell caught a puzzled glance across the room from Morgan's aide.

Morgan hurried Nell through the door. "Does anyone else know you're here?"

"I beg your pardon?"

"I meant, once you arrived in town did you discuss your plan to call upon me with another person? We may be a while with the marshal. I don't wish to cause undue concern if someone expects you presently. Must I send a message to explain your absence?"

Nell stared at him. A prickle of alarm crept up her spine.

"Anyone at all, Miss Bishop?" he pressed.

An unsettled feeling gripped her chest. "No one. I came alone."

"I don't wish Daisy to worry," he said. "Is she still at Fort Braddock?"

Nell forced a smile. "Yes. Daisy is at Fort

Braddock." Daisy's name was never mentioned. Nell slid her hand into the hidden pocket of her skirt and felt for the derringer.

The blow from Morgan's fist sent her reeling. Before she recovered, an arm encircled her throat cutting off the air. "I'm glad to hear that," he whispered harshly in her ear. Nell struggled in his iron grip, gasping for breath, but Morgan remained rooted in place. "You should have stayed out of this, Miss Bishop," he hissed. "Now, you've forced my hand."

Her vision blurred and dimmed. In the distance, an eagle screamed, and then Nell's body went limp.

Chapter Thirteen

Sam buttoned the shirt and then crammed the black hat on his head. "How do I look?"

Mateo made a wry face. "Like a walking dead man."

"*Muchas gracias.*"

"*De nada.*"

Both men returned the way they came, moving with deliberate caution in the dark. They reached the incline and slowed to a near crawl, aware the location of the sentries was no longer plain at night.

The glow of several campfires and a few kerosene lanterns lit the camp. "Many outlaws still about," whispered Mateo. "How do you plan to get inside unobserved?"

After examining the ground with a practiced eye, Sam marked a lone man with a rifle pacing off his rounds near the corral. "Over there. I only note one guard and can choose when to slip into the camp."

"What if he happens to turn his head at the wrong moment?"

"I can also shoot him and then run as fast as a jackrabbit."

Mateo grunted an accord. "I'll bide my time by the horses. If you are not here by mid-morning, I'll come for you. I rather not. The only other black shirt we have is on a bullet-ridden corpse that will fester by then. It's not to my taste." He clapped him on the shoulder. "Good luck, my friend. May our next meeting not be at heaven's gate."

Sam crawled down the incline and melted into the cover of the woods. Darting from tree to rock, he edged closer to the perimeter. From a hiding place behind an acacia, he kept a wary eye as the sentry paced off his route.

Sam mentally counted. *One…two…three…four…*

At thirty-five seconds, the man disappeared past a tent. He reappeared five seconds later on the return sweep. Sam timed the length of the guard's round for several circuits. Each figured roughly the same. He had between five and six seconds to make a break from the woods and get to a hiding place out of sight of the guard. The surroundings offered little cover, but stacked haphazardly by the tent were a few small barrels and crates. With luck, he could hunker down there and keep his body from view while deciding the next move.

The sentry neared the tent again. Sam tensed, waiting for him to disappear. "Now or never," he muttered. The instant the man rounded the corner, Sam broke from cover. He slid to a halt and ducked behind the stacked crates.

"You there!"

Sam froze, heart pounding, as footsteps approached the tent. He drew his revolver from the holster and cocked the hammer.

"Yes, sir," came the sentry's response.

Sam relaxed and cautiously spied around the barrels. The new arrival carried a lantern and had six men at his heels. He wore a black shirt as the others, but with one chevron stitched over a pocket—the same as the dead man at Fort Braddock.

"Got word from headquarters to increase the guard at the perimeter." He motioned to two of the men. "Stay here on patrol with him."

Sam stifled a curse. The extra men made it impossible to leave the compound at the same place without being seen. Not to mention, his hiding place became less secure by the second. A single idle glance from a guard in his direction meant discovery. He needed another exit point, but not before a good look at the camp.

"The rest of you," the man with the chevron barked, "come with me."

Sam squatted low and holstered his revolver. As the men strode by his hiding place, he slipped from behind the barrels and silently joined the end of the line. They passed another group of dark riders. He pulled down the brim of his hat, but no one paid any attention to him.

As the group walked across the grounds, Sam made a mental note of the number of men, revising his estimate to over seventy. He lagged farther and farther behind and then peeled off to the right. Sam headed for the center of the compound where riders gathered at a mess tent. He stifled a grin. No better place to pick up gossip. Besides, he missed dinner and was a mite peckish.

Sam filled a plate with beans and bacon and took a tin cup with coffee. Nearby were several campfires. He joined a circle of men eating dinner. Sam dug into the meal pretending to pay no attention while listening to their conversation. The talk concerned the addition of new guards.

"Heard tell something's up at headquarters," said one man.

Sam's ears pricked up. *Headquarters? There's a second compound.*

"What about it, Edwards?" demanded another. "We moving out?"

Across from Sam, a man with a black bushy mustache mumbled a response. "Not yet. Word got sent a prisoner came in rousing trouble for Doyle."

"Who's the prisoner?" asked the first man.

"Don't know," grunted Edwards. "Don't much care. As long as the money keeps coming."

The other man's concerns weren't so easily dismissed. "You think the Army suspects the attack on Fort Braddock?"

Sam's fork froze halfway to his mouth.

"If they did, the hills would crawl with cavalry," said Edwards. "Extra sentries are just a precaution. Doyle's plans are tight." Edwards motioned to the well-guarded tent where men had earlier removed crates of rifles and ammunition. "With what we got in there, the soldiers don't stand a chance."

"Reckon the women will need comforting," rasped another with a harsh laugh.

"Won't be nary left," grunted Edwards. Sam's blood chilled at the offhand comment.

"Don't worry about the prisoner," Edwards continued. "Anybody in Doyle's way is soon gone, dead already or will be by morning." He squinted in the dim light of the campfire, peering directly at Sam. "Ain't seen you around."

Sam swallowed a sip of coffee. "Name's Lambert.

Just got in."

He narrowed his eyes. "Didn't hear about new arrivals."

Sam chewed slowly, considering whether to pitch his plate in the fire and go for his revolver. "Don't reckon you know everything."

"You got something to say?" Edwards growled.

"Rein it in, Edwards," one of the men growled. "You savvy the rules. Start trouble, and the captain will dish it out to all of us. I ain't getting shot over your temper."

"He ain't never been no captain," Edwards snorted out. "Just another god-damned outlaw who was once a scout."

"What's your beef? There's plenty to eat. Money's good and will get even better. Doyle named McLaren captain. Lest you want to cross his decision, I reckon you keep your mouth shut."

Sam nonchalantly poked with a fork at the beans on his plate. "Reese McLaren? Heard tell he went to Mexico."

The man let out a guffaw. "You mean with the rest of us?" The others at the campfire echoed his laughter. "That was right smart of Doyle to spread that rumor. Ain't nobody searching these hills when the law thinks we headed south."

Edwards eyed Sam with suspicion. "He a friend of yours? Reckon to pull in a favor with McLaren?"

"Nope," Sam answered smoothly. "He owes me fifty dollars silver."

Edwards sneered. "Don't figure him to pony up anytime soon. He took a wagon to headquarters. My advice is leave him be. McLaren ain't likely to care about squaring old debts now. Crossing any officer is grounds for getting shot."

The men went back to eating. When the conversation turned to more mundane topics, Sam edged from the campfire and stole into the shadows. He had heard enough. No need to press his luck any more. The admission of an attack on Fort Braddock unnerved him. Maybe Edwards' words were just rough talk, but the cold in the pit of his stomach refused to go away. If the outlaw spoke the truth, the riders meant to kill every man there and then the women…death wouldn't come so quickly for them. An image of Nell flashed into his mind, but not as he left her. Her eyes pleaded for help.

Sam shook his head to clear his thoughts. Nell was safe for the present. He had to find a way out of camp to where Mateo waited with the horses. Together, they'd warn Abernathy about the attack on the fort.

His gaze drifted toward the ammunition tent. At once, a burning desire raged to see the number of outlaws' weapons. The entrance flap was securely tied shut. Two armed men were stationed at the ready. A lantern hung on a post next to each one, illuminating the grounds. Entrance was well-nigh impossible without gunplay. Sam kept in the shadows and crept to the rear. He scowled. The area was also well lit with two more sentries posted.

Front and back were covered, but another option arose. Pitched next to this was a second tent. The sides nearly abutted, only a few feet separated the two canvas walls from each other. Sam watched for several minutes, but the guards' attention remained fixed in front. None cast an eye at the narrow space in the center.

The finely honed edge of his hunting knife could make quick work of canvas. Sam's fingers gripped the handle as if the blade called him to action. He slipped silently to the rear of the second tent, hidden from view of the sentries. A glance showed no one in the vicinity. He picked out a spot with the deepest shadows. A single slice with the knife made an opening big enough to enter.

The interior was pitch black. Sam paused a moment to listen for any hint the guards detected him. All remained quiet. Satisfied, he pulled a match from the tin in his pocket and struck it against the sole of his boot. The light from the tiny flame revealed stacked wooden cartons marked with foodstuffs such as beans, coffee, and sugar. No weapons were in sight. Snuffing the match, he carefully felt his way across the space. Sam made another slit in the canvas and listened hard, but the guards stayed rooted to their stations. His lips twisted in a grim smile. The other tent was nearly close enough to touch.

Another quick cut and Sam eased inside the ammo tent. Faint illumination from the sentries' lanterns filtered through the canvas. It was enough to make out the rough shapes of boxes and barrels, but not for Sam's eyes to read any identifying words stamped on the wood.

One large crate dominated the center of the space. Sam felt along the rough wooden slats and then gingerly tested the hinged lid. It had already been pried open and moved freely. Wood shavings packed inside kept the contents from jostling.

Sam plunged his hands through the shavings. His fingers snagged a piece of paper, but the light was too poor to read. Sam dug deeper. This time he grasped something hard and metallic. Sam ran his hand along a smooth pipe-like shape. Bigger than a carbine muzzle. Much bigger. He frowned. What was it?

Cold sweat broke out on his forehead as an awful thought occurred. *It couldn't be.* Sam stared again at the paper in his hand, striving to read the words, but to no avail. He must chance another match. From outside, two of the guards made conversation. The other two were silent. Paying more attention to the tent? Sam sent a silent prayer to the Apache spirits that all four kept their backs turned so no one would notice one little flicker of light.

Sam struck the match. A sick knot of fear formed in his stomach when he realized he held a U.S. Army shipping invoice for a Gatling gun. Sam stuffed the paper in his shirt and then frantically brushed aside wood shavings. Gunmetal steel reflected the gentle illumination of the tiny match flame. He had seen a Gatling gun in action once. The damage one of these weapons could do to the soldiers and their families at the undermanned fort chilled his blood.

Fury rose in a tidal crest. The attack on Fort Braddock will be a massacre. He could no longer delay a return to Mateo. Abernathy must be warned at once.

A curious pricking jabbed at the nape of his neck. His hand went to his revolver. Someone was in the tent with him.

"*It'sa.*"

His head jerked toward the sound of the voice. A coyote stood not six feet away. Golden brown eyes peered into his.

"Help me."

****

It'sa sailed high over the settlement. Far below, people scurried like insects, oblivious to the hunter patrolling the clouds. Humans held no interest for the eagle. Nothing in their worthless piles of sticks and mortar assuaged his hunger. Game was plentiful elsewhere. He cast one last glance to earth. A woman with golden hair peered into the sky. One hand shielded her eyes from the sun and obscured her face. Her other arm extended and the index finger pointed to the western hills.

Flapping powerful wings, the eagle flew west. Soon both the town and its inhabitants were out of sight. Trees instead of streets blanketed the landscape. Boulders dotted the hillside. Faint impressions in the dirt drew his attention. A game trail?

The eagle dove from the sky in a quick pass. The trace was newly made, but well hidden. A combination of acute vision and instinct marked it as the work of man, not animals. His wings beat a silent cadence through the air. It'sa soared over a field filled with orderly rows of tents.

As the eagle spied from above, heavily armed men in black shirts struck camp. They saddled horses in haste and hitched others to wagons. The humans hurried as if called to action.

Regarding the scene with disdain, the eagle hid from their sight in the glare of the sun. Game had long since fled from here, and the actions of men served no purpose in his world. The eagle banked upon the breeze, reveling in the warmth of the sun on his back. The hunt would take him elsewhere.

It'sa flew northwest. From high above, he marked

a peaceful stream bordering a clearing. Here was a smaller group of men and tents, but still no game. The eagle shrieked in anger.

"It'sa!"

Keen eyes scoured the landscape. "Who calls to me?"

A dark-haired man dragged a coyote from a tent. Ropes bound Baya tight. Blood left a sticky trail from her wounds.

Rage boiled within the eagle. The man had dared touch Baya. "Release her," the eagle demanded. "She is mine!"

The dark-haired man laughed. "You have no claim. You are wing, she is claw. Baya belongs to me. I use her as I will, discard her when I choose." His laugh turned into a howl, his teeth transformed into fangs dripping black poison. He was the Devourer of Souls. "This is how I deal with any who stand in my way." The monster slashed at Baya tearing her skin.

It'sa let loose with a war cry. He dove at the creature, raking it with talons of steel. The Devourer screamed and dropped the rope.

"Run, Baya!" cried the eagle.

"No!" She shook off the bindings and leapt at the Devourer, sinking her teeth into its leg. "I fight with you."

The Devourer roared and swatted her body aside as if nothing. Poison spewed from the creature's mouth blighting the land. A horse caught in the venomous wave, died in an instant as flesh seared from bone. The terrified creature's final screams echoed through the hills.

"Kill them all," the Devourer commanded.

The power of the monster's voice infected the men in the encampment with a lust for death. The black-shirted horde mounted.

"Come with me, Baya," said the eagle. "There are too many. We must sound the alarm."

The coyote staggered to her feet and dashed after him. The Devourer thrust a finger toward her. A shadow fell on the land and transformed into a solitary dark rider.

"Her life is yours," said the Devourer to his servant. "Her body is yours. She must suffer."

Foul corruption filled the dark rider's soul. "As you wish."

"To the heights," It'sa cried. "Faster, Baya." He flew overhead urging the coyote to greater speed. The lone dark rider raced toward Baya, drawing his revolver.

Baya's steps faltered. "I cannot run any farther. Go on alone, It'sa," she pleaded. "I only slow you."

"Never!"

"Please, It'sa. The evil spreads too fast. Give the war cry." They reached the crags. Coyote stumbled with weakness, the dark rider nearly upon her.

"I won't leave you."

"You must. Others need your help. Rouse warriors against the coming evil. If the Devourer triumphs, my death will be in vain."

The eagle spotted a notch high in the rocks, big enough to shelter coyote. He swooped down and lit on a triangular boulder. A long zigzag-shaped mineral streak discolored the surface. The rock's position disguised the sight of the opening from anyone below.

"Here," he cried. "Follow me."

With a final burst of energy, Baya staggered up the cliff and into the cave. The man dressed in a black shirt scoured the base, unsuccessfully searching for her trail. Relief flooded It'sa. For the moment, coyote was safe.

The eagle beat his wings. "Stay hidden," he ordered. "Make no sound. I swear to return for you. Stay alive, Baya!"

The coyote made no answer. Her eyes closed.

At the bottom of the crag the black-shirted man seized upon her path and let out a victorious cry.

****

Sam leaned against the wooden crate, legs shaking, shirt drenched in sweat. He stifled a curse at a searing pain. The matchstick had burnt to his fingertips. He shook out the flame and took a deep gulping breath of air. Never was a vision so intense. Never was a warning so straightforward. Nell was in trouble. Big trouble.

Damn it, he left her at Fort Braddock. Why did she leave? Where was she now? Images danced through his mind in a dizzying pirouette. Concentrate. Learn their meaning. As he fought to bring them into clarity, they spun away, maddeningly out of reach. So many impressions; sights, sounds, smells collided into each other in wild abandon. He couldn't force any order from the chaos. As Sam braced against the crate, the images faded. Dread gripped his heart. Soon nothing would be left other than the misty residue of dreams. Nell would be lost.

The time to decide had come. Face the power or turn away. Sam let out a breath. Whatever the outcome, he'd no longer fight the visions. Lenna Tanner's words rang in his head. *Embrace who you are, It'sa.*

"I am Sam Tanner of the white men," he

whispered. "I am *It'sa* of the Apache. I am two. I am one." He cleared his thoughts. "I will use my great-grandfather's gift and do it all honor."

It is done. Something within him acknowledged approval.

Clouds parted in Sam's mind. He saw with the eye of an eagle images clear and distinct. Tents filled an open space surrounded by trees. Was Nell held captive near him? No…the camp in his vision was different, near a stream and smaller. He brushed away the disappointment and concentrated. The second camp must be the headquarters Edwards mentioned. Located west of Prescott, hidden in the hills along an unmarked trail. Doyle was there, preparing to spread his poison across the land.

Sam clenched his fists. The Devourer wasn't alone. He had also seen the face of Reese McLaren. The outlaw captain left for headquarters only that afternoon. Nell was now with them and death most assuredly dogged her footsteps.

Not yet, please not yet.

Sam took a deep breath to still the rising fear that muddied his thinking. He must stay calm. The dreams always came as a warning—she was still alive. Baya was smart, a trickster. She fooled even him. Coyote Woman would use her wiles, weave her clever words. Time was against him, but hadn't run out.

"Halt!" One of the guards shouted outside the tent.

Edwards' voice barked. "Got orders to move on Fort Braddock. Load the ammo."

The flaps whipped open. Lantern light spilled in. "You there," said Edwards. "Grab those casks along the side."

Sam froze. Over the tops of the stacked boxes heads bobbed and weaved toward the slit in the tent. The men blocked his avenue of escape.

"Move your feet," Edwards growled. "We ain't got all night. Load the Gatling gun first." Sam pressed flat against the crate as the men approached.

With no place to hide, Sam's gaze lit upon the open crate. He grasped his revolver, jumped in, and lowered the lid. His rangy muscular frame squeezed painfully against the weapon. Sam kept a tight grip on his gun. If anyone looked inside, he'd take them by surprise and make a run for it.

Footsteps shuffled closer. Sam tensed, ready for them to lift the lid. Instead, the entire crate rose several inches, and then slammed down with a thud. Sam winced as his head banged against the side. Stars danced in the dark interior.

"Shit, this thing weighs as much as a dead mule. You, two," Edwards shouted, "get over here and help."

More shuffling footsteps joined them. With a chorus of muffled grunts, and a then a jerk, the crate rose again.

"Easy, easy," snapped Edwards. "Any of you sonuvabitches lets go and you'll answer to me."

Men's shouts now mixed with the neighing of horses. They were outside the tent. The shrill creak that followed signaled the release of the rear gate on a wagon. With a sudden heave, the crate thumped onto a hard surface. A sliding motion jockeyed it in place. Inside, Sam jostled back and forth with the movement of the wagon bed. Thumping noises hinted at cargo piled on the crate and along the side. Sam's heart hammered wildly. If the outlaws packed too much weight on top, he'd never be able to raise the lid and die from slow suffocation.

Breathing became difficult. The dark closed around him, cutting off air. Hands sweating, Sam swallowed hard. *Don't panic, you fool. Keep a cool head. You don't dare open the crate until the wagon is away from the campfires.*

Sam forced himself to draw steady breaths. He shut his eyes, envisioning Nell. She was in trouble and needed help. If he succumbed to death in this makeshift coffin, her life was also forfeit.

The rear gate was hoisted and latched. The floorboards bounced again as the driver climbed into the seat. Wheels lurched and moved forward at last. Sam burned with impatience as the wagon rolled at a steady pace. His fingers itched to test the weight piled on the lid. He let go of the pistol grip, his hand pressed overhead on the wooden surface.

Not yet…not yet…you only get one chance to escape.

Sam silently counted to five hundred. The sounds of bustling camp activity decreased as the wagon left behind the compound. The question remained how many riders were still in sight. Was anyone close enough to notice a man slipping out of a crate?

Only one way to know for sure…

Sam placed both palms flat against the lid and pushed hard. It didn't give at all.

Chapter Fourteen

A hard bump jarred Nell to consciousness. Her
eyelids fluttered open. Surrounded by darkness, she
tried to call out, but a gag prevented it. Her bonnet was
missing and rough scratchy cloth covered her face. Nell
struggled to move, but both hands and feet were bound
tight. Panic surged through her. Where was she? What
happened?

Think! What is the last thing you remember?

Nell stopped her futile struggle and took long deep
breaths through her nose, holding them for a count of
three before release. Her pounding heart stilled and
orderly thoughts emerged. She had been in the alley
with Morgan. He struck her. His arm went around her
neck cutting off air, and then she became dizzy and
weak. The remnants of panic subsided, replaced by
burning rage. Morgan assaulted and kidnapped her.
How could she have been so stupid not to see Morgan
was in collusion with Doyle?

Nell strove to sit up, but the bindings and the
incessant jostling made movement impossible. She
must be in a wagon. Where did he take her? They hit
another bump, and her head banged painfully against
the wooden slats.

She shifted position. A small object pressed into
her thigh. The derringer remained in the hidden pocket!
Morgan hadn't bothered to search her. Despite the

agony of her harsh confinement, Nell experienced a rush of grim satisfaction. Thank heavens for the arrogance of the man. He never expected a woman to be anything other than weak and defenseless. Once her hands were free, Thaddeus Morgan would curse the day they ever crossed paths.

The wagon jolted to a halt. Nell struggled once again to loosen the ropes securing her wrists, but to no avail. Footsteps crunched on the pebbly ground as another person approached.

"Why meet here?" called a man's voice.

"Trouble," Morgan answered from the driver's seat. He jumped into the wagon bed and roughly yanked Nell to a sitting position. The roll of burlap covering her body was tossed aside. Nell blinked and looked around. They must be in the countryside, several miles outside Prescott. The rugged trail was the only sign of civilization.

A man in a dark shirt eyed her coldly. "Who the hell is she?"

"Nell Bishop," said Morgan, "a newspaper reporter for *The San Francisco Dispatch*. She knows about Doyle and came to give me warning of his plans." He regarded her with haughty distain. "Wasn't that gracious? Miss Bishop was also kind enough to inform me she received her information from a servant in Doyle's household."

"Daisy? Well, now." The man's flinty gaze sent a chill through Nell. "Doyle got word the little whore traveled with another woman. Didn't suspect no reporter." He ripped off the gag. "Where is she?"

Nell's lips and mouth were dry. Her voice came out no more than a croak. "Safe—where you can't reach her."

"She let on Daisy is at Fort Braddock." Morgan spoke with smug assurance. "Isn't that convenient? She can die with the others."

Nell's heart sank as the truth set in. "The attack comes at Fort Braddock and not Prescott."

The other man leaned over to catch her in a piercing glare. "Who else in Prescott is wise to Doyle?" Nell pursed her lips together in a thin tight line. He withdrew his revolver. "I'm not a man known for patience."

"I spread the word to too many people to count," Nell said. "If you think your treachery won't be discovered, you're sadly mistaken."

His chuckle was a cold harsh sound. "If that were so, the hills would be awash with troops. Ain't nobody coming to the rescue." He cocked the trigger and then glanced around with a dispassionate gaze. "This is as good a place as any to dump a body."

"Can you be so certain I didn't alert others in Prescott after my arrival?" Nell glared at Morgan. "Can you? They surely plan retaliation even as we speak."

Morgan stayed the other's hand. "I doubt she tells the truth, but bring her to Doyle just in case. He'll want to question her. Take the wagon. I'll ride back to Prescott on your horse. I must return before I'm missed."

"I don't get my orders from you."

Morgan's face reddened. "You'll do as I say. Doyle put me in charge of matters in Prescott."

"Is that what you get out of this?" Nell spit out in disgust. "Prescott? I'm astonished you sold your soul to the devil so cheaply."

"The United States government has never seen fit to reward me adequately for my abilities, but Doyle offered a lucrative alternative."

Her eyes widened in understanding. "You think Doyle can garner you the Territorial governorship? All this blood on your hands for that? You're either as mad as Doyle or a fool."

Morgan back-handed Nell hard across the face. "Watch your tongue," he hissed, "before I forget I was born and bred a gentleman." Morgan mounted and heeled the horse ruthlessly in the ribs. Without a look back, he galloped away.

The other man climbed into the wagon bed. Nell froze as his gaze raked her body. "You got sand, missy, I'll grant you that. I'd just as soon kill you, so don't cause me no trouble—at least not until Doyle is done with you." He leaned in, his breath hot against her cheek. She flinched in disgust as his tongue made a long slow pass up the side of her face. "Very sweet," he murmured. "Maybe the two of us will have a go, if there's anything left."

Nell huddled against the wagon and turned her head away as if in complete defeat. He grunted his approval and then jumped into the driver's seat and slapped the reins against the horse's rump. The wagon took off with a jerk. Fortunately, he had either forgotten to replace the burlap on top of her or considered it no longer necessary.

They headed into the hills. Nell surmised they were west of Prescott, but how far she had journeyed while unconscious was impossible to determine. Shadows lengthened and deepened, stretching across the ground. Mile after mile the wagon bounced along, increasing the agony in her arms and legs. How much farther could they travel before night came? Would they ever stop? As if in answer to her unasked question, the driver halted to light a lantern and hang it on a hook attached to the wagon to illuminate the trail.

With each bump of the wooden wheels, white hot pain lashed across her shoulders and calves. Exhausted, Nell surrendered the struggle to loosen her bindings. Her hands and feet were numb. Even if able to untie her wrists, she doubted her fingers could grip the derringer.

Save your strength. Without doubt, every last bit will be needed soon.

Nell pressed her lips together to keep from crying out as another violent lurch slammed her to the floorboards. How much more of this torture must she endure? She gritted her teeth, stubbornly determined not to make a sound and give the driver any satisfaction. He was a man who reveled in cruelty. Better to let him think he broke her spirit and weakness completely claimed her.

Jolt after agonizing jolt brought total collapse ever nearer. The lantern light blurred and danced in front of Nell's eyes. She fought to keep her mind focused, but strength failed as darkness swallowed the woods. The sweet oblivion of unconsciousness was but moments away. At least, the pain would end.

An eagle's scream broke through Nell's misery. She forced her head up and locked gazes with a majestic bird perched on a tree limb. It dipped its wings as if in salute and then soared into the sky and disappeared from view. Her head sank low. It must have been a dream. Eagles don't fly at night.

The sight of the bird brought the memory of Sam's

kiss and the life that could never be. Filled with such tender longing, she envisioned him standing silent vigil over her in the dark.

"Just a dream," Nell murmured.

The image spoke with fierce intensity. "Have courage, *Baya*. Fight. All is not lost."

Nell drew in a breath. His likeness was so distinct, perfect in every detail. If her hands had been free, she could reach out and touch him. "Sam," she whispered.

His arms opened to her.

Nell blinked. The image vanished. Her body responded with renewed energy. *I will not give into them. I...will...not.*

The driver jerked the horse to a halt. A half dozen armed guards in black shirts blocked the trail.

"I've come with a prisoner for Doyle," said the driver.

Without a word, the men stepped aside and lowered their guns. The wagon wound through a small camp crowded with tents and horses. A quick count gave Nell twenty men. Was this the extent of Doyle's army? They could cause a great deal of damage and bloodshed, but the cavalry would easily defeat them. Doyle must be mad. Only his death was a certainty from this plan.

Two men stood guard in front of a tent larger and more ornate than the others. Stacked beside it were piles of lumber, bricks, and other building materials. The driver jumped off the seat into the wagon bed, reached into his pocket, and drew a switchblade. With slight pressure from his thumb, the edge popped open.

He leered at her. "Well, now, missy, didn't expect to see you awake after that jostling. I was right about you. Full of sand." His hand ran up Nell's boot to rest on her stockinged knee.

Nell recoiled from his touch. "Get your hands off me."

He snickered. With a flick of the wrist, he sliced through the rope binding her legs. A groan escaped Nell's lips. Spasms of hot searing torment coursed through her as blood rushed into numbed limbs. Another quick cut and her arms were free. Painfully swollen, they hung limp and unresponsive at her side. He grabbed one arm and yanked her off the wagon. As Nell's feet touched the ground, she collapsed in a heap. Her weakened legs refused to support any weight. Escape was impossible until strength returned.

The two guards took Nell's arms. They dragged her past the tent flap and dropped her in front of a large desk. "Where's Doyle?" the driver demanded.

"Far side of camp," said one of the guards.

"I'll fetch him. You two get to your post. Our guest ain't going nowhere." The driver watched the men leave and then crouched beside Nell. Without warning, he yanked her head back by the hair and kissed her hard. Nell fought to lift her arms, but couldn't. She bit his lip.

With a yelp, he pushed her away and swiped one hand across his bloody mouth. He raised an arm as if to strike, but then dropped it to his side with a smirk. "We'll have us some fun when Doyle is through. Yes, we will." He strode from the tent.

Nell's heart pounded out a drumming beat. She rubbed her lips viciously against a sleeve, attempting to remove the foul taste of his mouth. The extra burst of adrenaline provided enough energy to regain her composure. With a moan, she stretched out her stiff and sore legs. Burning jabs laced with fire danced against her skin as feeling returned. At least the sturdy leather boots prevented the coarse rope from tearing into her flesh.

The same couldn't be said for her arms. Her wrists were bloody. Nell flexed her fingers, grimacing at the excruciating spasms. She briskly massaged her thighs to encourage circulation. One hand felt for the reassuring shape of the derringer.

As strength improved, Nell's spirits rose. Fighting temperament returned in full force. Her focus turned to escape, but the tent sat in the middle of the compound with guards stationed at the front flaps. She could hardly waltz through unnoticed. In any case, her legs were unable to support a dash for freedom just yet. Nor did she know Prescott's location in relation to the camp.

Wincing, Nell forced herself to rise. She examined the surroundings, at once taken aback by the rich display of furnishings. Instead of bare earth, a luxurious Persian carpet in vibrant colors covered the ground. The desk wasn't standard camp issue, but mahogany wood burnished to a high gloss, the surface inlaid with ebony and mother of pearl. Expensive accessories, including a silver inkwell and a solid gold letter opener studded with green gems, lay out in a row as if soldiers at morning call.

Along one side of the tent was a long wooden table and chairs also of mahogany. A silver coffee service and an array of crystal decanters filled with brown and red liquids sat on top of a chest of drawers. A hand-painted oriental screen in the rear obscured the foot of a bed. The coverlet was no ordinary woolen blanket, but embroidered Chinese silk.

Growing up privileged had advantages. Nell easily made an accurate judgment of the value of the tent's furnishings. Colin Doyle had very expensive tastes. A gilded mirror over a dressing table drew her eye. Underneath a silver tray held matching combs, brushes, and other toiletry articles. They shared space with an assortment of creams and pomades.

Nell raised an eyebrow. "Well, well, Mr. Doyle. Not only elaborate furnishings, but an extensive toiletry as well. A monster who wishes to appear a gentleman. Yes, very interesting. You can tell a lot about a man by his surroundings."

Footsteps approached. The guard held back the tent flap, and Colin Doyle entered. He wore an elegant tailored jacket. The outfit conformed to his athletic physique without a solitary wrinkle. Self-assurance wove around him like a mantle.

Nell brushed her fingers across the handle of the derringer. A single shot and the smug arrogance vanished forever. She forced her hand to her side. An attempt on his life now was pointless. Her fingers barely flexed enough to pull a trigger, and she only had one bullet. If by chance she got off a lucky shot, the next would surely come from a guard's revolver pointed at her head. Death wasn't in Nell's plans.

"Nell Bishop?" said Doyle with obvious surprise. "You plucked my little Daisy from the garden? That was an impressive feat. I never assumed her chaperone was a reporter."

"Whom did you expect?"

He shrugged. "Another worthless whore."

Nell stifled a caustic retort and instead answered

smoothly. "Not so worthless, it seems. You put a five thousand dollar reward on Daisy's head."

A flicker of interest showed on his face. Had he expected her to whimper in a pile at his feet, begging for mercy? "Are you looking to collect, Miss Bishop?"

"Hardly. You aren't the only one to admit to surprise. While the furnishings reflect taste, a canvas tent isn't the usual domicile for a gentleman rancher."

Doyle gave a casual wave of the hand. "These are merely temporary quarters. I have plans to build a much finer and more permanent residence."

"You'll remain in the Territory? I'm surprised to hear country life suits you. What of your businesses in San Francisco? Who will supply whores and opium to the needy?"

He narrowed his eyes. "You have a clever wit, Miss Bishop."

"And a good eye. I must admit, Mr. Doyle. I am impressed by this opulence."

"I pride myself on maintaining a sense of elegance, no matter the location."

"Your surroundings speak of a gentleman." Nell held out her injured wrists. "Your subordinate's rough treatment does not."

The violent change in Doyle's personality stunned Nell. He grasped her wrists, roughly pulling her toward him. "I don't take kindly to criticism, Miss Bishop. It is by my will alone you live or die. Don't forget that or try my patience."

Hair trigger temper. Tread carefully. Don't antagonize him further. "I apologize," Nell said, imbuing her words with all the sincerity she could muster. "I meant no disrespect. Please, my skin is quite painful…" The pressure on her wrists brought tears to her eyes. "Please, I-I beg you to let go." Doyle released his grip. Nell collapsed into a chair, heaving shuddering breaths.

Doyle held her in icy regard. "You caused a great deal of trouble to my plans by helping Daisy slip away. Where is she?"

Nell hunched over, cradling her wrists. "I already told Morgan she was at Fort Braddock. You're a successful businessman, Mr. Doyle. What possible reason can you have for attacking the cavalry?"

He appeared startled. "So you know?"

"Morgan let it slip. The man is a fool. I'm surprised you tolerate him at all."

His expression changed to amusement. "He has his uses."

"He doesn't strike me as the type to bloody his hands."

"You'd be surprise how easily money can cure the delicate nature of even the most squeamish man."

"It isn't just money, is it? He thinks you can hand over the territorial governorship to him."

Doyle raised an eyebrow "Very clever, Miss Bishop."

"How can you possibly accomplish such a scheme? Morgan isn't known beyond the Territory and not highly regarded here. The president will never appoint him as a replacement."

"But he will." Doyle's words rang with absolute confidence. "Public opinion will demand it after Morgan's acts of heroism. So will the railroads. They hold powerful sway in Congress and will insist upon him as the new governor."

"Heroism?" Nell scoffed. "Morgan?"

"Indeed, the people and the railroads will back him to the hilt. Even the Army will be grateful after he avenges the deaths of the soldiers and their families. A train arrives directly to Prescott carrying a delegation of railroad executives. They plan to announce the construction of a new line from Prescott to Tucson by way of Fort Braddock. Unfortunately, outlaws will attack the train at the station in an attempted robbery. Morgan will thwart the attack and mount a pursuit of the nefarious dark riders who dared to commit such a heinous act."

Nell paled. She regarded him with disbelief. "The marshal in Prescott will step in."

"Sad to say, he and his men will perish in the attack. Naturally, I'll offer my own men as posse."

"Why Fort Braddock?" she demanded. "What can be gained by those deaths?"

"I'll create not just one hero, but two; Morgan and myself. Our posse will come upon the attackers at Fort Braddock and in a bold and fearless move engage the dark riders and destroy them."

"Gunman won't sit still to be slaughtered."

He shrugged. "In the heat of battle, who is to say which person killed another? I have handpicked men here and at the compound loyal to me. They have their orders. Enough bodies wearing black shirts will make the story believable. An investigation will discover they are wanted men. No one will question their deaths. Morgan's valor will get him what he wants—the territorial governorship." His lips formed a cruel smile. "Why I can see the headlines now, Miss Bishop—all the way to *The San Francisco Dispatch*. His bravery in the face of such impossible odds will no doubt bring a tear to every reader's eye."

Nell eyed him askance. "All this to make yourself a hero? You have more to gain than that. The railroads will undoubtedly be consumed with gratitude. Thankful enough to run the line through your land, instead?"

"You are sharp, Miss Bishop. In truth, I have more than a few social acquaintances employed by the Burlington Northern Santa Fe. Opium, alcohol, and the company of beautiful women can do wonders to loosen lips. I discovered the railroad planned to add a spur from Prescott to Tucson. Spurs are big money, bringing development to an area, but after the slaughter at Fort Braddock no one will want to build on the site of a massacre. It's bad for business. My dear friend, Governor Morgan, will step in and offer every manner of political and economic incentives if the company runs the line through my property instead. They will, I assure you, and control of the entire western part of the Territory will be mine."

His cunning look sickened Nell. "Oh, don't be modest. I think you'll achieve more than that. Morgan is a puppet and you pull the strings. With him in office, you'll be the power behind every move he makes."

A flicker of respect marked Doyle's appraising look. "Well done, Miss Bishop. You deduced correctly. California is a state bound to Washington, and San Francisco is a city bound to a state, but Arizona remains wide open. I see a huge opportunity to expand my business empire. Nothing stands in my way, except you and Daisy." His eyes bored into her. "Who else did you appeal to for aid?"

"Only the captain in charge of Fort Braddock," she

lied. "He refused to take any action, so I decided to press my case directly to Morgan. Obviously, that was a mistake. I never suspected he was your man. You can't believe Daisy is still a threat to your plans."

"No, but she and I have unfinished business. I don't forgive betrayal. You should think on that, Miss Bishop."

Doyle leaned over her. "You tell a very pretty story, but I'm not convinced. Not long ago, I received word Daisy was spotted dressed as a nun. You can imagine my amusement. Daisy? A nun?" The cruel smile had no hint of mirth. "She was in the company of another woman. I dispatched a troop of men to intercept. Two women against a dozen of my well-armed riders, and yet, they seemed to have no trouble eluding them."

Doyle drew a pistol from his holster and cocked the trigger. "You can understand my predicament. You say, you traveled alone, but I'm inclined to believe you had help escaping my riders. Who else here in the Territory besides Morgan and the captain at Fort Braddock know of me?"

Nell took a steadying breath to keep her voice from shaking. "No one."

Doyle pressed the pistol against her temple. "Two females eluded the riders?" His voice dripped with scorn.

Nell gave silent thanks she only told Morgan the bare bones of the story. "Yes, for a time. Daisy and I left the stage at Spirit Ridge and secured horses. On the road to Fort Braddock, dark riders gave chase, but we managed to make the fort. The Army engaged them in battle and killed several, but some escaped. The cavalry pursued them the next day, but I don't know what happened as I left for Prescott before they returned. The only help we received came from Captain Abernathy. Ask Morgan. Captain Abernathy wired the report to him."

"Morgan's tale is the same," said Doyle. "However, I'm not as easy to convince. There is still the matter of Daisy Tremaine. You say she's at Fort Braddock. I may be persuaded to keep you alive until I discover if you speak the truth."

Nell swallowed hard and tried to look suitably cowed. Any display of anger was sure to antagonize him further. "You won, and I have no wish to die."

He ran a finger along the side of her face. Nell's smile froze in place, her stomach twisting in revulsion. Doyle slipped the revolver into its holster. His finger slid to her neck. He loosened the top button of her jacket. Nell's aching fingers futilely tried to ball into a fist.

"You might care to know," he said, "two of the men escaped from the cavalry's pursuit, but died in the hills. The cavalry has no one left to trail and will return to Fort Braddock. No one will come to your rescue." He unfastened another button. "How much do you wish to live?"

Nell steeled herself. "A great deal."

"I may have a use for you yet," he murmured. "You have the most unusual colored eyes. Has anyone ever told you?" The last buttons gave way to his agile fingers. "I tire of a woman quickly, but Daisy had a way of pleasing a man that kept her around longer than most. Almost with regret I ordered her killed, but I can't have disloyalty." He opened the jacket and slipped his hand over her breast. "I wonder how long you will please me enough to keep you alive."

Nell's hand inched toward the pocket of the skirt with the derringer. *One shot...make it count.*

The flap whipped back and the black-shirted wagon driver entered. He smirked as Doyle turned around. Nell fastened the buttons as quickly as her swollen, shaking hands allowed.

"Messenger just arrived from Morgan, boss."

"I'll see to him." Doyle jerked Nell to her to feet and shoved her toward the dark rider. "We shall continue our conversation at another time. Take Miss Bishop to one of the spare tents. Make sure the guards are men you trust. I don't wish her disturbed."

The dark rider grabbed Nell by the elbow. Outside, he barked an order to two guards, and they fell behind. Nell struggled to walk on her numb feet.

"With all these supply wagons headed in," he muttered with callous amusement. "I wondered when Doyle would fetch himself a toy."

Nell's face burned hot. "I don't belong to Doyle."

"Everything here belongs to Doyle, bought and paid for. Including us...ain't that right, boys?" The guards guffawed.

They arrived at a smaller tent, and he parted the flaps. "Get in," he barked to Nell and then ordered the two guards to take up their stations. "No one comes or goes. She's not to be trifled with or you'll answer to Doyle. Savvy?"

"Whatever you say, Reese."

Nell stopped halfway past the tent flap. She raised an eyebrow. "Reese McLaren?"

"You know my name?" McLaren said with

undisguised pleasure. "Hear that, boys. I'm famous."

"I saw the wanted poster at a stage depot," Nell said. "The law speculated you headed to Mexico."

"I got a better offer." He looked her over with a smirk. "If I were you, I'd take whatever Doyle offered, too. He's a man who hears the word no as an insult and don't forgive one who done him wrong."

Nell eyed the black interior with a sinking feeling. She cast her eye at a lantern hanging near the entrance. "May I have it?"

He shrugged indifferently, and Nell took the lantern. McLaren followed. She froze as he pressed his body against her. Nell's heart pounded in her ears.

"Anger in your eyes." The raspy whisper dripped with ruthless savagery. "That's good, hang onto that." He inhaled. "I ain't had me a woman in a long while. This close I can smell the fear, even in a fighter."

Nell forced her voice to stay calm. "Doyle said I wasn't to be disturbed."

McLaren backed away. "He'll tire of you soon enough. I can hold on a while longer, missy." He shut the tent flaps, leaving her alone.

"You should have headed to Mexico while you could, McLaren," Nell whispered. "Sam Tanner doesn't forget anyone who did him wrong, either."

Chapter Fifteen

Nell hugged her arms tight to keep from shaking. The rough touch of Doyle's hands turned her body to ice. Would warmth ever come again? Exhausted and alone, her arms and legs throbbed in pain. She wanted nothing more than to sink to the ground and never rise.

You'll get your wish when Doyle returns. He'll surely use you first and then discard the remains. McLaren will take what's left.

She forced her hands to her side. "I refuse to succumb to such pathetic weakness. Think. An escape from the camp must exist."

Nell reached into her pocket and retrieved the derringer. The swelling had decreased on her wrists. She could flex her finger on the trigger but the tiny pistol was only an effective deterrent at close range. Even fired from ten feet away, the bullet was more likely to wound than kill. With two guards at the door, the derringer's single bullet wasn't enough to shoot her way to freedom. Yet, the knowledge of one meager defense at hand buoyed her spirits. Nell returned the pistol to her pocket with a silent vow. If need be, Doyle would feel its sting.

With lantern raised high, Nell walked a slow circuit of the tent and examined the surroundings. This one was more modest than Doyle's and obviously used for storage until recently. Discarded crates lay scattered on the ground. Only a few barrels and burlap sacks remained, stacked against the side farthest from the flaps.

Nell ran her hands over the rough burlap of one of the sacks and discerned a few hard, round shapes…coffee beans. Stenciled on the side of the largest barrel was FLOUR. The smaller one said SALT. The lid on the salt had been removed and placed on the ground. Nell peered inside. Visible at the bottom was a shallow coating of white crystals, enough for two handfuls. Her heart sank. Not much of an arsenal. Even a small paring knife would have been useful.

Next to the salt barrel was another pile of discarded burlap sacks. Nell's despair increased as each proved empty. Expecting more of the same, she hefted the last sack buried under the others, but something remained inside. Nell upended the bag and spilled out a cluster of jalapeño peppers tied together with string. She sank to the floor, hope dashed at finding a weapon.

Off in the distance a coyote howled. The plaintive cry sounded particularly mournful as it echoed through the night air. Nell's heart tugged in sympathy. What so distressed the poor creature? Did it call for another of its kind or suffer in pain?

Pain?

Nell's lips formed a sly smile. "Many thanks for the inspiration, Sister Coyote," she murmured.

Kneeling beside the sturdy wooden lid of the salt barrel, Nell tore the peppers off the string and laid them on top. Using the butt of the derringer, she ground the green flesh. Juice dribbled over the cuts and abrasions on her skin. Nell sucked in her breath, wanting to cry out at the searing pain. Her hands ached before, but now they blazed fire. Agony shot right to the bone.

"Damnation. Damnation. Damnation..." Nell uttered every curse word she ever learned in English, Spanish, and then Chinese, both Mandarin and Cantonese. Tears sprung up and trickled down her cheeks as acrid vapors rose. She dare not wipe them away for fear of juice getting into her eyes to blind her.

Nell worked the peppers into a slimy pulpy mass. With a grunt, she dumped the contents of the salt barrel into the mixture. Gritting her teeth, she kneaded the granules and jalapeños together to produce a mushy paste. Addition of the salt increased the burning agony on her skin. The irony of the situation wasn't lost on Nell. The pain in her hands made the misery from other wounds now seem inconsequential. Even her mind cleared with each inhalation of the peppers' fumes.

The mash was done. Grimacing, Nell flexed her arms and bounced on her toes. Her feet regained full circulation. She balled her hands into a tight fist. The fingers bent freely. Although her skin was still painful, the heat did more good than harm to her limbs.

Nell carefully wiped off the butt of the derringer and slipped it into her pocket. The mess of salt and peppers barely filled two handfuls, but had to do. She then placed the lid with the pepper mash on top of the flour barrel so the mixture was within quick reach. The lantern went on the ground near the entrance flaps in order to keep her figure on the other side of the tent wrapped in the shadows. Fiery torment rained down on her hands, but now the misery was welcome—a steady reminder she had a fighting chance.

Time ticked by with agonizing slowness. Nell paced back and forth, growing impatient. The blistering heat in her hands abated. The desire for action increased with each step. How much longer must she wait for Doyle? The best opportunity for escape was before the sun rose and dawn was but minutes away.

Scuffling footsteps neared the tent. Nell darted in front of the barrel to keep the pile of mash from sight. The flap whipped open, and McLaren entered. "Doyle sent for you."

Nell grabbed two handfuls of the mash. Pain exploded from her skin again, reinforcing her nerve. She crossed her arms and walked to the opening, hugging her body tight to hide her fists.

The sight of Nell's face, still tear-stained and red-eyed from the pepper fumes, seemed to please McLaren. She brushed past him pretending to limp. Murky half-light dressed the world in somber hues of gray. Although this side of camp was quiet, a muffled ruckus from across the compound signaled other inhabitants began to rouse. With every step, Nell's heart threatened to pound through her ribcage.

They approached Doyle's tent. Next to a sapling, a dark rider finished saddling a horse. Nell slowed her footsteps and made the limp more pronounced.

McLaren shoved her. "Come along, missy," he growled. "Doyle ain't a man who cottons to waiting."

The dark rider untied the reins and prepared to mount.

Now! Go now!

Nell's fists shot out slamming the pepper mash into McLaren's eyes. The scream satisfied her to the core. As he doubled over in pain, she snatched a revolver from his holster.

Nell fired point blank at the dark rider. He dropped

without a word, wearing a look of dumbfounded surprise. The horse shied. Dodging flailing hooves, Nell snatched at the reins. She grabbed the saddle horn when an arm encircled her neck and yanked her to the ground. "Where do you think you're going?" Doyle hissed. His other hand wrenched Nell's wrist, forcing her to drop the revolver.

Nell struggled to breathe as his grip around her neck tightened. She kicked at his ankle. Doyle slammed her against the sapling. Stars danced before her eyes. He jerked her head up by the hair. "Nobody gets away from me."

McLaren staggered on his feet. Tears streamed down his cheeks. With a wolfish howl, he fired wildly. The bullet ricocheted off the tree. Startled, Doyle loosened his grip. Nell jabbed her thumb, still smeared with pepper mash into his eye.

Doyle's head drew back with roar. Nell fumbled inside her skirt for the derringer. Her fingers clasped the handle. Doyle lunged at her again, expression twisted in fury. Nell's finger tightened on the trigger and the shot tore through her pocket. With a grunt, Doyle fell against McLaren, blood pouring from a wound in his thigh.

Nell snatched the reins and leaped into the saddle, hitching up the cumbersome skirt around her knees.

"Stop her!" Doyle yelled.

Half-dressed men stumbled from tents, fumbling for their rifles. Nell gave the horse a savage kick in the sides, and they bolted into the semi-dark. Behind her came gunfire.

She bent low over the horse's neck urging it to full speed. Men scattered as she raced past, heedless of anyone in her path. A startled sentry had no time to do anything other than leap aside as Nell's horse thundered straight at him.

Nell galloped into the woods. With no idea of her location, her one hope was to outrun any pursuers. She reached a stream and reined to a halt. Which way?

From upstream, came the shriek of an eagle. Nell dug in her heels, following the cry. From the camp came pounding hoofbeats and the shouts of men. Disregarding safety, Nell pressed the horse faster, knowing one slip now and she was done for. After a quarter mile, the sounds of pursuit faded in the distance, but Nell had no confidence in a clean escape. A man who killed for pride would never willingly set her free. Most assuredly, he ordered dark riders on her trail. How many and how far to the rear was unknown.

Nell pulled on the reins, bringing the horse to a trot. Riding her mount to exhaustion only delivered her into enemy hands. If most of the dark riders were gunslingers, then their tracking skills may be poor. The water blurred the impression of the horse's hooves in the ground. With luck, pursuit slowed even more.

For miles, Nell rode at a steady pace. Sunlight filtered low through the treetops doing little to offset the morning chill. After the flat of the camp, the landscape began a slow steady incline to the foothills. The topography steepened. The stream narrowed and deepened. Scattered boulders slowed the horse's passage. The once gentle current increased in strength, whipping around the horse's legs. She couldn't keep to the water much longer.

Nell reined to a halt at the bank and dismounted, allowing the horse to drink. She cupped her hands, also, and took in deep gulps of water. Her stomach growled. Damnation. Why hadn't she stolen an animal outfitted with provisions? She considered her two options; continue along the stream or change direction and head up the incline. The wrong choice meant disaster.

Overhead, the eagle's cry sounded once again. A majestic bird circled in the sky, dipping wing as if in salute. With a single mighty flap, it banked toward the heights. Sam's image came to mind, strong and powerful as the eagle. She almost heard his voice calling, *Baya, follow me.*

An overwhelming desire took hold. Nell swung into the saddle and urged the horse after the eagle. The land became rockier. Small boulders and pebbles littered the ground. She slowed the horse to a walk. Now and then she cast a fearful glance over her shoulder. Death followed behind, steadily closing in. She felt its dark presence as plainly as the sun on her back.

The cry of the eagle drew Nell even as her own body succumbed to weakness. It had been far too long since she ate or slept, and she was weak and dizzy. Despite the drink at the stream, her lips were cracked and parched. She ached for another sip of water. The side of her face was tender and bruised where Doyle slammed it into the sapling. She craved sleep and the chance to rest, but to stop now allowed death to close the gap.

Footing became treacherous as the land rose to craggy heights. The horse's hoof landed on a slick rock. Nell grabbed at the mane as the animal slipped and stumbled. Blowing hard, he regained balance, but the next step came with a limp. Nell dismounted to examine the injury. Blood oozed from a deep laceration. Her stomach sank. The leg didn't appear broken, but the horse couldn't carry her weight any longer. Her escape must continue on foot. She slapped the animal's rump and sent him on the way.

The eagle screeched, soaring to the top of a rocky peak.

"I'm coming," Nell grumbled. She started up the rise. Soon, muscles trembled with the strain of the ascent. Her arms and legs seemed filled with lead. Sweat poured into her eyes. Nell gulped a deep lungful of air. How much farther to the summit? And then what? She was nearly spent.

A rock came loose in her hand. Her gaze followed as it tumbled down the slope with a shower of pebbles. She pressed flat against the cliff face as her stomach gave a sick heave. One slip meant death.

Nell peered at the sky and ignored a wave of vertigo. "Keep going, you ninny. Don't look down and the problem is solved."

After another twenty feet, she came to a dead stop. Boulders loomed ahead leaving her nowhere else to go. Clinging to the rise, Nell fought a tide of panic.

An insistent screech drew her attention. The eagle perched on a triangular-shaped boulder streaked with a zigzagged mineral deposit. The bird's piercing gaze focused on a narrow shelf carved out of the rock by eons of wind and water. Half-hidden by the boulder and steeped in shadow, it was invisible to all but those who unwittingly stumbled upon it.

The only way to the shelf was a narrow ledge. Nell swallowed hard and took a step. The width barely matched her boot. "Surely, you jest." The bird impatiently tapped its beak on the boulder.

Nell inched along, hugging tight to the crag. "Don't look down," she murmured with a trembling voice over and over again. "Don't look down." The ledge ended short of the shelf requiring her to leap the last two feet. Nell gritted her teeth. "This is what you get for following the advice of a bird." With a final bolster to her courage, Nell jumped. She let out a cry of relief when her boot once again hit solid ground.

"I made it." She panted. Every limb shook with fatigue. "Where do I go from here?" The eagle cocked his head and with one beat of its wings launched into the sky.

"Don't leave now!" Nell raised her hand as if to snatch the bird from flight.

Her arm dropped limply to one side as the eagle disappeared. Nell leaned against the rockface to wipe sweat from her eyes, then noticed a cleft behind the triangular boulder. She staggered with leaden steps to the opening of a cave. Nell sank to her knees. Legs gave out, arms barely obeyed. With the last of her strength, Nell crawled into the dark and collapsed.

"*It'sa*," she whispered as her eyes closed.

****

Inside the stygian dark of the wooden crate, Sam struggled against panic, fighting the urge to pound on the lid and demand release.

Drawing a deep breath, he stilled his thumping heart. "Damn it, think. You ain't a goner, yet."

Sam's fingers wrapped tight around the pistol grip. A heavy weight rested on top of the crate. The men who loaded the wagon hadn't bothered to nail the lid shut, so he only had to raise it enough to slip through the gun's muzzle. With luck, the weapon could become a lever to force a larger opening.

And if the weight on top was too much or tied so it didn't shift?

Well, then I reckon the dark riders will get a big surprise when they open their Gatling gun and find a dead man.

With gritted teeth, Sam twisted in the crate, rearranging his body so a knee now pressed against a round hard surface. The tip of a pointed metal gear bit into his thigh. He grimaced at the pain, but the position provided necessary leverage. With a grunt, he raised his head and one shoulder to rest against the top of the crate.

One…two…three…now!

He strained against the lid. With a sudden jerk, the weight above shifted. Sam nearly shouted as the lid budged half an inch. He struggled to force the muzzle of the revolver in the gap. The next instant a wagon wheel hit a rut, jarring the crate. Sam lost his grip. The lid slammed shut as his head banged against the side.

Stifling a curse, Sam tried again, but the jostling had moved the cargo. He shoved against the lid again and again, but it stubbornly refused to budge. The air was now thick and stale. His breathing labored as sweat poured down his brow. The dark became a shroud wrapping tight around him, cutting off the air. Alone…he was all alone. He couldn't think. He couldn't breathe. Panic threatened to exert control.

A wave of anger surged. "You will not die in this goddamned crate."

The wheel hit another rut. As the wagon bed bounced again, Sam shoved with every ounce of strength. A weight slid across the top, and the lid cracked open. He rammed the barrel hard into the slit.

Sam pressed his face against the narrow opening. Gulping breaths of fresh air sent his spirits soaring and renewed both energy and determination. He took a few minutes to listen for any sounds of guards nearby, but heard nothing above the rumble of the wagon. Most likely, the bed held cargo, not gunmen.

"Most likely" wasn't a term to offer much comfort. Sam squinted, straining to make out shapes in the dark. No guards were apparent, but the truth of the matter would only be revealed once free. With the revolver jammed under the lid and his knife tucked in a boot out of reach, he was an easy target for anyone with a view of the interior. Sam snorted in disgust. He'd sure got himself in one helluva fix.

The only choice was to make a break for it and hope for the best. With the gun barrel now in place as a lever, Sam shifted the lid. Slowly, he forced out one hand and then an arm. He froze as something slid along the top. A weight crashing to the wagon bed definitely attracted unwanted attention. If he held fast until the wagon bounced again, the sound might be less noticeable.

The lid pressed on Sam's arm, cutting off the circulation. Stabs of numbing pain shot to his shoulder. If he didn't move soon, he wouldn't move at all, making defense impossible. The wagon hit another rut, and Sam shoved hard. A large object rolled along the top of the crate. The lid shifted, and he wiggled out both head and shoulders.

An ammo casket balanced precariously on the edge. Sam eased out his body. Once boots hit the ground, he placed the casket on the floor, and then secured the lid.

Luck was with him. A tarp had been loosely tied over the contents in the wagon, obscuring Sam's exit from the crate. Other boxes and barrels piled against the sides left little room for him to maneuver. Out of the confines of his cramped prison, Sam now clearly heard horses. Revolver in hand, he crept to the rear gate. Peering under the tarp, he drew back with a curse and then slammed his gun into the holster. No way out there. A dozen feet away rode a line of dark riders with Edwards at the lead. Even in the dead of night, he couldn't miss Sam jumping from the wagon bed. Edwards was the type to shoot first for the hell of it.

Sam burned with frustration. Nell was in trouble. Every minute wasted brought her closer to death. He couldn't delay any longer. He must chance an escape now.

The wagon halted. A man outside shouted, "Let'm pass." Sam pulled out his knife and slit a peephole in the canvas. The wagon rolled by a squad of armed guards on horseback. Sam's convoy was now at the gap where the trail bordered an incline. With careful timing, he'd drop into the scrub with none of the riders behind any wiser. He widened the cut in the tarp and then jammed the knife into his boot. The wagon bounced over another rut. Sam held his breath and slipped over the side.

He hit the ground hard and rolled down the hill. Pressing flat to the dirt, Sam drew the revolver and tensed, half-expecting a shout of alarm from the guards followed by gunfire. None came. Above, noises from the wagon and the horses drew farther away. As silence descended upon the woods, he crawled up to the trail. Not a dark rider in sight.

Every second now was precious. Sam backtracked, moving with haste as the sun rose. He approached the rendezvous point with caution and then pursed his lips, mimicking the call of a black phoebe.

Seconds later, Mateo appeared leading two horses. Relief showed on his face as he holstered the revolver. "You were gone a long time, my friend. I almost decided to come for you."

Sam filled him in on what he learned at the compound.

Mateo let out a low whistle. "A Gatling gun."

"The wagon carried the stolen Army supplies. Doyle's men were behind the robberies. You don't have much time. The dark riders are on the way. They mean to slaughter every man, woman, and child at Fort Braddock."

"What about you?"

"I ain't coming." Sam vaulted on his horse. "Nell's in trouble. She left Fort Braddock."

Mateo raised an eyebrow. "How do you—oh, a vision?"

Sam gave a terse nod. "A bad one." He reached into his shirt and pulled out the piece of paper he found with the Gatling gun. "Give this to Abernathy. It backs my story."

"Go," said Mateo, without hesitation. "I swear to get word to the captain. The troop has just a few hours head start."

"The fastest way to Nell is to cut through the dark riders' compound. I'm still wearing one of their shirts. The guards will let me pass. If not…" Sam's hand rested lightly on the pistol grip. "I saw only two men."

"Probably trigger-happy ex-gunfighters," Mateo noted wryly. "Not that the knowledge will stop you. Make sure you don't give them time to draw first."

"I won't." Sam gripped the reins tight. "There's something else. I've reason to believe Daisy is no longer at Fort Braddock, either. In my vision, I glimpsed a woman in Prescott who bore her resemblance. I can't be sure as her face was obscured. If Daisy traveled with Nell, she may still be there. I wanted you to know."

"Was she harmed?" he said anxiously. "A prisoner of Doyle?"

"I couldn't tell. I'm sorry."

"I understand. Be careful, Sam."

"You too, *amigo*."

Sam dug his heels into the horse's sides and cantered along the trail. As he approached the compound, he tensed, waiting for an order to halt, but to his surprise the entrance to the camp was unguarded. The entire grounds were deserted, not a single man remained. The dark riders apparently had no intention to return. Sam galloped away. He cast back to his dream and held a picture in his head of Nell's location. Her hiding place was off to the north high in the rocks.

Before long, the camp was far behind. Sam reached a stream mimicking the one in his vision. His tension lifted with the knowledge Nell was close, and he paused for a quick bearing. The landscape looked different at ground level than from an eagle's view in the air, but he was certain the spirit's message held true. Nell veered to the heights. A strange sensation of dynamic energy formed in his chest. It drew Sam ever forward as if a taut rope lassoed his body, and the hand at the other end tugged him forward with unrelenting determination.

The incline in the rocky landscape steepened. Sam reined in at the sight of a fresh hoofprint in the dirt. Judging from the depth of the impression, a slight rider recently traveled this way. Elation at finding Nell's trail quickly turned to dread when he discovered a second set of much deeper hoofprints. A larger and heavier person tracked Nell's horse.

Rough boulders dotted the landscape, slowing Sam's horse and making the path treacherous. He dismounted, gnawed by frustration at the now plodding pace. The tug on his chest became a steady pull. He was close, very close.

A disturbance in the earth dropped him to a crouch. He ran his fingers lightly over the soil. Something happened to one of the riders. Pressure in the hoofprints altered. He dabbed at a splash of color on a rock. Fresh blood spatter smeared under his touch. The horse carrying the smaller rider had slipped and gone lame. A sick feeling hit his stomach. Did the blood belong to Nell? Had she been thrown and injured? A petite heel print on the ground drew his attention. Nell was on her feet and climbing up the crag. Nearly on top of hers was the impression of a larger boot—the mark of the second rider. The black shadow of death closed the gap.

Sam scrambled up the heights. At the halfway point, he spotted two horses below along the bottom of the rise. One was lame. The other sported two white fetlocks.

Chapter Sixteen

Nell's eyelids fluttered open. Her lips parted in a groan. A memory surfaced of a weary crawl into the cave. While an effective hiding place, the interior was hidden from the warmth of the sun. Now, her body shivered with uncontrollable chills and ached as if she had slumbered on a bed of ice.

A shaft of bright light beamed into the narrow recess and bolstered her confidence. Sleep had consumed her for no more than a few hours. The misery of the frost seeping into her bones would increase with sundown, but for now daytime offered the promise of renewed warmth.

Nell stirred, overused muscles screamed for relief. Her skin no longer burned with the pepper mash, but even a slight movement sent throbbing lashes of pain across her body. She sat up and blew on her chilled hands. Every fingernail was either chipped or torn during the ascent up the crag.

She crawled to the sunbeam and then closed her eyes to bask in the newfound warmth. The heat absorbed by the rock wall soaked into her aching shoulders. Nell's head cleared. She had avoided Doyle's clutches, but was far from safe. The cave proved an effective hideout, but not forever. Fort Braddock was in danger. Captain Abernathy must be warned.

Where to go was the nagging question. Her escape had been nothing more than an unplanned mad dash. Now she was lost somewhere in the Arizona Territory and her horse was lame. How many miles to reach help on foot? Nell's heart skipped a beat. How close were the dark riders?

"You'll find no answers moaning on the ground," Nell muttered in disgust.

Her voice came out as a near croak. The stolen sips from the creek were hours ago and thirst now a searing ache. With thoughts of water once more running down her throat, came an intense desire to leave the crag and return to the stream. The ascent of the heights had been strenuous and terrifying, the descent promised the same or worse, but no respite from hunger or thirst ever came from huddling in a cave. She could either move or spend the day sitting against the rock and dreaming of a steak dinner at one of San Francisco's finest restaurants.

Nell struggled to her feet with a groan. Dreams wouldn't fill the painful hollow in her stomach. Although cramped and aching, her legs supported her weight without a tremble. She scrutinized her dirty, disheveled clothing and managed a wry grin. "If Aunt Agatha saw your disreputable state now, she'd have choice words."

To call her surroundings a cave was an overstatement. The break in the rock was little more than a cleft. The low ceiling and narrow interior offered barely enough room to stretch out full length. Nell squinted in the dim light at scratches on the wall. She wasn't the first traveler to pass this way. Her fingertips traced distinct impressions. Carvings of ancient hieroglyphics danced across the surface. That one was most definitely a sun…then those wavy lines must be water…and what's this? A canine figure bayed at the moon. A bird soared above them watching from on high.

Her heart tugged with yearning. "Sam," she whispered.

What happened to him? Had the cavalry returned to Fort Braddock? Had the attack begun? Was he safe? She swallowed hard. Of course, he was safe. Nell refused to consider an alternative fate.

"Did you send your eagle to guide me, *It'sa*?" Nell murmured. "If so, I thank you."

The belief his spirit hovered protectively over her lit a fire in her soul. Nell closed her eyes again, cracked lips formed a smile. "You gave your heart to an impetuous woman, Marshal Tanner. I hope you have no regrets." She imagined his anger when he learned she left for Prescott. The anger wouldn't last, of that she was certain. He made his intentions plain.

What of her own?

Nell felt the strength of his arms around her once more, the touch of his lips against hers. "I intend," she croaked, "not to die on this blasted peak before I see the face of Sam Tanner once more."

Stumbling from the cave, Nell's confidence increased with each step. Hunger, thirst, and weariness had taken hold and refused to let go, but she was only weaker, not helpless. A trip to the stream wasn't impossible after all.

Not yet, though. Arms and legs lacked the necessary vigor. A single misstep spelled doom on the rocks below. Her descent could begin only after she completely warmed. Nell raised her head to the sky drinking in the sunlight. She wondered idly if the eagle was nearby. A compelling desire to offer thanks filled her heart.

"My deepest gratitude," she murmured. "I could never have made it to the rocks alone."

"God may have led you this far," McLaren snarled, "but the devil's been beside me my whole life."

Fear stole Nell's breath. With gun drawn, McLaren approached the cleft in the rocks. The black shirt was now gray with dust. He panted from the exertion of the climb, his face streaked with grimy sweat, eyes still red-rimmed from the pepper mash. Nell's heart pounded wildly. She never saw an expression so twisted in hate.

"You led me on a merry chase, missy, but now it's done." McLaren jumped to the ledge. He took a long slow look at her torn clothing and then holstered his gun and pulled out a Bowie knife. Sunlight glinted off the razor sharp edge. "Doyle ordered you returned alive, but we got us a score. No woman gets the better of me. You ain't gonna make it off this ridge."

Nell pressed flat against the rocks, striving to keep her voice from trembling. "Doyle won't approve. Failure doesn't set well with him."

"I'll take my chances. I reckon he's got more on his plate to worry about now. Morgan sent word the train he's been expecting is on the way to Prescott. Doyle and his riders left to do the deed."

"You must realize Doyle is insane. It's only a matter of time before he's stopped."

"By then, I'll be a rich man in Mexico with none the wiser. The wanted posters believe I'm already there.

Doyle can have his power. Money is all I ever craved, and Doyle has been mighty generous with pay." He ran his thumb along the side of the blade. "I'm a man of simple tastes, and I'm done talking." Without warning, he lunged.

Nell sidestepped, but he snagged her waist and threw her against the rocks. He pressed his body tight against hers and raised the knife to her throat. She spit in his face and kicked him in the calf.

His lips formed a smile that held no warmth. "Still got the fire," he murmured, rubbing away the spittle. "Don't make it easy. I savor a good fight."

"Let go of me," she shouted.

He grabbed her by the hair as she struggled to break free, and with a savage jerk, slammed her to the ground. "Death will be slow misery. Mighty slow." The outlaw bent over her, his voice a harsh whisper. "First, I'm gonna have me a little fun."

McLaren dragged her into the alcove. "Let's see what you got hidden under that skirt." He threw himself on top of her, pinning Nell beneath him. McLaren's hand slid along her calf, hitching the skirt over her thighs. "All women ain't nothing but whores."

Fear gave way to blind rage. Hunted and cornered, feral strength coursed through her body. Teeth or fangs, nails or claws, both coyotes and humans had their own weapons. Nell bit hard into his cheek.

McLaren drew back with a maniacal howl. Blood seeped from teeth marks in his skin. "Bitch!" he snarled.

Nell scrambled past him and out of the cleft. McLaren tucked his knife into the boot. "Where you headed, missy?" he growled. Darting after Nell, he caught her by the wrist. "Ain't no escape from me."

"Let her go!"

Nell's heart hammered in her chest. Sam inched along the ledge. McLaren went for his pistol.

"No!" Nell screamed, throwing herself at McLaren. She grabbed for the gun as the outlaw squeezed the trigger. The bullet exited with an explosion of sound that rang in her ears as it ricocheted off the rocks. She wrestled for the weapon, but he swatted her aside. Sam leaped off the ledge onto the shelf. McLaren pulled back the hammer and aimed as Nell dashed in front of the muzzle. The trigger released. Sam shouted her name.

Snick.

The chamber was empty. McLaren shoved Nell toward Sam, lunging for the marshal's gun. Nell sidestepped. The two men grappled with each other, rolling ever closer to the brink. McLaren slammed Sam's hand into the ground. His grip loosed, and the gun dropped. Both men lunged for it, but it skidded across the surface and disappeared over the edge. McLaren squirmed free of Sam's hold and jumped to his feet. He pulled the knife from his boot.

Sam drew his blade and faced the outlaw. Each man circled the other, gazes locked, searching for an opening. Nell's breath caught in her throat. They were perilously close to the rim.

"Tanner," McLaren snarled. "How the hell did you track me? Well, I reckon it don't matter none as it'll be the last thing you do."

Gaze glued to McLaren, Sam continued the slow circle, nothing but cold, hard intent marked his features.

"You're a mite out of your district, Marshal,"

McLaren jeered. His gaze widened with understanding. "You weren't tracking me. You came for the girl. She means something to you. Well, ain't that romantic. I'll tell you what," he taunted. "I'll keep you alive long enough to watch me take my pleasure."

McLaren struck with stunning speed. The knife tip grazed Sam's cheek. Pinpoints of blood oozed down to his jaw. At the sight of the wound, McLaren's eyes took on a rabid gleam. He thrust the knife forward, but Sam dodged as the edge swished past his neck.

"You ready to quit your little dance?" McLaren jeered. "I'm ready for your woman. Bet she's a sweet little thing. You seen what I done with that whore in Amarillo. This one will squeal twice as loud." McLaren moved with the fluid assurance of a man who killed many times, and only needed a careless opening for a clean thrust of the blade.

"Have at it, coward," McLaren growled, as Sam avoided another pass. "Let's wind up this business."

McLaren baited him, but Sam stayed tantalizingly out of arm's reach. Then with an impatient roar, McLaren charged. Sam sidestepped the blade and slashed at the outlaw's chest. McLaren swerved, but not fast enough. The point of Sam's knife ripped through his shirt. The dark material showed no blood, but red droplets spattered the ground.

The outlaw's expression twisted with rage. "Think that'll stop me? 'Tain't nothing but a scratch."

They squared off. The knives were a blur of motion. Each step in the lethal dance brought them one step nearer the rim. Both drew blood again, but the cut made from Sam's knife ran deeper. A stream of red gushed down McLaren's arm.

Both men breathed hard, exhaustion marked their movements. Nell held her breath. How much longer could they continue? As if of like mind, they attacked. Knife edge met knife edge, and then Sam's fist collided with McLaren's jaw. The outlaw's head snapped back. Sam hurled the blade as McLaren pivoted. It missed the heart, but drove into the outlaw's shoulder up to the hilt.

McLaren roared. He yanked at the handle with a clean jerk and then tossed the knife over the side of the drop. Clattering against the rocks, tinny clinks faded away as it plummeted to the bottom. Blood streamed from the wound, but McLaren wore an expression of crazed indifference. Madness took hold, delivering him beyond pain. Lips pulled back to contort his face with a feral smile. "Got you now, boy."

Sam charged, wrestling McLaren to the ground. He gripped the outlaw's wrist tight to keep the knife from his throat. Nell gasped as they rolled to the brink. McLaren shifted his body and now bore his full weight on the blade. The tip pricked Sam's skin and then raked across his neck.

"Gonna cut you apart," McLaren spit out. "Bit…by…bit."

Muscles straining, Sam heaved McLaren from him. Nell screamed as the two men slid past the brink. McLaren dropped the knife. Both men's arms flailed, striving for a grip. One of Sam's hands snagged the rim. Nell threw herself at him and grabbed his wrist. Her feet skittered across the pebbly surface inching toward the cliff's edge.

"Let me go," Sam shouted. "You'll be dragged over."

"Never!" Nell strained to keep her grip on his wrist. "I'll die with you." Her boot lodged in a small crevice. She pulled with every ounce of strength. Sam's other hand snagged the rim. With a final tug, Nell hauled him over the side. Shaking with fatigue, Sam staggered to his feet.

One of McLaren's hands grasped the ledge, but his feet dangled free. The two men locked eyes. The dark rider begged no mercy. None was given. Sam's boot heel landed hard. McLaren grimaced as the weight ground into his fingers. He let go without a word, hitting the ground far below with a thump and a scattering of pebbles.

Sam drew Nell from the rim, gathering her in his arms. She fell into his strong embrace, pressing her head against his chest. "Sam."

"*Baya*," he whispered. "Still finding trouble."

Nell's heart flooded with joy. She rose on her toes, lifting her face. He pressed his lips against hers and then covered her face with kisses. Her heart pounded wildly as tears streamed down her cheeks.

"Don't cry, *Baya*," he murmured. "I have you. You're safe."

"I-I'm happy is all," she stammered. "I feared to never see you again."

"The devil couldn't keep me from your side, *Baya*." He took her hand in his and kissed the fingertips. His eyes went wide. A quizzical look came over his face as he licked his lips.

Nell laughed and cried at the same time as she gasped out the words. "Hot p-p-pepper mash."

****

Sam and Nell sat against the rockface, clinging to

each other. As they spoke, their stories spilled together.

"A Gatling gun," she said with a horrified whisper.

"Mat will get word to the cavalry. The dark riders can't travel fast with loaded wagons. Abernathy has time to evacuate civilians."

"What of the soldiers and Mateo?" said Nell. "What will become of them? If they choose to stand against Doyle's army, they'll die."

"Abernathy is no fool. We must hope for the best." His jaw tightened. "It ain't no surprise now Morgan didn't cotton to your tale. He was in collusion with Doyle all along."

Nell breathed out a sigh. "I'm still in wonder how you found me. I assumed the eagle was simply luck, but now…"

Sam nuzzled her hair. "The spirits brought us together. It seems they wish to keep it so."

Nell wrapped her arms around his neck and kissed him. "Please tell the spirits I'm extremely grateful for their help."

"As am I." He glanced up at the sun. "We're safe here, but have little daylight left and no kindling to start a fire. Nights are cold, and the heights too difficult to scale once we lose the light. We must climb down now and retrieve the horses." Sam eyed her with tender concern. "You need food and water."

"So do you," insisted Nell. With an amused expression, Sam rose to his feet and offered a hand. Nell staggered up with a groan. "I don't relish tackling the crag again. By chance," she added hopefully, "did the eagle hint at an easier way to descend?"

He chuckled. "Perhaps, in all the excitement the location of a secret stairway slipped my mind. I'm afraid I only recall one safe path to the bottom."

Nell sighed with regret. "Very well, then. Lead the way."

They approached the edge. Nell glanced over the side and swallowed hard. *Can a cliff grow in size overnight?* It seemed to have spontaneously sprouted dozens of additional feet. Sam eased to the rim and then hopped onto the narrow ledge. His face pressed tight to the rockface, boot heels hung over the side. He held out his hand. "Keep your eyes on me and don't look down. I promise, I won't let go."

Nell grasped his hand. The gentle pressure of his fingers fortified her courage. Sam chose a longer route than her previous ascent. Inch by inch, they descended the treacherous slope. When she finally arrived at the bottom, sweat dripped from every pore. Nell threw herself into Sam's arms, panting hard with exertion, "I don't know who to kiss first, you or the earth."

Sam's eyes gleamed. "Then I'll decide for you." Sam kissed Nell again and then took her to a flat grassy spot. "Rest a spell. I'll gather the horses and return directly."

Some darker emotion reflected in the depths of his eyes. As he strode off circling the slope, the truth hit her. The route from the cliff took longer because Sam led her away from where McLaren landed. He went to assure the outlaw's death.

Sam returned shortly leading two horses. "Luck was with us. Neither my horse nor McLaren's were far. The other wandered off, but we've no time to chase it now." He handed her a canteen. "Drink."

Nell gulped the water with relief as the cool liquid bathed her parched throat. She stopped herself before draining the canteen dry and handed it to Sam. "You, too." He opened his mouth as if to protest, but she shook her head. "I won't swallow another drop until you do." As he drank deeply, Nell's gaze went to the holster with the revolver and the knife now tucked firmly inside his boot.

Sam eyes met hers. "Found them at the base of the crag. The gun works. Blade is undamaged."

Nell placed a hand on his arm. "I know why you led us this way. You wished to spare me the sight. Is McLaren dead?"

His jaw tightened. "Yes. I take no pleasure in killing, but if he still drew breath I'd have ended him. I didn't want you to see."

"I take no pleasure in killing either, but won't mourn his death, nor would have stopped you. If I had a gun in the cave, I'd have killed him myself. As far as I'm concerned, Reese McLaren got better than he deserved. Most of his victims weren't afforded a quick death." Nell blinked. Even to her own ears, her voice sounded harsh. "Oh, dear, I don't suppose that was very ladylike."

Sam chuckled. He stroked her cheek with a gentle hand. "Perhaps not, but my grandmother would approve." His gaze turned to the sky. "We have to go now. Only a few hours of daylight remain before we must make camp. After we lead the horses off the mountain, we can mount up again. I got jerky in my pack. We'll eat on the trail."

"Where are we headed?" said Nell. "I confess, I'm completely lost."

"We can make Spirit Ridge before sundown tomorrow, but," he warned, "it's a hard ride."

"Not when you're with me," said Nell stoutly, "but what of Daisy, Sam? I feel as if I abandoned her in Prescott."

"Mateo knows where she is. Daisy is gifted with enough sense to stay out of sight. Doyle won't order his men to seek her under his nose. You told him she remained behind at Fort Braddock. He'll expect to see her there."

Nell shuddered. "I fear for them all, Sam. Even if Mateo reaches Captain Abernathy, they have no defense against a large armed force."

He gathered her into his arms. "As do I, *Baya,* but we can't do them good from here. Once in Spirit Ridge, I can telegraph for help and organize a posse."

"What chance does a posse have against a Gatling gun?"

"I got no answer, but can't believe the spirits guided us this far only for us to abandon hope."

They led their mounts from the cliff face. Sam retrieved the packet of jerky from his saddle bag, and they ate in silence. The bites of dried meat were enough to assuage the worse of Nell's hunger. Renewed strength filtered into her limbs.

When they reached level ground, they mounted and nudged the horses to a gentle trot. They halted at the creek bed. Sam dismounted to scout ahead on foot. Nell tensed in the saddle with nervous anticipation, but he returned shortly with heartening news. "No sign of tracks others than yours, mine, and McLaren. Doyle must have reckoned McLaren could do the job without help."

They stopped long enough to fill the canteens, then pressed deeper into the woods. As the last of the daylight disappeared in the west, they arrived at a small clearing. "We'll camp here," said Sam "but I can't build a fire. Doyle may have sent others after McLaren failed to return. If so, I don't aim to make the search easy for them."

She nestled against his chest. "Hold me close, then. We'll keep each other warm."

They settled under the stars wrapped in saddle blankets and each other arms. "I know you plan to stay awake all night to protect me," said Nell, "but I won't be able to rest unless you do. Promise to wake me before dawn. I'll watch for us until we have enough light to ride."

"*Baya*—"

"Don't you '*Baya*' me," she scolded. "This is the way of it. I'm not a fragile china doll placed upon a shelf and guarded from harm. You had less sleep than I and need rest."

He nuzzled her ear. "Ah, Coyote Woman has spoken. Will she set teeth and claw at me if I don't obey?"

"Coyote Woman has been known to put up a fight."

"All right then, I promise." His lips found hers. "Sleep well, *Baya*. Know that my love is with you."

I love you, too. Nell bit back the words. She closed her eyes, sensing his anticipation. He wanted to hear her say it. Her heart urged her forward, but saying the words aloud bound him to her.

Aren't you already bound?

She was, tighter than the earth to the sky, but a reckoning with Doyle loomed ahead of them. Her fate at the end of that road was hidden. Death may wait with open arms. Was it better to leave Sam wondering than for him to know Nell died with his face etched into her heart? Would his pain heal faster? And what if they survived? Did Sam only love a dream? Could she bring him the peace he deserved? So many questions and she was too exhausted to face them tonight. Nell surrendered willingly to sleep.

As promised, Sam woke her a few hours before dawn. Nell sat and insisted he lay his head in her lap.

"We must rise before the sun reaches the horizon," he cautioned.

"I promise."

Without a word, he pressed his revolver into her hands. He took out his hunting knife and put it within arm's reach before closing his eyes. Nell bathed in the warmth of his trust and placed an arm protectively across him. She watched the slow rise and fall of his chest. The lines in his face softened. His breathing slowed. She gripped the gun tight and kept fierce vigil as he slept.

Shadows went from black to gray. "Sam," Nell whispered, "it's time to go."

His eyes opened instantly. He sat up and smiled. "I was dreaming."

"About eagles arguing with coyotes?" she teased.

"About a large plate of scrambled eggs and bacon washed down by a pot of coffee."

Nell chuckled. "You had to mention food. I'm famished."

He jumped to his feet and took her hand. "Then let's make tracks."

Sam helped her into the saddle, and they headed out in the gray morning light. Although still stiff and sore, the rest had done her well. The chill in the air didn't cut nearly so fierce. Sam rode in front setting the steady pace. They exchanged few words, each to their own thoughts.

As the day wore on, the rises flattened to lowlands. The forest thinned. They increased the pace, stopping occasionally to rest the horses. The sun had long since passed the high point when they came upon a spring and dismounted to stretch their legs and water the horses.

The burst of energy Nell had upon waking was now a distant memory. Fatigue sank into her bones. Her empty stomach ached. She could barely hoist herself into the saddle when Sam announced time to go. Nell patted her horse's neck in sympathy. It had been weary days for both of them. At least they weren't followed. The horses couldn't keep to a gallop for long.

Sam reached over and squeezed her hand. "We're not far, now. See that path?" He pointed to a worn spot on the ground. "It's an old hunting trail my grandparents and I used often—" His voice broke off as he peered ahead.

Nell shaded her eyes from the sun to follow his gaze. Far in the distance, she made out a dark speck. "What is it?"

"A rider," he said, reaching for his rifle, "and he's coming our way."

Chapter Seventeen

Nell scanned the surroundings. Cover was scant, no place for them to hide. Her heart hammered against her ribs. "Who is he?"

"Can't say yet. Could be an advance scout for a party of gunmen. Don't plan on you being here to find out." Sam pressed the knife into her hand. "Follow the trail. It'll take you straight to my grandparents' cabin."

"No, I won't—"

Sam ignored her protest. "We can't make a stand. I'm near out of ammo. If they're unfriendly, I can lead them from here and lose the riders in the hills. I know this country better than any."

Nell eyed him with horror. "Your horse is hardly fresh."

"Nor are theirs." He spoke with confidence. "They'll not have an easy time of it. Find my grandparents." He lifted her into the saddle and slapped her horse on the rump.

The horse raced away. Nell glanced over her shoulder at Sam as he took off after the rider. She dug in her heels, fear rising as a wave with each pounding hoofbeat. They came so far. To be stopped right on safety's doorstep…

"It won't end here for us, Sam Tanner." Nell bent over the horse's neck urging him to top speed.

The trail disappeared into the brush. She reined in,

her throat closed in panic. Which way?

"Hey, there!" A gray-haired rider with one arm in a sling approached at a gallop.

"Hurry!" Nell shouted. "Sam Tanner…riders are upon him…he needs help."

The man pointed. "Trail's that way. Get on to the cabin." He spurred his horse in the side and raced past her.

Nell kept to the trail, listening hard for the crack of gunfire. No sharp retorts resounded from the hills, but silence proved as unnerving. After several miles of hard riding, she came to a cabin. A woman with long braided hair streaked with gray stood on the porch holding a rifle. Her face showed neither surprise nor concern, as if she expected her arrival.

Nell slid from the horse, her legs barely able to support her weight. "Sam…he's back there. He's alone."

The woman put aside the rifle and gathered Nell in her strong arms. "Frank will find him. Have no fear, little one. You are home."

The built-up tensions flowed from Nell. "Are you Lenna Tanner? I met a man with his arm in a sling."

"My husband. Sam's grandfather."

"Riders are after Sam. I have to help him—"

"No one knows this land better than my husband and grandson. They will return."

She spoke with such quiet confidence, Nell's fears vanished. "H-he made me leave," she stammered. "I didn't want to go."

"Come inside." Lenna picked up the rifle and draped the other arm around Nell's shoulders. "You wished to stay and fight by my grandson's side?"

Nell gripped Sam's knife. "Yes, I do. I will." She peered at the blade, surprised by the fierceness in her voice.

"It is well." Lenna regarded her with approval. "The time comes upon us, but is not yet here. Frank and Sam can avoid trouble." She motioned to the door. "You need food and rest. Have something to eat and we will talk."

"Thank you." Nell entered the cabin and sank into a chair. "Forgive me. I didn't introduce myself."

"You are Nell Bishop, reporter from *The San Francisco Dispatch*."

Nell gaped at her. "How did you know?"

Lenna's eyes twinkled. "We received a telegram from Mateo yesterday."

"Mateo?" she gasped. "He's unharmed?"

"For the moment. He caught up with the cavalry and passed Sam's message to Captain Abernathy, but that was the last we heard before the telegraph wires were cut. Many civilians reside at the fort. Abernathy may decide to evacuate and head here, so Frank went to town earlier to organize a defense. This morning I sensed Sam neared the cabin and sent Frank to watch the trail." She squeezed Nell's hand. "Now we must be patient for their return."

Nell nearly exploded with frustration. "Patience isn't one of my virtues."

"Nor mine," she said with a soft chuckle, "but trust in their skills. Eat while you tell me of your adventures with my grandson."

Lenna ladled out a large bowl of thick rich stew that Nell devoured. In between bites, the story spilled out. With the combination of food, the warm comfort of the cabin, and Lenna's calm assurance the men would return soon, Nell's spirits rose as quickly as the steam from the coffee pot.

"You accepted Sam's gift of the visions," said Lenna. "I see the truth in your eyes."

Nell was taken aback for a moment and then smiled. "Sam found me hiding on the cliff. He said spirits led him. I don't pretend to understand the ways of the spirit world, but am grateful for their help."

"As am I, but now you need to rest."

"I can't. Not until Sam returns."

Lenna's sharp eyes caught Nell's gaze. "Your feelings for my grandson run deep, but a barrier guards your heart."

Pink rose to Nell's cheeks. She had no wish to plumb the depths of her emotional whirlpool with Sam's grandmother. "There are complications."

"That he is of my blood?"

"No!" Nell let out a vehement protest. "That's not it at all."

"Good." Lenna nodded approval. "Hatred of skin cannot be easily overcome."

The flush deepened. "I can't argue my aunt Agatha won't have objections, but I don't."

"Others in society oppose a union."

Nell managed a wry smile. "I've battled society's disapproval of unorthodox behavior my entire life. The older I get, the less it concerns me."

"Something else disturbs your heart, then." A knowing smile played about her lips. "You are not the only one to find the path to love strewn with thorns."

Nell's gaze widened. She leaned forward. "You, too?"

"Did you think my people welcomed a white-skinned husband for me with open arms? I had to leave my tribe behind—everything in my life, including the man already chosen as my husband. Sam's mother was disowned by her family when she married a man with Apache blood. They refused to accept Sam or speak to Alice again, even as she lay dying. Tanner women have always been forced to make difficult choices to be with the men they loved."

The kind concern opened Nell's heart to Lenna. Her words tumbled out in a rush. "My life had no meaning until I found purpose at the newspaper. I'm not sure I can change into a marshal's wife. I'm afraid to become someone else and in the end cause him nothing but disappointment and pain."

Lenna snorted in disbelief. "You believe Sam wishes you to lose your spirit? He does not. Nor should you. You accept his gift. He will accept yours."

"Mine?"

"Your courage and strength, your sense of duty and honor. The same qualities that served you well in San Francisco are needed here, too. Sam won't begrudge use of them as Frank does not begrudge me when I'm called upon to help others with my healing skills—" Her head jerked toward the door. "A rider approaches." She snatched up the Winchester, Nell at her heels.

Nell's heart sank at the sight of only Frank Tanner. She brushed aside her fear. Sam's grandfather would never allow him to face danger alone.

Frank dismounted and doffed his hat to Nell. "Sam is fine. The rider you saw was sent ahead by the cavalry."

Her heart nearly exploded in relief. "The people

from Fort Braddock are safe?"

"For the moment, all is well. They evacuated the fort. The soldiers and families will arrive by morning, but the dark riders ain't far behind. Sam rode to Spirit Ridge. He'll spend the night in town, and we'll meet him tomorrow."

"I need to go now, please."

Frank chuckled. "He said you'd say that. He also said you must rest."

Lenna placed a kind hand on Nell's shoulder. "Sam is right. Rest first and then fight."

"But—"

"We head to town at first light. When the time comes, I promise neither of us will cower in a cabin."

Lenna ushered Nell to Sam's old room and brought soap and hot water. After Nell washed, Lenna spread a cooling ointment over the rope burns on her wrists. As Nell got into bed, Lenna returned with a steaming cup of herbal tea.

"Drink it and rest," she insisted before closing the door.

As Nell sipped the comforting liquid, her aches and pains drifted away. Healing medicine, indeed. She drained the last drop and nestled under the covers.

"What would Aunt Agatha say," Nell whispered, "if she heard I climbed into Sam's bed without a twinge of hesitation?" An image formed in her mind of the elderly woman with a look of frozen horror on her face. She clutched her chest with one hand and a vial of smelling salts with the other. Nell chuckled. "Be at peace, Aunt Agatha. You won't hear the truth from me."

With warmth came contentment, surrounding Nell

as if Sam's tender embrace still held her tight. Her restless spirit never had such tranquility in the noisy bustle of San Francisco. She gazed on the portrait of Alice Tanner and smiled in affinity.

Outside, a coyote howled at the moon. "Watch over *It'sa* for me," she said with a yawn and then closed her eyes.

****

Sam flagged down his grandfather as the rider approached. "Good to see you, Grandpa. Nell is safe?"

Frank reined in beside him. "Good to see you too. Put your heart at ease. The little gal is at the cabin by now. Your grandma will see to her comfort." He rested a hand on the butt of his revolver. "We running or fighting?"

"Neither, I hope." He motioned to the rider. "He's wearing cavalry blue, lest it's a trap to draw us in."

"Reckon we'll know soon enough." He related the details of Mateo's telegram.

As the rider approached, Sam relaxed. "It's Corporal Romero. He rode with us on the trail of the dark riders."

Romero reined in beside them. "Perez caught up to us with the warning. Once at the fort, the captain sent a telegram to the Army command at Fort Denning. Perez sent his telegram to Spirit Ridge, and then left for Prescott. The wires went down before we got word from Fort Denning—Doyle's work we reckoned. Captain Abernathy figured the dark riders were fixing to make their play. They'd be at the fort pronto, and we couldn't be sure of reinforcements. The captain ordered the fort to evacuate and dispatched me ahead to warn they're coming. The troop will push hard for Spirit

Ridge, but they got woman and children and can't travel with haste."

"Neither can the riders." Sam spoke with confidence. "Their wagons are loaded down with ammo and that Gatling gun. They should be at least half a day behind the cavalry."

Romero chuckled. "I can picture the outlaws' faces when they ride into an empty compound. I bet they let loose with a choice word or two."

"Think they'll follow all the way to Spirit Ridge?" said Frank.

"Reckon they got no choice," said the corporal. "They realize by now we figured out the truth and mean to stop us from spreading word."

"We started preparations," said Frank to Sam. "I gave Jeb orders to round up the best marksmen."

"I'll take Corporal Romero with me," said Sam, "and ride in to secure the rest of the town's defenses. Will you go to the cabin—"

Frank's eyes twinkled. "I'll see to your little gal. We'll meet you in the morning."

Sam grinned. "Nell will put up a fuss. She needs rest, but will press to come right away."

"I reckon so. The women who fall for Tanners always have a mind of their own. Don't worry. Lenna will talk sense to her if I can't."

Sam wheeled his horse around and headed into town with the corporal at his side. Jeb stood in front of the marshal's office talking with a dozen men and women. Relief spread across his face when he spotted Sam. "Damn good to see you again."

"Thanks, Jeb. Where do we stand?"

"I passed the word. Everyone is on the lookout for

riders, but we expect them to come by way of the ridge. Got Tom and Ned posted on the high ground keeping watch. They'll alert us if anyone approaches."

"Good. We need to barricade the main street and keep them out of town. We're outnumbered, and the dark riders shoot to kill."

"I got to tell you, Sam, we're all a mite jittery. I'm not sure how many aim to stay."

"They must," protested Corporal Romero. "We are severely outgunned."

"Their first duty," said Sam, "is to their wives and children. I ain't telling them otherwise."

The crowd clustered around the men, faces drawn tight with nervous apprehension. "What news do you bring?" demanded Mrs. Bonifay. Sam relayed the information on the cavalry's arrival.

Earl limped up to him. "You expect us to stay and fight? Mateo's wire said the riders got a Gatling gun. Ain't it smarter to leave before they get here?"

"I can't leave," sputtered Mrs. Bonifay. "I have a business to run. Where will Martha and I go? Everyone must stay and protect the town."

Earl stared at her with wide-eyed disbelief. "From an army of gunmen? Hell, even the cavalry hightailed it out of Fort Braddock."

"Captain Abernathy had to think of the women and children," insisted Corporal Romero. "The fort had little in the way of defenses, but the men will bring whatever arms and ammunition remain."

"What of our families?" Earl asked. "We got to do what's right by them."

"What of ours?" argued Romero. "They come here seeking shelter. Will you abandon them to the riders?"

Sam watched the agitated faces. Tempers ran high. Not tempers—fear. "The people of Spirit Ridge ain't cowards, Corporal, but ain't soldiers, either. They're ranchers, farmers, and townsfolk. They never planned to fight a war on their own doorsteps." He turned to the crowd. "I know what's at stake. I won't stand in front of you and tell anyone to stay. Those who want to get your families away, leave now." A murmur rippled through the group.

"What are you and your grandparents fixing to do?" said Jeb.

"We ain't ready to surrender Spirit Ridge just yet. Those who stay will give the rest as much time to make a getaway as we can, but I won't lie. We're in for a desperate fight, and the odds ain't in our favor. The more men, the better." He gazed into the hills. "If the riders win here, death will spread throughout the Territory. No one will find a safe place, and a body can't run forever."

Jeb raised an eyebrow. "What are you saying, Sam?"

Sam clapped him on the shoulder. "Much as I love this town, dying in the street ain't part of my plans. Captain Abernathy will arrive in due time with reinforcements. We know this land. The riders don't. If I didn't believe we had a fighting chance, I'd straight up say so."

"Enough of a chance to hold off an army of hired killers?" said Jeb.

"I can't know the truth of that either, but I'm staying."

The people of Spirit Ridge looked at each other. One by one faces reflected the same resolve, a decision without words apparent to all. "We're with you, Sam," said Jeb. "What do you want us to do?"

"Spread the word. Any folks who aim to leave need to go now. Barricade the streets with wagons, barrels, and whatever we got to keep out the dark riders and give our people cover. We need to find shelter for the families once they arrive. Mrs. Bonifay, I'll leave that to you."

"I'll see to them," she said, drawing up her shoulders. "I assume the Army will make recompense for their room and lodging."

Sam stifled a grin. Death prepared to ride hellbent into town, and Mrs. Bonifay worried who'd pay her bill. "If we survive, you can give an accounting to Captain Abernathy. I'm sure the Army will oblige."

They spent the rest of the night securing the town. Even as Sam stacked barrels, he couldn't fend off growing dread. Brave words were spoken earlier, but now their preparations seemed so inadequate for an attack by well-armed men. Yet Sam's heart held the certainty of the vision. If they didn't stop the riders here, Doyle's plan would come to fruition. The shadow would sweep across the land, devouring all life in its path.

After completion of the barricade, Sam returned to the marshal's office. A few minutes later, Martha Bonifay entered and left a supper tray on his desk. Sam raised an eyebrow at the holstered revolver on her hip.

"Mama told me to leave," she said stoutly. "I'm staying."

"Ain't that Jeb's gun?"

Martha blushed. "Jeb wanted me to go, too, but I won't without him."

"Your mama knows of you two?"

Martha chuckled. "She does now. We kept it quiet before as Mama didn't approve. Jeb's only got that bit of land outside town, and she doesn't think it's enough to keep a wife. I don't care. He's a good man. Mama and I got into a big old row when I told her I won't leave Jeb. Then Jeb jumped on her side."

She shook her head in disbelief. "That's the first time they ever agreed on anything. I told them both I was staying, and that's the end of it. So then Jeb gave me his gun and told Mama to hush. She did." Martha eyes widened in wonder. "No one's ever got the last word with Mama. Well, I best get back to work."

Sam watched as Martha flounced out the door, a new spring in her step. Damn, he loved Spirit Ridge with all its little dramas and characters. No other place like it existed on Earth, and Doyle planned to reduce it to ash.

Not my town. He'd die to protect them and give folks like Jeb and Martha a chance at happiness.

After downing supper, Sam checked the barricades one more time. The guards had everything under control so he went to his room behind the marshal's office to catch some shut-eye.

Sam lay on the bed and closed his eyes. Thoughts drifted to the desperate escape in the hills and then the night on the trail. His hand stroked the empty space beside him yearning for Nell's warmth pressed against his side. The touch of her lips had filled him with the sweet comfort he never dreamed to have with a woman of his own.

Had he found Coyote Woman's heart yet? No, not quite. Hesitation lurked in those eyes. Perhaps, it was just as well. He might have one more daybreak in his future. Regardless of the time granted, Sam vowed the end wouldn't come before a reckoning with Doyle. Nell didn't elaborate on her captivity, but Sam saw the truth. By the bruises on her face and the tightness around her jaw when she spoke, Doyle tried to take what only should be freely given. Sam had showed no mercy to McLaren. He held none for The Mick, either.

Sam awoke before sunup and checked the barricade. It appeared sturdy enough, but how long could any makeshift defenses hold against a Gatling gun? Restlessness griped him. He headed for Mateo's barn and spied his grandparents as they rode in with Nell. Her welcoming smile lifted his heart.

"I'm going to the ridge to await the cavalry's arrival," he told them.

"I'll come with you," said Nell.

Frank dismounted. "In that case, I reckon you don't need us. We'll stay here and see to the townsfolk."

"He means," grunted Lenna, as she slid off the saddle, "we keep Earl from the whiskey so he doesn't get trigger-happy and shoot himself in the other leg."

The Tanners left. Sam and Nell gazed at each other, an awkward silence between them. Nell turned away and retrieved his knife from the saddlebag. "I was most thankful I didn't have to use it."

He slipped the knife into his boot. "Before we go to the ridge, I've something to show you." They rode out of town on the same trail that went to the Tanner's.

"Are we returning to your grandparents' cabin?" asked Nell.

"Not that far." Sam turned his horse to the narrow path to the glen. Nell followed at his side. Sunlight dappled the grass. Soft breezes rustled the treetops. Sam took in the peaceful scene with a contented smile. His land.

They dismounted. Nell gazed in delight. "It's so beautiful. I've never seen a place lovelier. Is this part of your grandparents' spread?"

"They set this land aside for my father many years ago, expecting he'd bring his family here after he left the Army. He died back East and never made it home to Spirit Ridge. Everything you see belongs to me now."

Nell smiled at him. "This country suits you. It's as if I hear the very earth calling your name."

Sam motioned to the dale. "My mother is buried over there. She's part of the land, now, as I've always felt this place is part of me. Now it's yours."

Nell startled. "What do you mean?"

He took her hands. "I ask nothing of you, *Baya*, but dark days are upon us. If this battle is the eagle's last, it pleases me to know a place so dear is in your keeping. It may bring your spirit comfort."

Nell paled. "Did you have another dream? Does death come for you?"

"No, *Baya*, but—"

"If death tries to take you, Sam Tanner," she cried, "it'll have to fight past me first. Don't think after everything we've been through I'll let you go freely."

His breath quickened. "What happened to Coyote Woman's heart?"

Her smile lit a fire within him. "*It'sa* found it to claim as his own."

Sam gazed at her hands, rope burns visible around her slender wrists. "This ain't an easy country. You felt its harsh nature. I won't hold on if you have any doubts.

Don't give me your heart out of gratitude. If that's the way of it, I set you free."

She laughed. "I have no doubts. Don't you see? My heart hid here all along. You pulled it from the dark recesses and into the light. I'll never keep it from you again."

Sam pulled her close in a tender embrace, joy flooding him. She slid her arms around his neck. He felt the last wall between them crumble. The kiss was long and deep, filled with yearning from both.

"I love you, Sam Tanner," Nell whispered. "Now and always, but I ask are you ready to accept me with all my faults? Your future could well consist of continuous apologies to the town for my unconventional behavior."

"I accept you with every breath of my being." He nuzzled her hair. "Don't change for me, *Baya*. I want nothing more than to fill myself with your warmth and wake to your face next to mine each day—my first sight to be the golden light in your eyes."

They clung to each other as if that action alone could keep the coming storm at bay. Finally, Sam pulled back, expression filled with regret. "We must go."

"First, I wish to pay my respects at your mother's grave."

A lump rose in his throat as he led her to the stone cairn decorated with the single hand-carved wooden cross. "I've always felt more comfort than loss here. I believe her spirit resides in this place. You ain't afraid?"

"No. I can't imagine the spirit of Alice Tanner doing anything but bless this land for her son and anyone who cares for him." Nell bowed her head for a moment. Then she slipped her hand into Sam's, and they returned to the horses. "I told your mother I'll love you always." She peered up at him, expression full of tender concern. "If I don't return, bury me beside her."

"*Baya*, don't speak of such things!"

"I must. Did you think I'd stay out of it? When the riders come do you expect me to hide in your grandparents' cabin, cowering in fear under the bed? Will Lenna? I never thought to find love, Sam Tanner. Now that it's mine, I'll stay with the other women in Spirit Ridge and fight to keep it."

Sam kissed her once again. "The eagle attacks from above while the coyote nips at their heels below. All is as it should be."

They galloped to the ridge, buffeted by a chilly, damp wind. Clouds from the north had blown in since their arrival in town. They filled the sky, blocking out the warmth of the sun.

"Another storm brewing in the mountains," said Sam. "Rain heads our way. Good for the cattle and the crops."

His comment brought a smile to Nell's face. Sam shot her a questioning look. "Your words are a comfort," she explained. "They make me believe life is destined to return to normal."

He chuckled. "Will it rain or won't it? Will the crops fail or won't they? Will the cattle fetch a good price at market or not? Spirit Ridge don't exactly have big city worries."

"No, but they're important and worth the fight."

A gust of wind swirled a pile of dry, crackly leaves. Before collapsing, the tiny spinning vortex danced across the ground.

"Do you hear?" said Sam. "The spirits whisper."

"What's that?"

"The town's name is from an old Indian legend. The tribes who settled in these parts believed the wind through the hills was the voices of the spirits. Only those with open minds and hearts recognize the words and receive their guidance. With their teaching comes peace."

Nell smiled. "Let's hope your people were right."

They dismounted at the base of the ridge. A man flagged them from above and then skittered down the pebbly slope to greet them.

"Seen anything, Ned?" said Sam.

"Naught but a few deer since Corporal Romero passed yesterday. We got the ridge covered, but can't stop an army here with two men."

"You'll have more once the cavalry arrives. Right now, I need a look 'round." The three of them scaled the incline. "Any sign, Tom?" Sam called to the other watcher.

"Not a peep. Shouldn't they be here by now? You sure they're coming?"

"They got no place else to go."

The top of the ridge had an expansive view. Sam surveyed the terrain. The widest part of the trail was about twenty feet. One side abutted the rocky incline, the other led into scrub and then forest. Difficult for horses and supply wagons to traverse, but not impossible.

"I'm hardly a military strategist," Nell said, "but this appears a defensible position."

"It is," said Sam. "We've plenty of cover, and can

pick them off from above until ammo runs out. Problem is a horde of well-armed men can still charge up the ridge and overrun us or rush by under cover of darkness. They can even ride south and skirt the rocks entirely, but I don't reckon so. Doyle is a man dead set on a course."

"If we block the trail," said Tom, "they'll have to take to the woods. It'll be tough going and slow them some."

"But not stop them," said Sam. "It'd only be a matter of time before they make their way to the other side of the ridge."

"How many men do the riders have, you reckon?" asked Ned.

"At least seventy."

Ned rubbed his chin. "We can cause them trouble for a spell, but keeping them pinned won't be easy."

Sam tensed, his attention drawn to movement on the trail. "Riders are coming."

Chapter Eighteen

As the riders neared, Nell stomach knotted with worry. "I don't see anyone else. Where are the rest from Fort Braddock?"

Sam peered at the riders, and then his lips parted in a grin. "One of them is Mat. The boy riding next to him is on Rio." He rose and held out his hand to Nell. "We'll greet them and find out what happened."

Together they scurried down the incline and mounted their horses, spurring them to a gallop. As they approached, Mateo raised an arm in greeting. He spoke to the boy beside him and then pointed out Nell and Sam. The boy removed his hat to wave in the air. Golden blonde curls spilled from underneath.

"Daisy!" Nell shouted.

A smile lit the young woman's face. She and Mateo reined in and dismounted. Nell jumped off her horse and ran to Daisy's outstretched arms.

"I was torn up with worry," said Daisy. "I didn't know what to do when you never returned from the meeting with Morgan."

"How did you escape Prescott?" demanded Nell. "Where did you find Mateo?" She pulled Daisy to arm's length and eyed her with wonder. "When did you learn to ride, and what on earth are you wearing?"

Sam interrupted. "First, tell us what happened at Fort Braddock?"

"Thanks to your warning," said Mateo, "everyone escaped barely ahead of the riders. We've been pushing hard. Abernathy and the rest are right behind us."

Nell snorted. "The dark riders ordered to attack the fort should be thankful for your escape. Most were meant to die with the cavalry so Morgan could proclaim himself a hero."

Daisy's eyes went wide. "What do you mean?"

"Best save it to tell at once," said Sam. "Here they come now."

Horsemen in cavalry blue along with wagons of women and children hurried along the trail. The four remounted and rode to meet Captain Abernathy.

Abernathy's face flushed with anger. "Miss Tremaine told us of Morgan's treachery. With luck, my message reached Fort Denning. The Army will move on Prescott and wrest control from Doyle and Morgan's men. I had no desire to abandon my command, but saw no other recourse with little ammunition and weaponry at our disposal."

"You couldn't stand against them," said Sam. "The deaths of everyone at the fort would have been meaningless and a boon to Doyle's plans. The truth of their evil lies in our telling."

"Any news from Fort Denning?"

Sam shook his head. "Telegraph lines are still down."

Abernathy's voice hardened. "So we must act as if we stand alone. Gentlemen, we need a strategy. I see you have watchers posted on the ridge."

As he spoke with Sam and Mateo, Daisy pulled Nell to the side. "If you don't start talking," she whispered, "I'll burst with curiosity." Nell related her adventures since Prescott.

Daisy shivered. "Doyle always had a knack for attracting evil men, but at least with McLaren's death the world has one less devil."

"Amen to that, Sister Mary. Now it's your turn…an escape from Prescott…those clothes…how in heaven's name are you riding Rio without protest? I haven't heard a peep about smarting nethers."

Daisy shot a shy glance at Mateo. "Oh, they're smarting right enough, but not so I care to make a fuss in front of others. After hours in the saddle, I started to get the hang of horseback. Rio is a real gentleman—hasn't tried to throw me once."

"What happened in Prescott?" Nell demanded.

"I figured the talk with Morgan might take a while as he was a man not easily swayed from his opinions. The longer you were gone, the more this fear in me grew. I couldn't shake the worry something was jiggered right enough. I determined to bide my time for you outside the territorial offices."

Nell's eyes widened in understanding. "You secured a disguise."

"I fooled folk as a nun, so could surely fool them as a boy. I swiped clothes off a wash line, but left a dollar behind as amends," she hurriedly added. "Then I returned to the livery for loan of a saddle and bridle for Rio, and explained a boy would come for him. I told the owner I fancied his hat and bought it for a fifty cent piece." She rolled her eyes. "Lordy, that man gave me a peculiar look. While he busied elsewhere, I changed clothes in the stall and then got on Rio. I gave him a good talking to first and asked him kindly not to throw me as I was a poor rider and liable to break my neck."

Nell swallowed back a chuckle. "I see he obliged."

"Rio was most amenable. He gave his all to you and Sam and must have figured I was set to do the same. So I patted his nose and said we were of like minds. When we returned to spy out Morgan, Doyle was gone. I went inside and found Morgan's aide. I told him I had a message for you from the telegraph office, but he said you left with him out the back door."

Daisy shuddered. "That didn't sit right. Many of Doyle's visitors who left that way were never seen again. On a hunch, I asked the man if he knew Doyle. Oh sure, he knew Mr. Doyle. He was a regular visitor to Morgan. They were good friends.

"I went cold all over and searched the alley. My throat near closed in fear when I found your bonnet muddied and lying to the side. I spoke with a man sitting outside a barber shop. He remembered seeing Morgan leave not long before driving a wagon. I was frantic now and scoured the town. As darkness set in, he returned alone on a horse. Morgan had a look on his face. I'd seen that look before on Doyle after he killed a man and got away with it."

Daisy's voice trembled. "He dismounted at the territorial office. The aide hailed him to say he got word the railroad men arrived before long. When Morgan spoke, I recognized his voice as the man in the other room that day talking to Doyle. I hoped Morgan took you to Doyle's ranch, but had no idea how to get there. I considered going to the marshal, but he had no reason to believe me and might be in Doyle's pocket. I decided to chance a return to Fort Braddock, hoping Sam and Mateo returned and could mount a rescue."

"You rode in the dark?" A lump formed in Nell's

throat. She left San Francisco with high hopes for Daisy's rehabilitation, but never imagined such loyalty. "I continue to marvel at your courage."

Daisy gave Rio an affectionate pat on the neck. "We had enough moonlight to go by and took it slow. Rio seemed to understand what was expected. I have to say, my heart near jumped out my throat when we came upon a lone rider outside of Fort Braddock. Thank goodness, it was Mateo though." Daisy blushed. "He had quite a look of surprise. Mateo headed to Prescott to pick up my trail. He explained Sam went after you, so we hurried to the fort. I handed over the rest of the invoices to Captain Abernathy. One was for a shipment of black shirts from San Francisco with Morgan's signature on the bottom. They readied to evacuate, and Mateo volunteered to lead them to Spirit Ridge."

Daisy eyed Nell in awe. "Mateo described Sam's vision. It's a wonder, ain't it? My heart lifted right then filling me with hope for your safe return."

"Yes, Daisy," said Nell with a smile. "The visions are a wonder."

Her friend shot her a knowing look. "Something changed betwixt you two. Why, Miss Bishop," she teased, "I do believe you're blushing. Didn't reckon anything could bring such high color to your cheeks."

"Am I? Then it's from happiness, although Sam and I have hardly had time to do other than admit our love. What of you and Mateo? He came in search of you. Feelings must run deep."

It was Daisy's turn to blush. "Riding with a cavalry troop ain't exactly the most opportune place to hold private conversation, but I told him of my life with Ma and Stepdaddy and how I was in Doyle's employ. I wanted him to hear the truth. Mateo spoke of his hard times before the Tanners. We didn't talk of feelings, but he acted most gentlemanly toward me. I ain't used to such concern."

They arrived in town. Frank and Lenna waited at the barricade. Abernathy dismounted to eye the makeshift blockade. "Sturdy enough, but not much of a defense against a Gating gun if they breech the ridge."

"They're your families, Captain," said Sam. "Do what you think is best. If you wish them evacuated, we can hide them in the hills until help arrives. Only…"

"Help may not arrive," said the captain, "and even less protection exists for them there."

Eliza laid a hand on her husband's arm. "We'll stay, Micah."

His eyes went wide. "Eliza, what are you saying? You don't understand what's at stake."

"Don't I? If the riders aren't stopped at the ridge, they'll descend upon the town, killing everyone in their path and then pick off the rest of us one by one. Hiding only delays the inevitable."

"Eliza…" He placed his hand over hers and seemed at a loss for words.

Nell stepped forward. "You are short of men, Captain. Defend the ridge. The women will stay behind and protect the town from any who break through the line. We can shoot."

"Better than Earl," Lenna muttered.

The captain eyed Sam with a helpless expression. Frank chuckled. "Must be a contagion in the air here. Makes the females a little loco."

Abernathy's eyes pleaded with his wife, but Eliza held firm. "It's the only way, Micah. You know this."

He gently stroked her cheek. "I know. The rest of us will man the defense of the ridge." He turned to Sam. "Your thoughts, Marshal?"

Sam opened his mouth to speak and then froze. His face reddened. "I was only acting marshal during my grandfather's convalescence, but he's on his feet again."

Frank clapped him on the shoulder. "No, Sam. You're marshal now. I'm right proud of your actions. No one can do better. I won't take back the badge, so I reckon you better get used to wearing it." He grinned. "I warn you, it's a heap heavier than it looks. I'll stay in town. I can't move as fast as others with an arm in a sling, but can still shoot one-handed."

"Better than Earl with two," Lenna murmured under her breath.

"Captain, we'll see to your families," said Sam. "Get your men and horses fed and then we'll talk strategy."

Nell helped Daisy and Lenna find room for the women and children in Mrs. Bonifay's boarding house. As they got settled, Nell left to walk the perimeter. As a defensible position, the building had merit. The structure was in the center of town in the middle of the barricades. Second floor windows offered unobstructed views of the terrain. She peered overhead, shielding her eyes from the sun's glare. The flat roof promised an even better post. Mrs. Bonifay directed her to a ladder behind the house. Nell climbed to the top and then balanced precariously on the last rung. She grasped the edge of the roof and with an unladylike grunt, hauled herself over the side.

Nell eyed the vista with satisfaction. Her range of

vision markedly improved with the added elevation. If dark riders broke through, her stand was here. Tension instantly knotted her stomach. *Don't I mean when the riders break through? They're surely on the way.* She shivered with a sudden chill. When it came to the fight, how long could the defenders hold them at bay? The town's stockpiles had food and water to last, but ammunition stretched thin.

Movement on the horizon drew her attention as a cavalryman galloped to the boarding house. He shouted for Captain Abernathy, and Mrs. Bonifay directed him inside. Nell's hands balled into fists. Were dark riders upon them already? She scoured the ridge, searching for any evidence of their approach and then let out a breath in relief. No, not yet. They still had time.

"I should have suspected when danger called, you'd take to the heights." Nell startled as Sam clambered onto the roof. "Perhaps you're the true eagle, not I."

Nell ran to his outstretched arms. "How did you find me here? Have you had another dream?" She flashed a teasing smile. "Or did the spirits advise I fell on my nethers as Daisy says? Please ease their fears and attest to my surefootedness."

"The spirits are silent. This time Mrs. Bonifay told me you asked for a ladder." Sam nuzzled her ear sending shivers of delight along Nell's spine. "I then said to myself—where is the most improper place to find a young lady of San Francisco society? Naturally, I came straightaway to the roof." He kissed her and then pulled back, peering into her eyes. "I'm fixing to leave and return to the ridge with the others. I can't go without saying goodbye."

Her breath faltered. "A cavalryman rode in. Do the dark riders come?"

"Not yet, but they're close upon us. The man you saw was a scout sent by Abernathy to spy on them. Doyle and his men press hard and will arrive at Spirit Ridge before sundown."

"That gives us a little more time to prepare, at least." Sam averted his gaze. Nell placed a hand on his chest. "What happened? Tell me. We're not a couple to hide truth from each other any longer."

Sam brushed a wisp of hair from her face. "No word has come from Fort Denning, and the wires remain down. The scout reported Morgan and his men joined with Doyle. They number well over a hundred now. Abernathy and I discussed the situation with the others. Despite encouraging words before and your desire to stay, we decided the women and children must go."

"There's no point in running," Nell argued. "Even now, Doyle and Morgan can escape into Mexico, but choose to attack Spirit Ridge. They are committed to evil and dare not leave a single person alive to tell of their treachery. Fighting is our only chance."

"The men accept death," said Sam, "but not for their wives and children. I can't tell them to fight with the threat of their families' destruction hanging in front of their eyes. They must hold fast to the belief of their safety even if it's only the faith of fools. The women and children need you to lead them. *Baya*, I ask this of you."

Nell clung to Sam. Was this her last moment with the man who meant more to her than life? "It can't end here. Did the spirits give new warning of death?"

He held tight. "I spoke the truth. I had no dreams. I choose to believe this means we have hope."

Anger boiled in her. "Hope? That's all they offer in our darkest hour? What good are the spirits then? I wish I could confront them and demand help."

Sam eyed her in surprise. Nell flushed. "Forgive me, I didn't mean to offend your beliefs."

"I take no offense, but your words brought to mind my grandmother. She told me her father communed directly with the spirits beyond random dreams."

"How?"

"She couldn't say." His brow furrowed in thought. "I never sought them on my own. Only recently did I even accept the gift. To me it has always been a curse."

Nell gazed at him in wonder. "Are you saying it can be done?"

"I don't know, but am inclined to try."

She swallowed. "Is it dangerous?"

"Another question I can't answer *Baya*, but now have the pressing need to set my feet upon this path. I require a quiet place so my mind opens to the spirits without distraction."

Nell sat. "Put your head in my lap. No one will disturb you."

Sam lay down and closed his eyes. A smile played about his lips. "Coyote Woman stands guard with bared fang and outstretched claw."

"'Til death claims us both," she whispered.

Sam's breathing slowed. Lines of weariness around his eyes relaxed. Nell stroked his brow. He pushed himself so hard these last few days. He'd push even harder to keep this town safe. Protective warmth spread like a blanket from her to cover Sam. Her mind opened as well. Apache god or white god, what did it matter? All life was one and should forever unite against the threat of evil.

Whatever strength I have is his. Whoever is there, please hear both our pleas.

****

It'sa soared overhead. He raised his beak to the sun and screamed a war cry. "A shadow poisons the light. I call to the ancestors, to the spirits who walk this land. Rise up!"

"Rise up!" echoed the coyote as she raced across the plain. "Before the shadow engulfs us all." Baya's howl was deep and guttural, a hunter on the prowl.

It'sa shrieked approval. Their combined cries sent shock waves across the earth. Boulders trembled in their resting places on the mountain. Thunder rumbled in the distance.

A presence stirred. "We are here. Who rouses us from sleep?"

It'sa beat his powerful wings. "The eagle and coyote join in battle against the coming darkness. We beseech your help."

"You are of the sky, she is of the earth." The voice resonated with doubt. "You come from separate worlds. How can you hunt together?"

"We are one!" they shouted in unison.

"United in life," declared It'sa. "United in fight."

"United in death?" boomed the voice in scorn. "Words...only words. Be gone from us."

A blast of icy air slammed into It'sa and pushed him away. He flapped his wings, fighting the wind's relentless power. "Always together," came his defiant cry, "until light no longer shines from our eyes. We will never yield."

Far below, Baya howled. Her claws dug deep into the ground, holding her steady against the gale that threatened to toss her body like a dry twig.

"Why do you fight?" taunted the voice. *"For fame? For glory?"*

"Never!" They shouted above the roar of the storm.

"We fight for life," said It'sa. *"For peace. For each other and all our people. For the very land itself. See us, know us,"* he challenged. *"We have no fear."*

"As you wish."

The wind stopped. From the sun, spears of light plunged into the hearts of eagle and coyote. Deeper and deeper they burrowed, stripping away any barriers of mental defense until they reached the farthest corners of eagle and coyote's souls. The light touched their spirits, the essence warm and welcoming.

"This is not the easy path," the voice warned.

"We accept the danger," said It'sa, *"and heed the call to battle."* Without hesitation, eagle and coyote drank in the brilliance as eagerly as the thirsty take water in the desert.

The splendor of the light faded. *"Your hearts have been weighed and measured. Judgment is passed. Will you carry the burden and protect the innocent no matter the cost?"*

Coyote bowed her head in acceptance. *"With my life."*

The eagle eyed her with pride and dipped his wings in salute. *"With our lives,"* he vowed.

"Welcome defenders of the light." The voice transformed into a brilliant being whose glory radiated

as the sun. Eagle circled around, awed by the presence.
Was it male? Female?

"Neither and both." *It spoke with the resonance of*
a thousand voices. "We are those who walk in the light.
Behold the shadow." *Through the gap in the ridge*
poured an oily black river of death.

"We go to the high ground," *the being cried.*
Clouds billowed around the mountaintops. Lightning
blazed across the sky and struck the cliffs. Rain gushed
in a frenzied deluge off rocky flanks. The torrents
gathered to a single roiling cascade. The sun dipped
toward the horizon—one hour until nightfall. With an
Apache war cry, the water surged from the peaks,
striking at the tail of the shadow. The streak of seething
evil bellowed in rage as a third of it savagely tore
away.

"Eagle to the sky!" *commanded the being.*

It's a beat his mighty wings, stirring up the wind.
The force of the air currents hammered against the
cliffs. It shook boulders from their resting places where
they kept sentry upon the ridge for millennia. With a
deafening roar, they crashed down the incline,
dislodging a river of dirt, gravel, and rocks. The
landslide slammed into the shadow. Another third
disappeared. It's a dove from the heavens into the
heaving mass and was lost from view. The shadow
screamed more in rage than pain and sighted on the
town.

The being called once more. "Coyote to the land!"

The coyote tore across the earth nipping at the
heels of wild-eyed creatures with long pointed horns.
She herded them toward the shadow. Hooves flashed
sparks upon the ground. They stampeded, eyes blazing

flame, goring out chunks of the dark and tossing it aside. Coyote howled a call to arms, leaped into the heart of battle, and disappeared.

The being's voice dropped to a whisper. "Forever the light."

Chapter Nineteen

The vision faded to misty gray.

Sam opened his eyes. Sweat beaded on his forehead. He gulped a deep breath to still his pounding heart.

Nell's concerned face hovered over him. "Are you all right?"

"I am." He sat up, rubbing his eyes.

"You saw something. What was it?"

"A plan to fight the riders only…" He dropped his gaze.

"Death is the result?" she whispered.

Sam took her hand and pressed it to his heart. "I can't say. They sent a vision of the coming battle, but not the end." The image of Nell devoured by the villainous dark made speech difficult.

"Then perhaps the end isn't written," she said gently. "Tell me what you saw."

"The end isn't written." Nell's words brought strength. Eagle and coyote would fight together no matter the outcome. Sam described the vision.

"I'm glad the spirits have use for a coyote," Nell said in all seriousness.

"Even the spirits," he teased, "know in times of trouble you won't sit idle."

Nell wrinkled her brow. "I don't understand the entire meaning of the vision. Do you?"

"Yes." Sam rose and helped Nell to her feet. "Now I must convince Abernathy to adopt a new tactic. How long was I here?"

"Spirits work with speed. You've been with me but a few minutes, and I haven't heard any horses depart. The captain is surely still below."

They found Abernathy in the parlor poring over an area map with the Tanners, Mateo, and several other townsfolk and soldiers. The captain looked up as Sam entered the room. "Marshal, we concluded our final preparations and are ready to ride out."

"I have another way." Without mention of the vision, Sam described his plan. As he spoke, his grandmother regarded him with a piercing gaze. She said nothing, but nodded her approval.

Abernathy gaped at him in disbelief. "Marshal, your tracking skills are beyond reproach, but forgive me, sir, if I'm skeptical of success. You rely solely on luck and wishful thinking. I can't in good conscience agree to such a mad scheme."

"It ain't luck." Sam spoke with quiet assurance. "There's rain in the mountains."

He raised an eyebrow. "How can you possibly know?"

Lenna stepped forward. "Sam speaks the truth. I, too, have read the signs."

"Even if true," Abernathy sputtered, "you can't be sure of the timing. These are your friends and neighbors. They're ranchers, for God's sake." His voice rose in anger. "How can you consider risking their lives in such a foolhardy manner? You doom everyone. They must evacuate."

"Marshal, listen to the captain," said Corporal

273

Romero. "Your people ain't soldiers. You can't fight a war."

"Speaking as one of those people," said Frank wryly. "I say the plan is sound and the best chance we got."

"No," said Abernathy. "I've made my decision. The cavalry holds them at the ridge giving my wife—" He swallowed. "Giving our wives and families a chance to escape."

"For what purpose?" said Mateo. "Every man on that ridge will die. I'm not against sacrificing myself for the good of others, but I want to believe my death has meaning. This doesn't. Those that leave will never make it to safety, and we can't hold back a storm of riders for long with the guns and ammunition at our disposal. Our deaths play into Doyle's hands. That's the truth. Deep down, everyone here knows it." The other townspeople muttered support. The rigid disapproval in Abernathy's expression wavered.

"Mateo's right," argued Nell. "Even if you stop half the riders at the ridge, the rest will sweep through the pass with the Gatling gun. When that happens…"

"No one will be spared." Daisy stood in the doorway. "You don't know Colin Doyle the way I do. Man, woman, or child don't matter. He carries neither mercy in his heart nor kindness in his soul. His mind is always focused on the prize, but now also bent on revenge. He's a man who kills for pride, and we dare stand in his way. Doyle will give no more thought to our deaths than swatting a fly buzzing about his head."

Abernathy exhaled slowly. "Engaging experienced gunmen long enough to slow a river crossing is damned near impossible. I recall the area. It has little ground cover."

"I won't argue that," Sam said, "but this is our land. Every rock, tree, and blade of grass, is known to us, but not to the dark riders. The scant cover is more to our advantage, not theirs."

Abernathy paused as if to consider Sam's words. "How many men will you take?"

"Eight including myself. If we don't make it back, you still have enough men left to cause them trouble."

He raised an eyebrow. "Eight to slow an army? Marshal, while I maintain the utmost admiration for your optimism, I'm inclined to judge you either a madman or a fool."

Frank grinned. "I'll let you in on a secret, Captain. A good marshal is a bit of both." He turned to Sam. "How long must Doyle be delayed?"

"We'll hold the riders on the other side of the wash until one hour before sunset. I reckon to engage them a half mile away. We'll fall back and keep to cover, drawing them slowly with us."

Frank rubbed his chin in thought. "The setting sun will be at our men's backs, shining in the eyes of his gunmen. It yields a small advantage."

"Very small," scoffed Abernathy. "Have you ever seen a Gatling gun fired?"

"Hope not to today," said Sam. "I ain't saying there's no risk, but Doyle and Morgan know we're outnumbered and expect an easy fight. We use the element of surprise and concentrate attention on the wagon. If we stay out of sight and move quickly enough, we can keep them from engaging the gun." He cocked his head and flashed a sudden grin. "Captain, what's your decision? Ready to lead the good folks of

Spirit Ridge into hell?"

Abernathy peered at their set, determined faces. Abruptly, his stern expression lightened, and he cracked a smile. "I do believe I am. Your men delay them long enough for the floodwaters to act. I'll command a defensive line at the ridge."

"Can you use this?" Earl reached into his jacket pocket and pulled out a stick of dynamite. "Got one left."

Sam's gaze went wide. "Where the hell did you get that?"

"My cousin works a mine near Tucson." Earl shuffled his feet. "I cajoled a few sticks to use for fishing in the river. Didn't work nearly as well as I'd hoped. Blowed most of the fish to pieces."

Abernathy gingerly handed the stick of dynamite to Corporal Romero. "One stick isn't enough to block the trail, but a well-placed explosion can rain boulders and force them to the woods. Marksmen can make a good dent in the outlaw's numbers, but if this foolhardy plan has even a chance of success—"

"We understand what to do," said Nell as if in anticipation of his concerns. "Have no fear. I'll wait for the signal before stampeding the cattle. Then, gentlemen, Colin Doyle will rue the day his mother had the misfortune to give birth."

With everyone in accord, Frank and Lenna volunteered to round up cattle from neighboring ranches. "Most have gone to market," said Frank, "but we might be able to corral thirty head."

Lenna pulled Sam aside. "You spoke with the spirits. I'm proud of you, *It'sa*."

"Let's hope I correctly interpreted their words."

"You have. I know this. Trust in your heart and all will be well."

"I'm proud of you, too," said Frank. "I chose a good man to succeed me as marshal so I can retire in ease. That is," he added with a twinkle in his eye, "if he don't get the rest of my cattle killed first."

From the men who volunteered to head to the wash, Sam picked Mateo and the six best marksmen. After plans finalized, Sam walked with Nell to the barn. He had so much to say and, yet, words refused to come. Sam saddled Rio and then slipped a hand into his pocket to retrieve a small wooden box. The contents made a rattling sound when he shook it.

"How much ammunition is there?" Nell asked.

"About thirty rounds for each man."

She gasped. "That's all? Sam…"

He drew her close. "I'll make every bullet count."

"Then, I'll pray the spirits warn you when to duck." Nell's voice held steady, but he read the fear for his safety in her eyes.

Sam cradled Nell's face in his hands. "I'm not the only one who needs to take care. A stampede is as deadly as a bullet. The idea of leaving your side is hard to bear."

"I feel the same, but am more useful here. You're the best marksman in town and needed at the ridge. Destiny demands we fight alone."

"Not alone, *Baya*," he whispered. "I hold you in my heart."

"And you in mine, *It'sa*."

With one long last kiss, they parted. Sam joined the company of marksmen. He sensed Nell's gaze on him as he galloped from town. The desire to turn back almost overwhelmed him. How could he ride off and leave Nell? His grandmother's words came to him again. *Trust in your heart and all will be well.* He sent a fervent prayer of thanks to the gods and tuned his attention to the ridge.

Captain Abernathy took charge of the company of defenders setting up position along the trail. He pointed to a spot near a rocky overhang. "I instructed your man Earl to place the dynamite up there. One stick of explosive won't bring down the entire cliff face, but in the confusion of battle the noise and debris will take a toll on the outlaws' nerves. Rattled men make mistakes."

Mateo eyed the cliffs. "Just be damn sure Earl doesn't set it off early. I rattle, too, especially with boulders crashing around my head."

"He won't light the fuse until the dark riders are beneath us." Abernathy shot them a wry look. "I assume you men will arrive first. If not, I suggest you urge your mounts to greater speed." He shook hands with Mateo and then turned to Sam. "It's been a pleasure to make your acquaintance, Marshal Tanner. May fortune favor you and your people."

Sam shook his hand. "And you, sir."

The group cantered along the trail. Mateo urged his horse to ride abreast with Sam. He leaned toward him and murmured. "Did you have another vision?" Sam nodded. "Any hints how the day ends for Daisy?"

Sam raised an eyebrow. "What happened between you two on that ride from Fort Braddock?"

Mateo gazed into the distance. "Daisy has suffered much. My heart grieves when I consider more pain in her future. In truth, I don't wish her to return to San

Francisco, but right now I'd give title to my livery to see her safely in that very spot. I sought Daisy out before we left and pleaded with her to leave town. She refused. Daisy is determined to face the riders with the people of Spirit Ridge. I can't help but fear for her. *Díos mio,* she can't even fire a gun."

"Daisy couldn't ride a horse before she got here. Don't be surprised if she's learning to pull a trigger right now."

"Your words are small consolation."

"I'm sorry, Mat. I wish they'd ease your heart, but I haven't foreseen how today ends for any of us."

"Then I take what little hope you've given and trust in the spirits' guidance—and pray God forgave us both for once lusting after nuns."

Before long, they arrived at the wash. Water flowed from the hills in a gurgling stream. At the deepest point, the level scarcely covered the horses' hooves. Mateo eyed Sam uneasily. "You're certain the spirits didn't pull your leg?"

"Have faith." Sam spoke with barely felt confidence. He had no doubt the flood would come, but had he correctly interpreted the time of arrival? A miscalculation spelled disaster for them all. He cast worry aside. Retreat was out of the question. Whatever happened, they were committed to the fight.

A half mile from the stream, the trail emptied into level land interspersed with rocks, scrubby brush, and trees. They dismounted and secured the horses out of sight. Sam eyed the landscape with a practiced eye and ordered the men to disperse. They took cover behind boulders. The scattered hiding places met Sam's approval. Each carried a Winchester rifle with an approximate range of two hundred yards. Their positions offered good coverage and an effective spread of firepower. The only strategy now was to keep moving and draw the enemy forward without giving away their own weak numbers. Once the riders determined only a few marksmen delayed the advance, they were sure to charge.

"Sam!" Mateo shouted from the top of a hill. "They're coming."

"Where are the wagons?"

"Middle of the company. Sam, the Gatling gun is assembled."

Sam's jaw clenched. He expected it, but the reality of such a fearsome weapon so close to town heightened his anger. "Sit tight for my shot. Make every bullet count, boys. Don't fire without a chance at a hit and then watch for my signal to fall back. Keep hard at 'em. Don't let the wagon with the Gatling come forward. I aim not to make this crossing easy for them."

The earlier cloud cover had dissipated and now the sun's rays were blindingly bright. Pressing the stock to his shoulder, Sam sighted along the barrel. His breathing slowed. A finger rested lightly on the trigger. As a gentle breeze brushed his cheek, he made an immediate mental adjustment in bullet trajectory for wind speed and direction. Body pressed against the outcrop, he sensed the faint vibration of movement; men, horses, and wagons headed his way.

The vibrations increased. Sam's ears picked up the distant rumble of wheels interspersed with the plodding clop of horses' hooves. A mouse skittered across the sandy soil toward a burrow, spooked by the commotion.

Men wearing black shirts spread like a rotting

infestation over the tranquil landscape. Sam stifled a curse. He had never met Doyle and hoped civilian clothing marked him within the group, but the outlaws dressed the same. If Doyle chose to come along, he blended with the others.

Sam's shoulders tensed. Doyle was there. He didn't have to see him. A man with his ego wouldn't ignore a supposed moment of glory. Sam glowered. Doyle must expect to ride triumphantly to Prescott after the slaughter, leading his own god-damned parade. Only death stopped such a man.

Closer now…four hundred yards…three hundred…Sam picked a target as the first riders came within range. He tracked their movement and automatically calculated distance—just as Frank Tanner taught him. Sam steadied his arm. One last wind check for speed and direction…lead on target…three deep breaths…pause on the down breath…brace for the recoil…gentle pressure on the trigger.

With a loud *crack,* the bullet exploded from the barrel. Two hundred yards away, a dark rider jerked in the saddle and toppled to the ground. A half dozen more shots followed in rapid succession from Mateo and the rest of the men. More bullets found their marks, more riders struck down. The outlaws fought for control as horses whinnied and shied.

Sam picked off the driver of the wagon with the Gatling gun. As he tumbled from the seat, another man took his place. Before he slapped the reins against the horses' rumps, one more bullet found its mark.

Men shouted orders as confusion spread. Several took aim, shooting in Sam's direction. He slid to the bottom of the rise and then up another outcrop to return fire. Mateo and the others were also on the move. He caught glimpses as they retreated, creeping from one hiding place among the rocks to another. Dodge and fire…move to new ground…keep the enemy off guard.

The outlaws took cover and regrouped. Sam and his men retreated. Ammunition was a precious commodity, and their targets weren't in the open now.

A group broke off urging their mounts forward. Sam returned fire, but the outlaws gained ground. The men of Spirit Ridge could no longer hold their position. Sam gave the signal to make for the water. Mateo and the rest slipped back. They kept to the scant cover, one eye on their pursuers.

"This way!" Sam shouted as the riders drew near. They reached a clump of trees, but the outlaws pushed ever harder. "Can't hold them any longer. Get to the horses."

Pistol shots cracked through the air. A man grunted in pain. "Tom," Sam called, "you hit?"

"Took one in the shoulder."

Jeb was already at his side, stanching the flow of blood with his bandana. "Get to Abernathy and the ridge," Sam ordered. "Mat and I will cover your escape and draw them away."

"Don't hole up too long," warned Jeb. "Once you break to open ground, they're sure to get a bead."

"We know. Ride hard. We won't be far behind."

The men mounted their horses. Sam and Mateo tensed in the saddle waiting for the front line of outlaws to appear. Sam tightened on the reins as Rio pranced a nervous step. He patted his neck. "Easy boy."

Mateo glanced at the sky. "The sun is low. Did we delay them long enough?"

"I reckon we'll soon find out," said Sam, as hoofbeats approached. "Ready?" Mateo nodded tersely.

Sam fired as the first of the riders appeared. They immediately wheeled their mounts to give chase. Hunkered low over their horse's necks, Sam and Mateo bolted from cover in a hail of gunfire and galloped downslope toward the stream.

As Rio's hooves splashed into the water, Sam's heart sank. The level hadn't risen so much as an inch. Shouts came from behind, followed by the thunder of pursuit. From the sounds, the whole company converged. Sam reached the opposite bank and pulled up short, staring in despair at the mountains. They removed a few of their enemies, but not enough to make a difference. Was his great plan ultimately just a dream?

Mateo galloped a dozen yards along the trail. He reined in his horse and shouted, "Sam! What are you waiting for?"

Sam peered upstream in anxious desperation. "Now," he murmured. "Please, send the water now."

"Sam, they're coming! *Vámonos!*"

Defeat pressed on Sam with a crushing weight. He misinterpreted the vision. A rifle shot split the air. Something splashed at the water's edge. He spurred Rio to a gallop and caught up with Mateo.

"The spirits didn't answer," was all he could say.

"You tried, my friend. What more can a man do?"

Sam nodded numbly. Fear tightened his chest. He'd failed Nell and Spirit Ridge. None of his actions mattered. The riders would attack with near full strength. Sam and Mateo kicked their mounts and raced to catch up with Jeb and the rest.

A brutal gust of wind from the peaks rocked Sam in the saddle. With a jerk of the reins, he halted Rio.

Mateo reined in next to him. "Why did you stop?"

Perplexed, Sam twisted in his seat and stared behind at the stream. The front line of dark riders reached the water's edge. "Don't you feel it?"

"Feel what? They'll be upon us in minutes. We can do nothing more here—"

Mateo broke off as a high-pitched keen whistled through the trees. "What the hell is that?"

Sam's expression filled with grim satisfaction. "An Apache war cry."

Instinctively, Sam and Mateo tightened the reins. Both horses' ears went back, near flat to their heads. Eyes wide, they snorted in fright as their hooves pawed divots in the ground. Through the air issued a low rumble followed by the gravelly clatter of rocks tumbling down an incline. The horses took skittish steps as the earth trembled.

Their pursuers' mounts sensed danger, too. From the stream came whinnied shrieks of terror. Horses bucked and reared. Two thirds of the dark riders had reached the opposite bank, along with the wagons, but now passage for the rest slowed. Men fought for control of panic-stricken animals as the low rumble surged to a roar. The wind billowed ahead as if propelled by an unstoppable force.

Mateo drew in a breath. "Sam?"

Sam's lips twisted in a humorless smile. "The spirits answered."

With an explosive boom, the flash flood slammed into the riders. Horses screamed in terror as their legs swept out from underneath. Stunned men cried for help.

The horde of dark riders became a seething black mass of twisted arms, legs, and broken bodies. Hands clawed fruitlessly through the air before dragged below the roiling surface. Within seconds, the raging torrent ripped off the tail end of the long line of men and horses and washed it from sight.

"*Dios mio*." Mateo crossed himself. "How many gone you think?"

"Maybe a third."

"Enough for a fighting chance, but not an assured victory? *Bueno*, I take the gift with gratitude, my friend."

"As do I." Sam uttered his own silent prayer of thanks. "Let's go. The riders will regroup and be on the trail before long. I don't reckon this setback will instill a forgiving mood."

They urged their horses toward Spirit Ridge.

Chapter Twenty

"Are you sure you want to do this, Daisy?" said Nell. "No one will think less if you choose to stay at the boarding house."

Daisy held firm. "I'm barely a passable rider and can't shoot. Bullets are scarce and needn't be wasted with me. All a stampede requires is whooping and hollering. Even I can do that."

Nell gazed over the landscape. Eliza Abernathy and the other women laid rags doused with kerosene around piles of brush. "Little cover exists. We'll be easily spotted when the dark riders come."

Daisy placed her hands on her hips. "Ain't stopping you."

"I can shoot back." Nell pressed a revolver into her hand. "I won't see you unarmed. Take care as it's loaded. Use both hands to steady the gun as you're not used to the recoil. Lock your arms, point, cock the trigger, and then squeeze."

"I-I ain't sure I can hit a moving target."

"Don't worry about aim. If you're far away, the shot may warn off an attacker. If you are close enough, whoever you fire at will sport a nice round bullet hole somewhere."

She tucked the revolver in her belt. "I do take strange comfort in that."

Nell eyed her with respect. "Well, look at you,

Miss Tremaine. I'm so very proud. This girl in front of me is not the same Daisy Tremaine who ran scared from San Francisco." Overwhelmed with sudden guilt, her voice faltered. "Forgive me. I've hardly delivered on my promise to lead you to a safe place."

Daisy caught her in a tight embrace. "Don't you dare beg forgiveness. I ain't a whit sorry and am grateful for what you done. I'd rather die here tonight than spend another second in San Francisco with the luxuries Colin Doyle offered." She gazed toward the ridge and sighed. "We had one grand adventure, haven't we, Sister Regina?"

"That we have, Sister Mary. God willing, it's not finished yet."

Nell examined the makeshift corral erected at the foot of the trail leading into town. Her plan was to stampede the longhorns into any dark riders who made it past the ridge. With luck, she'd thin their ranks enough to overcome their superior firepower. Even now the cattle seemed to sense what was to come. They shuffled in the pen, tossing their heads and lowing.

She turned from the setting sun and faced the ridge. Somewhere to the east, Sam engaged the enemy. Frustration and fear swirled together, was he safe? Would she see him again?

"Your thoughts run deep. Do they hold concern for my grandson?"

So mired in anxious feelings, she didn't notice Lenna's approach. A flush heated Nell's cheeks. "Yes. I wish I was at his side. Right now, I'd settle for the knowledge he's unharmed."

"Sam is a skilled warrior. Trust the spirits approve his actions and watch over him. Even though," she added with a twinkle in her eye, "I, too, often wished the spirits gave clearer answers. Frank and I will be on Mrs. Bonifay's rooftop and return fire if any riders make it into town. You're certain you wish to remain here instead?"

Nell nodded. "Sam's vision saw the coyote nipping at the hooves of great beasts and herding them toward the riders. I believe I'm supposed to guide the stampede."

"You have no experience with cattle and a stampede, by its very nature, is not guided."

"Well, as Daisy said, all I need to do is whoop and holler. That'll get them started in the right direction."

"Starting is not the difficulty," said Lenna. "Longhorns are dangerous and unpredictable. A stampede is liable to charge anywhere. A herd of terrified cattle are near impossible to get under control until the animals wear themselves out. I'm not certain the spirits' intention was to put you at close quarters to such mindless destruction."

"The plan is sound. Smoke and fire will force them to the trail while I ride from behind and urge them forward."

"Or make them so wild with fear they do not care if they bolt through the flames, or turn completely into your path." Lenna reached over and squeezed Nell's hand. "The burden Sam carries is heavy. Since the day I realized he had my father's gift of visions, I've prayed to the spirits to send him a woman to bring peace to his heart. When he spoke of the coyote with golden brown eyes, I knew the spirits had finally answered my prayers. I have no wish to lose a granddaughter before marriage vows are spoken."

Nell's blushed. "Thank you. I promise to be careful."

"Ride to the boarding house as soon as the cattle head in the right direction. Frank and I will cover you and Daisy from the rooftop. Join us there."

"We will." Nell mounted her horse and galloped beyond the outskirts of town, passing women standing ready to light the bonfires. The setting sun painted long thin shadows across the ridge. Nothing but the muted rustle of leaves through the trees broke the silence. Time passed with agonizing slowness. The shadows lengthened and deepened, but no word came from Sam or the others. Had they stopped any of the dark riders or been caught in the torrent themselves? Her mind formed a horrifying image of his body broken against the rocks.

From the distance came the fearless yowl of a coyote. Like the clarion call of a trumpet leading troops into battle, the animal's cry bolstered her courage. Nell pushed morbid thoughts away. "Have at us then," she murmured. "We're waiting for you."

As if in answer, gunshots rang out from the ridge, followed by a muffled roar. The screams of horses and shouts of men drew near. Nell jerked the reins and galloped to Spirit Ridge. The final battle was upon them.

****

Sentries passed word to Captain Abernathy of Sam and Mateo's arrival, and he rushed to meet them. "Did my men return?" Sam asked.

"They're safe and wounds being tended. The riders?" Sam gave a terse report. The captain's eyes shone with approval. "A third, you say? By God,

Marshal, we have a chance."

"We couldn't take out the Gatling gun."

"That gives them a heavy advantage. The bullets can tear through a sapling so use sturdy cover. If they get to Spirit Ridge, the dark riders can easily keep shooters pinned long enough for men to break through the doors and enter buildings."

Sam gave a terse nod. "We'll stop them here. Where do you want us?"

"My men are in position above with the dynamite at the ready. Take charge of your people in the woods. Slow the front until the rear arrives at the ridge. If they turn the Gatling toward you—"

"We know how to duck," Mateo noted wryly.

"Just keep behind rock and not brush. How is your ammunition?"

"Near played out," said Sam.

Abernathy signaled Corporal Romero to give them enough for a full load in both revolvers and rifles. "We have no more to spare, I'm afraid."

"We'll make do."

A sentry called, "Riders coming!"

Sam and Mateo galloped along the trail and then cut into the woods and secured their horses. Jeb and twenty other townsfolk with rifles crowded around. A grin spread wide across Jeb's face. "Tell me you washed all the bastards' sins away."

"Not all," said Sam, "but we made a dent in their numbers. Spread out. Dark riders will be upon us pronto. Mind yourselves. Keep to good cover and away from the trail."

"We got to get close enough to shoot," argued Jeb.

"Brush won't block a spray of bullets from a

Gatling gun. Make sure you ain't far from rock or thick wood. Keep their attention off the ridge, and we may stop a helluva lot more of the bastards. Watch your ammunition. We've got nary to spare."

They melted into the woods. Sam took point where the ridge ended and knelt behind a fallen tree. He glanced around. Mateo was off to his right. Everyone else took cover farther into the brush. The wait was short. Far off sounds of movement soon became black-shirted riders trotting along the trail.

Sam sighted down the barrel. The scrubby brush and the deepening shadows made homing in on a moving target through the trees difficult.

Difficult, but not impossible.

Sam took aim, held his breath, and squeezed the trigger. The shot rang out, signaling the other men. At once, rapid gunfire burst from their hidden positions. Shouts came from the riders. They returned fire, but couldn't get a bead through the underbrush. Sam ducked, smiling in grim satisfaction as the outlaws' shots went wide. He raised his head again and took aim.

Hellfire spit though the trees.

Sam dropped and rolled. Wood chips flew from the spot his head had been a moment earlier. He drew a deep breath and then crawled to a boulder. Bullets from the Gatling gun raked the woods in a steady stream of death.

As the spray swept another area, Sam flattened to the ground and peered around the rock. The wagon with the Gatling was at the front of the line. Mounted figures slipped behind it on the run to Spirit Ridge. Sam let out a curse. The outlaws had enough ammunition to keep them pinned as their own men advanced.

Sam fired in rapid succession. The man at the Gatling gun cried out and fell to the side of the trail. Within seconds, another outlaw jumped in the wagon bed and swung the muzzle to bear on Sam's position. He dove behind a rock, bullets thudding into the dirt.

More shots came from the woods as his men returned fire. Duck and cover…crawl to the next rock. Sam fired at any dark figure moving past. Dust from the trail kicked up around the riders. The outlaws regrouped as if preparing to charge. Sam's Winchester emptied. He pulled ammo from the revolver, reloaded the rifle, and fired again. Riders broke for the trail to town. He checked his ammunition—four bullets left.

Damnation, how long until they all pass under the ridge?

The blast was deafening. With an explosive roar, a cascade of boulders tumbled from the incline. The wave of deadly projectiles barreled through the outlaws' line, sending men and horses scattering. Sam rolled as a jagged rock as big as his head crashed through the underbrush, splintering a nearby tree trunk.

The cavalry attacked. Gunfire echoed along the ridge. Men shouted frenzied commands from every direction. A roiling wave of dust and debris engulfed the trail, dropping visibility to near zero.

The Gatling stopped firing. For a moment, Sam took heart the rocks destroyed it. He crept forward and cursed. From the turmoil, he glimpsed riders bolting toward Spirit Ridge with the wagon in escort. Sam brought the rifle to his shoulder, but they disappeared into a dust cloud before he squeezed off a round. Dodging gunfire, Sam dashed to the horses. Once in the saddle, he spurred Rio toward town.

****

Nell raced to the makeshift corral. "Light 'em up and get to cover! Riders are coming!" Matches blazed. Oily black smoke rose from one bonfire after another.

Eliza released the supports from the gate. "Good luck to you both."

Nell and Daisy took position on opposite sides of the corral. Nell raised a revolver in the air and fired. "Hyah!"

Daisy took the gun from her belt and pulled the trigger. Her free hand made a frantic grab for the saddle horn as the recoil knocked her back in the saddle. "Move your arses, ya dumb beasts."

Wild-eyed with terror, the cattle bellowed and then bolted toward the opening. In a blind panic, they crashed through the remains of the corral, tossing chunks of fence aside as if mere kindling. A living avalanche of horns and hooves swept across the land. Nell lost sight of Daisy. Even her voice was swallowed by the thunderous clamor.

Seeing the flames ahead, cattle skewed off the trail. Nell jerked hard on the reins as her horse nearly collided with a pair of horns. She fired several times in rapid succession. Bawling cattle crazed with terror lurched back on track.

The herd raced between bonfires. Nell finally glimpsed Daisy at the rear whooping and firing. Two hands now clutched the revolver to hold it steady. As the final steer passed the last smoky blaze, Nell reined in, heart pounding. They had done all they could.

"Now," Nell whispered. "Make them pay."

Dark-shirted riders boiled out from the trail to the ridge only to slam into the oncoming stampede. At once cattle, horses, and men collided. All around came bursts of gunfire. Men shot wildly as they attempted to force their bucking mounts through the herd. Cattle mad with fear, pressed forward.

From within the chaos, a man barked an order to regroup. Nell gripped the reins tight. She'd never forget Colin Doyle's voice. She sought him in the chaos, but instead glimpsed Morgan jump into the wagon with the Gatling gun and open fire. Cattle dropped in their tracks. Thrown by both the noise and the smell of blood, the remaining animals barreled forward in mindless frenzy. The wagon lurched and heaved and then upended in a crack of splintering wood.

A group of riders broke away and galloped toward Spirit Ridge. Nell wheeled her horse around. Daisy had stopped and waited for her.

"Run!" Nell shouted. "Get to town."

Daisy's boot heels dug into the horse's side as one of the riders veered to intercept her. She held the pistol with one hand and clung desperately to the saddle horn with the other, bouncing uncontrollably in the saddle. The rider quickly gained ground.

Nell fired the revolver. The shot went wide, but drew his attention. Recognition marked Colin Doyle's features and his expression twisted in rage. He dropped pursuit of Daisy and spurred his horse toward Nell.

She raised the revolver and fired again, but the hammer struck an empty chamber. The ammunition was spent. "Damnation," she muttered as Doyle took aim. Nell hunched low against the horse's mane as bullets whizzed past.

Doyle galloped at her, cutting off the route to Spirit Ridge. Heart pounding, Nell turned onto the trail to the

Tanner's cabin. If she could reach the cabin, block the door…

His horse gained with every stride. Nell made it to the perimeter of Sam's property when Doyle fired again. Her horse screamed and stumbled, pitching Nell to the dirt. Stunned for an instant, she scrambled to her feet. Doyle's horse thundered up to her. He raised the gun and sighted on her forehead. With a smirk, he pulled the trigger.

Click.

Nell took off running as Doyle cursed and fumbled to reload. She reached Alice Tanner's grave and sought a hiding place, but to no avail.

"No woman makes a fool of me." Colin Doyle limped toward her, a bloody bandage wrapped around his thigh. The gun's muzzle pointed at her.

"I'd say two of them already did," Nell jeered. "More than that if you count the women who, at this very minute, defend the town and lay waste to your riders. You're done."

"Done?" he spit out. "I'm not done. No one has proof I'm part of this. Why I'm only in a posse rounded up by Morgan. I was a pawn, you see. He had designs of being named new territorial governor. When I found out his terrible plot, I tried to stop him."

"You're insane. Both captured riders and Morgan will talk."

"Morgan is dead, and who'll believe any statement from a bunch of murderers and thieves? Before the truth is sorted out, I'll be long gone from here and into Mexico. But not you." He cocked the trigger. "You, I'm afraid, will be quite dead."

The gunshot ripped through the silence of the

clearing.

****

Sam's horse dodged the horns of the steer. Whipped into near madness, the cattle continued their mindless race across the earth. A rider with a neatly trimmed mustache attempted to right the upturned Gatling gun. The man drew his revolver. Sam fired, and the man dropped. Two more bullets stopped two more.

Behind him came a shout as Mateo circled the stampede. More gunfire erupted along the trail. The riders reached Spirit Ridge. Without a word, the two friends raced away.

"It'sa!"

Sam reined in Rio. Mateo halted beside him with a questioning look.

"I have to go. Nell went this way."

"Good luck, my friend." Mateo wheeled his horse to town.

A coyote trotted out of the scrub. She paused, eyes flashing amber fire in the dusk. With a flick of her tail, she bounded onto the trail to his grandparents' cabin. Without hesitation, Sam followed. The coyote's paws were a blur, barely touching the ground. She stopped at Sam's property. With a final flick of the tail, she disappeared into the woods.

Up ahead were two horses. One dripped blood from a wounded flank. Sam dismounted, running toward the sound of voices. Nell stood on Alice Tanner's grave, her back to Sam. The dark rider that faced her pointed a revolver at her head. Nell's body blocked a clear shot.

I told your mother I'll love you always. If I don't return, bury me beside her.

Sam raised the rifle to his shoulder. Sunlight was nearly gone. He could barely see.

"You, I'm afraid," said the man, "will be quite dead."

One bullet.

Sam held his breath and fired.

****

Doyle's head jerked. Blood spurted from a neat round hole in his forehead. He collapsed to the ground, his visage frozen forever in intense surprise.

Nell turned to see a rangy figure running toward her. She ran into Sam's arms, her face lit with joy. "You're safe. You're alive."

"As are you." They kissed each other, clinging tight as if neither could bear to let the other go first.

She wrapped her arms around his neck. "Has the fight ended?"

"Not yet. Spirit Ridge is still under attack."

Nell motioned toward the body. "The dark riders have no leader now he is dead."

Sam eyed the corpse with a raised eyebrow. "Colin Doyle?"

"Didn't you know?" She gave a shaky laugh. "That's right. You never met."

"Reckon it's a little late for an introduction," he said wryly. He bent over and retrieved the rest of the dead man's bullets from a cartridge belt. "Reckon he won't need these, either."

Nell mounted Doyle's horse and then she and Sam galloped away. Evening had descended on Spirit Ridge.

"I don't hear any gunfire," said Sam.

Nell sucked in her breath as they passed a body, letting it out when she saw the black shirt. Close by was another.

Four figures approached out of the dark. Sam's hand rested on the handle of the revolver. "Easy now," he muttered to Nell. "Get ready to run."

"Halt," cried a man.

"Grandpa?"

"Sam! Nell!" They dismounted. Frank caught them in a relieved embrace. "We been checking the bodies…" He swallowed hard. "I was worried about you two. Mateo told me Sam took off, and nobody's found Doyle—"

"We met by Ma's grave," said Sam tersely. "He won't cause any more trouble. What of the town?"

"Fighting's done. Less than twenty riders made it past the stampede. We took care of them right enough. Those not dead are crammed into the jail and damned uncomfortable."

"Casualties?"

"Two dozen wounded." He turned to Nell, sympathy etched his expression. "Miss Tremaine is one of them."

"Daisy!" Nell gasped. "Where is she?"

"At Mrs. Bonifay's. Lenna is with her."

Nell raced to town with Sam right beside. She burst through the door of the boarding house. The parlor had become a makeshift hospital where women tended to the wounded. Eliza Abernathy put down a pan of hot water and greeted Nell with open arms. "I'm so happy to see you safe."

"And I, you. Your husband?"

"Unharmed. A few injuries among the cavalry but no deaths, thank God."

"Daisy?"

"Upstairs, first door on the right."

Nell and Sam rushed into the room. Daisy lay on the bed with her arm in a sling. Mateo bent over, kissing her gently on the lips. They pulled apart with startled looks.

"Well," said Nell tartly. "I came to offer comfort, but am beaten to it."

Mateo flushed. "I-I was telling Daisy I was very glad to see her alive."

"Indeed."

Unlike Mateo, Daisy showed not the slightest discomposure.

"Where's my grandmother?" asked Sam.

"She went to the kitchen," said Mateo, "to fetch Daisy a meal."

Sam draped his arm around Mateo's shoulders. "Come, my friend, let me first assure her of both Nell's safety and my own. There is still much work to be done in town. We'll leave the women to the comfort of each other for the moment—if you can tear yourself away, that is."

Mateo grabbed his hat. Daisy held out a hand to him, and he pressed his lips to her fingers. "I'll return directly." She smiled happily.

"I see Mateo made his intentions plain," Nell said as the door closed.

Daisy blushed. "He has. I lost sight of you in the stampede with the riders upon me. One tried to grab me from my horse. I fell to the ground and ran. Another fired…I felt this pain. Mateo fought his way through, and then carried me to Mrs. Bonifay's, begging me not to die." Her voice softened. "He stayed here with Miss Lenna. When she left, Mateo said he had so little, but would share it all if I'd have him as my husband. If I'd have him…" She wiped away a tear. "I never imagined so good a man would want me as his own."

"You no longer have to live in fear, Daisy," said Nell. "Colin Doyle is dead."

Her eyes went wide. "Tell me what happened."

Daisy listened raptly. When Nell finished, she took her hand. "What of you and Sam? Will you return to San Francisco alone?"

Her gazed drifted out the window. "Yes. I made my decision. I must go."

****

Several hours later, Mateo sauntered through the door to say Sam was downstairs waiting for her. Nell and Sam slipped from the crowded boarding house and strolled the now quiet street arm in arm.

"The telegraph wires are repaired," said Sam. "We received word a cavalry detachment from Fort Denning will be here tomorrow. Better late, then never," he added wryly. "They can help us bury the dead and clear the trail past the ridge of boulders and debris."

"What of the attack on the railroad? Any word?"

Sam glowered "Morgan did the job well. The dark riders killed the marshal and several deputies. The railroad men lived, but are wounded. They described how Morgan rode to the rescue and then left with his posse supposedly chasing the dark riders. All were mighty shocked to hear of his treachery. He deceived them, right enough. They were ready to proclaim him hero of the day."

"So Doyle's plan would have worked," said Nell.

"Seems so. I reckon the railroad men feel powerful foolish about now."

"Naturally," Nell sniffed. "They don't wish to be reminded how close they came to supporting a madman for territorial governor."

"I have to escort the prisoners to Prescott and then assist the Army tracking a few escaped riders. I'll be gone several weeks. Do you think you can stay out of trouble that long?"

"It's not in the coyote's nature," she chuckled, "but I'll try." Her expression turned serious. "I must leave, also, and return to California to finish what I began. *The San Francisco Dispatch* will tell the adventures of the brave folk of Spirit Ridge. Even with Doyle's death, remnants of his criminal empire remain. The authorities need assistance to find them."

Sam wiped a stray lock of hair from her face. "I only need your promise San Francisco won't capture your heart."

"I keep it safely in your hands."

"When will you return?"

"In a month or so, depending on how often Aunt Agatha takes to her bed with the vapors after I explain my intentions. Daisy insisted on coming with me, to lend sympathetic support and keep me from throttling an elderly woman."

"I don't wish to cause your aunt distress. Stay with my grandparents until I return. We'll go together so I may ask for your hand."

"No. You and I have work to do that can't delay. I'll explain to Aunt Agatha my hand is my own to give and have already done so. Once she hears the rest of my plans, she'll be so horrified as to forget everything else."

Sam raised an eyebrow. "Which new scheme will

so distress you aunt?"

"I'll also…" Nell flashed a teasing smile. "I won't tell you yet. A woman must retain a little mystery or her man loses interest."

Sam pulled her close. "Have no fear of that, *Baya*."

Chapter Twenty-One

After working several hours, Sam and Mateo headed to the spring to wash off the grime and sweat. Mateo arched his back and stretched. He scrutinized the neat little cabin with approval. "Nell will be surprised her home is nearly finished, but not as surprised as the look on your face when the cast iron stove arrived. A most generous wedding present from Aunt Agatha. What exactly did you write to her?"

"Only a letter explaining my feelings for her niece," said Sam. "I told her I was building a cabin for Nell and me and requested her blessing for the marriage and nothing else. Didn't seem right not to. Said I'd take care of my wife on my own and didn't want a penny of her money. Didn't want nothing at all, but goodwill for Nell's sake."

"Your words must have won her over. Either that or she fears we are unwashed savages and doesn't wish her niece to live on a diet of raw meat."

"I don't bet against the latter," he chuckled, eyeing the cabin with pride. "I'm obliged for the help from you, Grandpa, and others in town."

"Do not think on it. We had to be certain the cabin had plenty of room for you and Nell with space to add on when the little Tanners begin to arrive. How soon will that be, do you think?"

"Nell and I will get hitched first, if it's the same to

you. What about the little Perezes?"

"The same. When did Nell's last letter say they'd be back?"

"Only that they were fixing to leave San Francisco directly. I told you three times already. Why do you keep asking? Daisy wrote you the same thing."

"I keep hoping you'll say something different. Did you finish the final chapter?" Nell sent copies to both men of a series of articles written for *The San Francisco Dispatch*. "Her words are imbued with a descriptive flair, no? At the time, I only tried to avoid getting shot and didn't realize our adventures were so riveting." Mateo regarded Sam with a deadpan expression. "Though, I'd never describe you as stalwart and handsome. I always reckoned you on the puny side with most unpleasant features."

"Nell wrote you were both vigorous and refined. You aim to argue that?"

"No, no. She's correct about me."

They saddled the horses for the ride to town. As Sam reached the edge of his property, a coyote darted across the trail.

It'sa, I am home.

Sam turned to Mateo with a grin. "C'mon!" He dug in his heels and urged Rio to a gallop.

"Where are we going?" shouted Mateo.

"The ridge!"

The horses' hooves thundered on the trail. In the distance, two figures drove along in a heavily laden wagon. As they caught sight of the men, Nell pulled the team to a stop and waved. Daisy tore off her bonnet and swung it over her head, letting out a whoop. Sam and Mateo reined in the horses beside them and dismounted. Both women jumped from the wagon, throwing themselves into the men's arms.

"Why didn't you telegraph you were coming?" said Sam after an exuberant kiss.

Nell laughed. "We wanted to surprise you, but it appears the spirits sent a hint."

"We came by train to Prescott," said Daisy, "and then secured a wagon and spent the night in Fort Braddock with Eliza and Micah. His new major's insignia is still bright and shiny."

"Well," said Nell, "they can't have a captain in charge of Fort Braddock any longer, not with the expansion planned for both the fort and the rail line. He'll make lieutenant colonel before long."

"The rail is coming to Fort Braddock?" said Mateo.

"Not just Fort Braddock," said Daisy. "Tell them Nell."

"They're extending the track to Spirit Ridge."

"Nell blackmailed the railroad," blurted Daisy with pride.

"It wasn't blackmail," she said tartly. "I simply explained to the Burlington Northern Santa Fe board of directors it would look poorly for the company if they didn't bring the line to the very town that saved the Territory from falling into the hands of Colin Doyle. People are aghast by The Mick's actions. Doyle's previous allies have a hard time of it right now in San Francisco. The railroad wishes to steer clear of any association with his name." She gazed upward with an innocent expression. "I may have also mentioned any story I write linking the railroad to Doyle will certainly interest *The Dispatch's* readers."

Sam narrowed his eyes. "You had no proof Doyle

and the railroad were in collusion."

"They didn't know that. When I suggested the extension to Spirit Ridge instead of newspaper articles critical of the railroad, they agreed. Officials arrive by the end of the week to secure right-of-ways. People owning property in the area will make quite a bit of money. New settlers will undoubtedly follow after completion of the rail line. I'm afraid, Marshal Tanner, in the near future Spirit Ridge won't be so sleepy."

Sam chuckled. "Coyote Woman is still a trickster." He motioned toward the wagon. "What's all this?"

Nell sighed. "Wedding presents. When I told Aunt Agatha I intended to return to the Arizona Territory to marry a marshal and live in a cabin, she took to her bed with heart palpitations. Then after she received your letter, she rose like Lazarus from the dead and decided it was time to shop. Don't be dismayed. Some of the trunks are my gifts for Daisy's trousseau."

"I'm relieved. I figured I'd have to build a second cabin to hold it all. What's in that large crate?"

Her face lit up. "That's my own purchase. Three guesses."

"Another stove. You'll need two. I have a powerful appetite."

"Wrong. Second guess?"

"A Gatling gun? The crate could make a bedroom for guests, tight but tolerable quarters."

"No, thank you. I hope never to see one of those infernal weapons again. Last guess."

"It's a printing press," burst out Daisy. "Nell plans to start a newspaper here in Spirit Ridge. I'm going to help her."

"*The Spirit Ridge Dispatch*," stated Nell with pride.

"So that was your secret?" said Sam.

Nell nodded with enthusiasm. "Another crate contains paper and ink—a wedding gift from Arthur. The newspaper will be weekly at first, but grow with the population." She eyed Sam with undisguised apprehension. "What are your thoughts? Newspaper stories are known to cause trouble."

As an answer, Sam kissed her. "All is as it should be. Coyote Woman continues to nip at the good citizens' heels, herding them in the right direction whether they wish to go or not. What did Aunt Agatha say about you becoming a businesswoman?"

"She took to her bed with the vapors this time, but only for a day. When Aunt Agatha rose, she told me if I was determined to go through with this mad scheme, she'd come to the wedding on the first train to Spirit Ridge. I promised to wait." Nell peered into his eyes. "We have to delay the ceremony. It'll be six months before the tracks are completed."

"Then we wait six months. I can't forgo the pleasure of seeing Mrs. Bonifay and your aunt together at the boarding house arguing which one of us is the worse influence on the town."

"Well, we're not waiting," said Mateo. "That is, if you're still of the same mind, Daisy. The circuit court judge will be here Friday."

The kiss left no doubt of her answer.

****

The eagle lit upon a rock next to the coyote. They both turned their faces to the sky. The sun's rays washed over Spirit Ridge, painting the crags with radiant hues of scarlet and amber.

"You have done well, children of the light." The

echo of the voice resounded across the land. "The shadow is defeated. I will grant a reward. State your desire."

"We wish a home with each other," said the eagle.

"To never be apart," said the coyote.

"So be it. I name you protectors of this place. May your hearts beat as one, ever vigilant against the dark."

As they gazed upon their new domains of land and sky, the eagle and the coyote's souls united.

A word from the author…

I live in Florida, where the heat and humidity have driven everyone slightly mad. In my spare time I call in Bigfoot sightings to the Florida Department of Fish and Wildlife. They are heartily sick of hearing from me.

If you enjoyed *Spirit Ridge*, please take a moment to leave a review at your favorite e-book retailer. No essay necessary, a few words is fine. Spelling and grammar will not count toward your final grade.

For more information about my books, visit my blog or drop me a line. I love hearing from readers.

Lurking spots:

http://lakelleythenaughtylist.blogspot.com

Twitter @AuthorLAKelley

Facebook www.facebook.com/l.a.kelley.author

l.a.kelley.author@gmail.com

www.ingramcontent.com/pod-product-compliance
Lightning Source LLC
Chambersburg PA
CBHW051516260626
47170CB00003B/650